Novelista
Girl

Books by Meredith Schorr

JUST FRIENDS WITH BENEFITS

A STATE OF JANE

HOW DO YOU KNOW?

The Blogger Girl Series

BLOGGER GIRL (#1)

NOVELISTA GIRL (#2)

Praise for Meredith Schorr

BLOGGER GIRL (Blogger Girl Series #1)

"What a fun book. The characters were incredibly well-written. I felt like I understood everyone's personalities and quirks, almost as if I knew them personally myself. Meredith Schorr is a talented author and I'm glad she has other books out for me to read!"

> – Becky Monson, Bestselling Author of the Spinster Series

"Sassy, sexy, endlessly entertaining, and full of laughs (as well as some heart-wrenching moments), *Blogger Girl* is one of those books that keeps you up at night because you can't wait to see what happens next."

> – Tracie Banister, Author of *Mixing It Up*

"America finally has its own version of Britain's Bridget Jones!"

> – *Books in the Burbs*

NOVELISTA GIRL (Blogger Girl Series #2)

"A strong and confident heroine, a sexy boyfriend you can crush on, supportive friends, and plenty of conflict leading to comical results, culminating in a very satisfying ending...Once you start this book, you won't be able to put it down."

> – Erin Brady, Bestselling Author of *The Shopping Swap*

"A perfect mix of romance, conflict, and humor, *Novelista Girl* solidifies Schorr's place among best-sellers Sophie Kinsella and Emily Giffin."

> – Carolyn Ridder Aspenson, Bestselling Author of *Unbinding Love*

"Absolutely brilliant chick lit, I couldn't put it down, and I highly, highly recommend."

> – *Chick Lit Plus*

JUST FRIENDS WITH BENEFITS

"Meredith writes with wit, candor, humor and vulnerability that illuminates the struggles of dating and relationships."
— Nancy Slotnick, Author of *Turn Your Cablight On*

"The perfect vacation read. The dialogue flows like beer at a beach party."
– K.C. Wilder, Author of *Fifty Ways to Leave Your Husband*

A STATE OF JANE

"I laughed my way through this novel. A must-read."
– *Chick Lit Plus*

"A witty true-to-life story that will not disappoint you, it is chick lit at it's very best!"
– *Jersey Girl Book Reviews*

"I am a huge fan of chick lit, but this book was so much more. It has become one of my favorite reads!"
– *The Little Black Book Blog*

HOW DO YOU KNOW?

"Meredith Schorr is an author to watch."
– Tracy Kaler, Founder and Editor of *Tracy's New York Life*

"You won't forget this delightful cast of characters or Schorr's sharp, candid insights about the plight of the modern woman."
– Diana Spechler, Author of *Who by Fire* and *Skinny*

"I think every woman will relate to Maggie and her friends, no matter her age or relationship status."
– *Chick Lit Club*

Novelista
Girl

Meredith Schorr

HENERY PRESS

NOVELISTA GIRL
The Blogger Girl Series
Part of the Henery Press Chick Lit Collection

Second Edition | February 2017

Henery Press, LLC
www.henerypress.com

Trade Paperback ISBN-13: 978-1-63511-165-1
Digital epub ISBN-13: 978-1-63511-166-8
Kindle ISBN-13: 978-1-63511-167-5
Hardcover Paperback ISBN-13: 978-1-63511-168-2

Printed in the United States of America

For Susan Goodman—thanks for being such a great mom and for inspiring so much material...XO.

ACKNOWLEDGMENTS

To the following people who either directly or indirectly made it possible for me to write *Novelista Girl*, please accept my heartfelt gratitude and a five-pink-champagne-flutes review.

Henery Press: Thank you for welcoming me into the Hen House with wide, open arms. To my editor, Erin George, you are amazing and I am truly in awe of how well you pinpoint where my books need extra loving care. I know my novels are in the best hands when I deliver them to you. Thank you to Kendel Lynn for designing the adorable cover. To Art Molinares, Rachel Jackson, and everyone else who had a hand in bringing me into the fold and supporting my journey, I am so grateful and consider myself truly blessed.

Vicky Sly and Aimee Oravec: Please accept my gratitude for all of your help editing and proofreading the first edition of the book.

My beta readers: Natalie Aaron, Hilary Grossman, and Samantha Stroh Bailey. Natalie, you know the characters in this series as well as I do and always help me keep them consistent and true to themselves. I am forever grateful to you—your honesty, your keen eye, your time, your friendship. Hilary, *Novelista Girl* might have been your first beta read, but you nailed it and helped me see where strengthening was necessary. More importantly, you've been a true friend since the day we met, and I'm so happy we've taken our friendship offline. Sam, I don't know where to start. Besides forcing me to dig deeper and answering all of my grammar-related questions on demand, you've been such an inspiration to me. The passion you possess for writing the best possible book and never giving up knocked me out of my writing funk and kept me going through the very last edit.

To my "real-world" friends: Ronni Candlen, Jenny Kabalen, Abbe Kalnick, Hilda Black, Julie Marie Shinkle, Shanna Eisenberg, Jennifer Baum, Jennifer Levin, Marisa Glaser, Elke Marks, Megan Coombes and many more. You are my gladiators in suits, the folks I'd risk my life for in a zombie apocalypse, and the best vacation and drinking buddies in the land. Although I don't see you all in equal measure, each of you is so special to me and inspires so much of my writing.

To Alan Blum: You may not be here with me anymore, but I'm never without you. You helped shape my voice and my sense of humor, and made me a better person. I owe so much to you, and that debt will never be paid. I love and miss you more than I can express in an epic ten-book series novel. Stay tuned for a book inspired by our friendship. It's coming!

To my family: Marjorie, thanks for being my sister, my sometimes-shrink, and my best friend. And thanks for giving me Sarah, Joey, and little Sarah. To my oldest sister, Melissa, thanks for encouraging my love of reading way back when I would have rather ridden my bike, and for Jared, Emily, and Olivia. To my brother, Jim, who will buy this book but probably won't read it, thanks for being one of the best men I've ever known, and for loving me. To my mom, words cannot express how much I love you and enjoy being your littlest M. No amount of nosy questions about my love life will ever change that. To my dad, our path has not always been smooth, but I love where we are right now. Thanks for all of your encouragement.

My fellow Beach Babes: Eileen Goudge, Francine LaSala, Julie Valerie, Jennifer Tucker, Josie Brown, and the aforementioned Samantha Stroh Bailey. I cherish our annual beach vacation and all of the Twitter/email exchanges in between. You are among the most gifted, witty, supportive, loyal women I've ever known (and often dirty and foul, but in the best way possible).

Deborah Shapiro and Laurie Buchanan: Thanks for making my "day job" a fun and supportive place, even as I work toward my goal of someday writing full time.

And, finally, to book bloggers everywhere who inspired the Blogger Girl series: Your support means everything to me! Special shout-outs to a few who have been on my side since practically the beginning: Kaley Stewart, Aimee Brown, Bethany Clark, Melissa Amster, Samantha Janning, Marlene Engel, Isabella Anderson, Ashley Williams, Mary Smith, and Kelly Perotti. And to the members of my street team, including Lily Barrish, Rebecca Moore, Lindsey Lowrimore—thanks for consistently cheering me on and spreading the word about Kim and the Gang.

Chapter 1

To: KimMLong@gmail.com
From: Libby_Knox@Knoxliterary.com
Subject: Re: Query—*A Blogger's Life*

Dear Ms. Long,

Thank you for your interest in Knox Literary. While I found the premise of A Blogger's Life *interesting, I'm afraid I wasn't sufficiently intrigued to ask for more at this time. Because this business is so subjective, and opinions vary widely, we encourage you to query other agents.*

After all, it only takes one.

Best of luck on your journey to publication.

Libby Knox
Knox Literary

I let out a deflated sigh before resting my head on my boyfriend Nicholas's shoulder. It was a Sunday afternoon in early December, and after a late lunch, we had come back to my place to watch television. Well, *I* was watching television—a romantic movie on the Hallmark Channel. Nicholas was doing work. As the in-house attorney for a cosmetics company, he often took work home with him.

Nicholas stopped typing furiously on his laptop. "What's the matter, Kimmie?"

With my eyes closed, I responded, "I got another rejection from an agent." Making it fourteen total for my chick lit novel, *A Blogger's Life*. When I gathered the courage to write a novel—a complete manuscript with a beginning, middle, and an end, as opposed to a partial story that I shoved in the back of my closet unfinished—I knew the journey to publication would be difficult. Now, I was thinking "impossible" was a more befitting adjective.

Giving my hand a gentle squeeze, Nicholas said, "I'm sorry."

I opened my eyes and sat up. "Me too."

"It's just one agent. Did you know Kathryn Stockett received sixty rejections of *The Help* before she got an agent?"

I jerked my head back in surprise. "I did know that. How did *you* know that?"

Nicholas smiled. "I did some research after your last rejection."

I kissed his cheek and ran my palm up against his ever-present five o'clock shadow. "How nice of you."

"I'm a nice guy." Nicholas paused for a beat. "For a player, that is."

When I first met Nicholas a little over a year ago, he was an attorney at the New York City firm where I work as a legal secretary. He was single, successful, hot, and flirtatious. Naturally, I assumed he was a player when we first hooked up. Either that, or out of my league. What would someone with his credentials want with me—a measly legal secretary with a nice rack? When Nicholas gently suggested my dreams might extend beyond book blogging to book writing, I worried maybe *he* was the one who wanted me to be a writer so I would be "good enough" to hang with all of his successful friends. I was blinded by my insecurity, but after some soul-searching, I concluded he was right, and I was wrong— something he enjoyed reminding me of on a regular basis. It had been almost six months since our reconciliation, and sometimes I still had to pinch myself to confirm that the guy I adored—the one who not only caused my knees to go weak and the butterflies to dance in my belly whenever he touched me, but also made me laugh and encouraged my dream to be a published author—was equally crazy about me. I was in love big time, but too chicken to be the first to say the words.

I playfully punched his arm. "Are you ever gonna let that go?"

Nicholas flashed me a sexy grin. "Not likely."

I shook my head in mock annoyance. Inching closer to him on my loveseat, I draped one of my legs over his and sighed. "Maybe I should have tried to publish *Read My Mind* first." *A Blogger's Life* was technically my second novel. I had given up writing *Read My Mind* in high school only to pick it up and finally finish it ten years later. Although *Read My Mind* was the novel that qualified me as a "finisher," I ultimately decided to shelve it and pursue *A Blogger's Life* instead.

Crinkling his brow, Nicholas asked, "I thought you said this one was much better."

Rubbing the opal pendant on my necklace, I said, "Do you not think so?"

Nicholas shook his head. "I can't say. I haven't started reading it yet." Probably noticing my face drop, he added, "I promise I will soon."

"It is better, but apparently, chick lit is dead among traditional publishers unless you're an established author in the genre. Young adult paranormal, on the other hand, is hot."

"Considering how many fans *Pastel Is the New Black* has, I'd say chick lit is pretty hot too." Patting my knee, he added, "Almost as hot as its founder."

Nicholas was correct that my book blog, *Pastel Is the New Black*, had thousands of followers. Unfortunately for me, none of those fans were literary agents, as far as I knew. "Why couldn't I have written *A Blogger's Life* ten years ago when chick lit was on fire?" I whined. Considering I didn't even know what a blog was when I was nineteen, it was a rhetorical question.

"It is what it is, Kimmie." Nicholas ran one hand along my thigh and then slowly up to the zipper on my black skinny jeans. "Anything I can do to make you feel better?" he asked.

"You can try, but it will be hard."

Placing my hand over his crotch, he said, "It's *very* hard, but you're worth it."

There was nothing I wanted more—besides an offer for agent representation—than to get down and dirty with Nicholas right then and there, but I was so behind on book reviews for my blog. I also wanted to make some revisions to my agent query letter based on suggestions from one of my author friends. And I knew Nicholas was swamped too. I decided a compromise was in order. "How about we do it in an hour?"

Nicholas frowned and tugged at my zipper. "But I want to do it now," he said, adopting the bratty entitled voice of Veruca Salt from *Willy Wonka & the Chocolate Factory.*

Sliding away from him, I said, "It's called delayed gratification. You should try it."

Nicholas got up from the couch and stood in front of me. Extending his hand, he said, "You don't want to make my brown eyes blue. Do you, Kimmie?" He frowned, drawing my eyes to his full and completely bitable lower lip.

I couldn't help but smile. "Don't It Make My Brown Eyes Blue" had become "our" song the night we got back together. I sang it to him at karaoke in a grand gesture when my two best friends, Bridget and Caroline, dared me to stop moping about and write my own happy ending.

I reached for Nicholas's hand and allowed him to pull me to a standing position. "I don't want anything of yours to be blue," I said as my eyes dropped down to his groin.

Leading me to my bedroom, he said, "That makes two of us."

As promised, Nicholas made me feel better. He had mad skills. But even as I writhed in ecstasy beneath him, I wondered if my fifteenth rejection letter had already landed in my inbox.

"Can I tell you how much I hate the commute downtown from here?" Nicholas asked later that night. He was sitting on the edge of my queen-sized bed and stood up to pull his jeans over his hips.

I gazed at his lean but muscular chest and reached forward to run my pointer finger up and down the happy trail of dark hair that extended from his belly to the button of his jeans. "Why don't you stay over?" I might have been preoccupied with catching up on my blog a few hours ago, but now I just wanted more Nicholas.

"I don't have work clothes here, so I can either go home now or stay and stop at my place before work first thing tomorrow." Crinkling his nose, he added, "But the thought of getting up extra early to go downtown just to go back to midtown is not at all appealing." He leaned down to plant a soft kiss on my lips. "Sorry, Kimmie."

I reclined against my headboard and sighed. "I suppose I'll do some reading. The exciting life of a book blogger."

Nicholas narrowed his eyes at me. "You love reading."

"Not as much as I love..." You. Not as much as I love *you*. "...spending the entire night with you."

"Then why don't you move in with me?"

I sat upright. "Wha-what?" My heart was beating rapidly, and I wasn't sure if it was due to excitement about possibly cohabitating with Nicholas or terror at possibly cohabitating with Nicholas. What would my parents say? I was almost thirty, and my younger sister was already married. They wouldn't say anything.

His brown eyes probing mine, Nicholas said, "Just think about it, Kimmie. We spend several nights a week at each other's apartments anyway, and mine is more spacious. Why pay the extra rent?"

I gaped at him, still in a semi state of shock. "Isn't it too soon?"

Nicholas shrugged and ran a hand through his short dark hair. "Later this month will be six months we've been dating. Would be longer if you weren't such a stubborn brat."

I opened my mouth to protest, but he put his finger to my lips and smiled. "Joking." Nicholas sat on the bed and kissed the top of my head. "I've been thinking about us moving in together for a while."

"You have?" This was news to me, albeit good news.

Nicholas nodded. "Unless you're not taking this relationship seriously." With a straight face, he went on to repeat verbatim what I said to him after the first time we had sex. "I'm not looking for a friends-with-benefits situation." And yes, I'm aware I should have mentioned that *before* getting naked with him.

I jabbed his elbow with mine. "Okay, I'll give it some thought."

While Nicholas continued getting dressed, I began thinking out loud. "My lease is up next month, so the timing is good. It would be weird living so far away from Bridget, but since Jonathan moved into her apartment, I don't see her as much anyway. At least your place is close to the subway, and the Village is hipper than the Upper East Side with more coffee shops for me to write—"

Chuckling, Nicholas said, "You keep thinking about it, Kimmie." He bent down and twirled a strand of my long, light brown hair around his finger. "I'll text you when I get home."

"Sounds good," I said. As I followed him to my front door, I visualized his apartment, already mentally redecorating it with splashes of femininity. I wrapped my arms around his neck and stood on my tippy-toes to give him a real kiss goodbye. At four foot eleven, I was still significantly shorter than Nicholas, who was also somewhat vertically challenged (but hot) at five foot seven. "Get home safely."

"I will, Kimmie Long." He gazed into my eyes for a moment and then gave me a soft smile. "I love you."

Before I could digest the magnitude of those three words— words we had yet to exchange in the entirety of our relationship— he turned his back on me and jogged down the two flights of stairs to the ground floor of my building, whistling to the tune of "Don't It Make My Brown Eyes Blue."

"I love you too," I whispered to the air before closing my front door and leaning against it with a huge smile on my face.

He loved me. I couldn't wait to tell Bridget.

Chapter 2

"Long!"

I rolled my eyes. I hated when Rob, my boss and prominent senior partner at the law firm where I worked, shouted to me from his office instead of calling me on the phone or simply walking to my cubicle right outside his door. I was convinced he did it on purpose to piss me off. I had worked for him at our current firm for just under a year and for nearly two years at our previous one. We secretly loved each other (in a totally non-scuzzy way), but publicly bickered nonstop because it was fun and because our colleagues enjoyed the show. I put my office phone on speaker and dialed his extension. "Yes, Boss Man?"

"Can you please come in here?"

"Of course." When I entered Rob's office, legal pad in hand, I noticed Daneen, Rob's junior associate, sitting on the other side of his desk in his guest chair. Rob's legal team comprised David (the paralegal), Daneen, and Lucy (another attorney). Although the rest of them also considered me a member of what Rob liked to call "the squad," to Daneen I was "just the secretary."

She angled her lanky body in my direction and gave me a phony smile, all the while not so subtly looking me up and down. I was wearing a Diane von Furstenberg black wrap dress with bright red pumps. I wouldn't have scraped together three hundred and twenty-five dollars for the dress if it wasn't flattering, and I stood up straighter in a show of confidence.

After returning her fake grin, I turned to Rob. "You beckoned?"

Rob nodded. "And it only took you half a lifetime to get here. Lost in a book, I assume? What's this one called, *Surrender to Love, Hearts and Flowers,* or some other corny romantic title?"

I narrowed my eyes at him. "I was revising your bills for the month. And I don't read that mushy stuff, and you know it." Most of the time. I was kind of digging some of the recent new adult titles, and they were definitely steamy, if not mushy.

"Yes, we all know your taste in literature is far more intellectual." Daneen snorted at her own attempt at humor while I glared at her.

Rob cleared his throat. "Can you please show Daneen the exhibit chart you created for the Orange Essence case?"

The Orange Essence case involved a dispute over a perfume scent. Normally, I went through the motions of my job without giving the details much thought, but since we were representing Nicholas's company, the plaintiff in the case, I gave it tender loving care. "Sure thing. Now?"

"If you can fit it into your busy schedule, then yes," he said, his dark-blue eyes twinkling under full brows.

A witty comeback at the ready, but knowing we could go all day, I motioned for Daneen to follow me to my desk. I sat down while she hovered over my chair, her head so close to mine I could smell the spearmint flavor of her gum over stale coffee breath. Locating the document on my computer, I said, "Am I just showing you the chart, or do you need me to email it to you too?"

"Rob said Nicholas will be sending more materials that will be added, but I want to see what we have so far. If you don't know to what the exhibit names correspond, don't worry about it. I'm sure I can figure it out or ask David."

I turned around to face her and smiled sweetly. "I know *to what* the exhibit names correspond," I said, mimicking her proper speech pattern. God forbid she end a sentence in a preposition, even in casual speech. "David and I have been going through the various materials together." I slid my chair back to give her better access to my screen. "And here it is."

"Impressive," she said. As her hazel eyes scanned the Excel chart, she tapped a finger along her narrow and, in my opinion after careful scrutiny, slightly long nose. "So, Nicholas tells me you're submitting your novel to agents."

My mouth fell open in surprise that Nicholas would share something so personal about me with Daneen, a woman he knew I hated. Not only was her crush on Nicholas beyond obvious to both of us, but his tendency to downplay her treatment of me like an intellectually challenged indentured servant, rather than have my back, was another contributing factor to our earlier breakup.

"That is correct," I said. Hoping to subtly change the subject, I pointed at the computer monitor. "The chart is organized with the oldest evidence first."

Daneen glanced at the screen briefly and nodded. Frowning at me, she said, "He mentioned you hadn't received any offers yet."

I was going to kill him. Or withhold blow jobs for a month. At least.

"But I think it's great you're putting yourself out there like that. You do know the average quality agent signs two, maybe three, new clients a year?"

From the look of pity on her face, I gathered she was not confident I would make the cut. Dryly, I responded, "I had no idea you were so knowledgeable about the publishing process." I pressed my lips together to avoid asking her the last time she shit herself while having sex—the one piece of dirt I'd managed to dig up on her. Although I dangled my knowledge of Daneen's "most embarrassing moment" in her face once in an attempt to get her off my back, I didn't have it in me to actually use the juicy gossip against her. A change of topic was in order. Hopefully one that would wipe the smug expression off her face. "Did Nicholas also tell you we were moving in together?" I hadn't technically given Nicholas my answer yet, but living with the man of my dreams was an offer I knew I couldn't refuse. When Daneen's eyes bugged out, I knew I'd caught her off guard.

"Congratulations. Although I personally would never move in

without a ring, it's a nice offer for a girl like you." Daneen flipped her long straight auburn hair and turned her attention to the computer. "I'd prefer the newest evidence on top." Glancing at her watch, she said, "And I'll need the amended document by lunch." With an exaggerated pout, she added, "Sorry for the extra work," before pivoting on her heel and walking away with long strides. As I observed her, I wondered how such a skinny woman managed to sound like a herd of elephants each time her three-inch black pumps met the carpet. Then, I turned back to the chart and with a single click of my mouse, changed the order of the exhibits from ascending to descending. For a talented attorney, Daneen was pretty clueless about some basic computer programs.

I was dying to prove how quickly I finished her petty assignment despite her obvious desire to ruin my day. I mimicked, "It's a nice offer for a girl like you." Seriously? Lots of couples lived together before they got married these days. It was the twenty-first century, not *Leave It to Beaver* Land. Daneen was a clueless and boyfriend-less workaholic. Why was I even listening to her? I swallowed back the morsel of doubt in my mind and returned my attention to the project at hand. I decided against sending the revised document immediately, knowing Daneen would probably pull another meaningless and oh-so-urgent project out of her ass in retaliation. After checking in with Rob to see if he needed anything and getting a muffled "no" in response, I pulled up my latest draft review for *Pastel Is the New Black*.

What if you were forced to play out the same day over and over and over again until you got it right, only you had no idea what wrongdoing you were required to fix? This is the plight of Starbucks barista Mariah Peters in The Daily Grind *by Hattie Angeles.*

As I continued to type, the Gmail icon on the bottom of my screen notified me I had received another email, and I sucked in my breath when I saw it was from an agent. I closed my eyes and muttered, "Please don't be a rejection. Please don't be a rejection." Then I opened my eyes, took a deep breath, and released it before opening the email.

Dear Author,

Thank you for your query. We apologize for the impersonal nature of this response, but rest assured, we read each and every query we receive. After careful consideration, we do not feel your project is right for our list, but we wish you success in finding another agent.

Sincerely,
Alex P. Keans Literary

I could have deleted the message after the greeting, "Dear Author," since any request for additional pages would have at least addressed me by my proper name. But I was a glutton for punishment, as well as an eternal optimist, who hoped maybe, just maybe, the agent would write something promising in the last sentence. Alas, he did not. I tried to take comfort in being categorized as an "author"—something that never would have happened if Nicholas hadn't forced me to face my long-buried dream of writing a novel, but all I wanted to do was go home and sulk into a bowl of ice cream. It only took one agent, but what if every single one of them rejected me?

I perked up when I remembered I had a girls' night scheduled with Bridget, my best friend since the seventh grade, after work. Substitute "ice cream" with Skinny Girl Margaritas, and my sullen mood was bound to improve. And at least Ginny Webber—my dream agent—hadn't passed yet. Ginny was bestselling chick lit author Olivia Geffen's agent, and I was waiting to hear back from her. Her response time to an initial query, based on what other authors posted on the *Absolute Scribe* website, was approximately four weeks. I refreshed my email. Any minute now.

While I waited, I still had an extremely successful blog to

manage and so, after telling Rob I was stepping away and sending Daneen the updated chart, I headed to the cafeteria, where I ate lunch and finished the four-pink-champagne-flutes review of *The Daily Grind*.

Chapter 3

"To cohabitation," Bridget said, clinking her glass against mine.

"To cohabitation," I repeated, before taking a sip of the white sangria Bridget had made from scratch. I smacked my lips together. "This is amazing, Bridget."

Grinning, Bridget said, "I know, right? I modified the recipe slightly to add more peach schnapps."

Taking another sip, I replied, "Whatever you did, it worked."

"Thanks." Bridget's fair skin beamed with pride as she placed her glass gently on the surface of her white antique coffee table. She leaned against her purple suede couch and sighed contently. "If I told you last December we'd both be living with boyfriends in a year, would you have believed me?"

"Um, considering I had yet to string two sentences together in conversation with Nicholas and was still sleeping with Jonathan, definitely not." I swallowed hard, wishing I could take back the last half of the sentence. I was definitely getting used to Bridget and Jonathan *in luurve*, but Jonathan was my high-school boyfriend, the first guy I slept with, and my on-again/off-again friend with benefits for several years. It came as a complete surprise when I discovered Bridget had a secret crush on him. It wasn't a "bad" surprise, since my lustful feelings for Jonathan were long gone, and I was already seriously into Nicholas by the time they started dating. But my best friend of over fifteen years in reciprocated love with my first boyfriend was still...awkward.

Fortunately, the comment appeared to go directly over Bridget's head. "I know. A lot can change in a year, huh?"

"Yeah, maybe I'll find an agent who actually likes *A Blogger's Life* in the next three hundred and sixty-five days." For instance, Ginny Webber. Frowning, I said, "But I won't hold my breath."

"I'm sorry, K," Bridget said, twirling a tendril of copper-red hair around her finger. "Any agent who doesn't want to work with my best friend is a dumbass."

I chuckled at Bridget's fierce loyalty. "All of them?"

"All of them. Screw 'em all. And it's only been fifteen. Did you know Kathryn Stockett got sixty rejections of *The Help* before getting an agent?"

"Nicholas said the same thing."

"Smart guy, that Nicholas. I always liked him," Bridget said, before taking a swig of her drink.

My phone rang. "His ears must have been ringing. Mind if I take this?"

"Not at all. I'll take the opportunity to grab a cig." Ignoring the dirty look I threw her way regarding her nasty habit, Bridget headed to the windowsill.

"Hi, baby," I said into the phone. I stood up and walked into Bridget's kitchen to pour a glass of water.

"Your best friend tells me you've decided to move in with me," Nicholas said in his deep, smooth voice.

"Bridget?" As I quickly realized my mistake, my stomach dropped. "Oh, you mean Daneen."

Chuckling, Nicholas said, "The one and only."

Remembering I was supposed to be mad at him, I said, "Speaking of the devil incarnate, why are you sharing my personal business with her?" I poured a glass of water and returned the pitcher to the top shelf of Bridget's refrigerator.

"What are you talking about?"

"She knows I'm looking for an agent. With no success, I might add." Returning to the couch, Bridget stretched her feet out on the coffee table and gave me a questioning look. I mouthed, "I'll tell you later" and returned my attention to Nicholas.

"Oh. I'm sorry, Kimmie," Nicholas said, sounding sincerely

apologetic. "I can't help myself from bragging about my future bestselling author girlfriend sometimes. But I'll stop."

I smiled, touched at Nicholas's faith in me. "I forgive you," I whispered.

"Thank you. So...is it true?"

Still feeling warm and fuzzy, I asked, "Is what true?"

"Have you decided to move in with me?"

"Oh, that. I have, in fact, made a decision."

"And?"

I yelped, "Let's do it," as my heart beat rapidly in a mixture of excitement and anxiety. I was afraid to get too excited in case he changed his mind. And even though it was true we already bunked at each other's places several times a week, having "overnights" with your boyfriend was significantly more casual than moving in together. Case in point—there would be bills to share, toilet seats to lower, hot water to hog...

"Good answer, Kimmie," Nicholas said, interrupting my self-imposed buzzkill.

"We'll have to sit down and figure out logistics, like how much closet space you're going to give me. And whose furniture we should keep. I don't want to throw out all of my stuff just because I'm moving into your place."

"Whoa. Slow down. We'll make it work."

"Promise?" I was particularly attached to the loveseat my mom finally gave me for my twenty-ninth birthday after I had begged for years. A family heirloom of sorts, it had been passed down from generation to generation. The fabric wasn't in great shape, so I'd had it reupholstered in a gorgeous shade of pink. I was afraid Nicholas would say pastel didn't go well with the otherwise "masculine" vibe in his apartment. I was a very pastel sort of chick, and if Nicholas wanted me, he needed to know I came with a lot of pink.

"I promise." Nicholas stopped talking, and I heard voices in the background before he returned to the phone. "I need to get back to work, but I'm glad we're doing this, Kimmie."

"I'm glad too," I said softly. I thought about adding, "I love you," since Nicholas had bolted from my apartment before I had a chance to reciprocate the day before, but I wanted to say it face to face the first time. Mostly because it was more personal that way, but also so we could have hot "we love each other" sex immediately after.

After we said our goodbyes, I rejoined Bridget on the couch. While we drank our sangria, she gave me the skinny on the ups and downs of shacking up with a boyfriend. The ups according to Bridget were someone to fix broken appliances, assistance carrying groceries, company while binge-watching television, and sex whenever you're in the mood. I flinched at the last one since I had taken to counting down my ten favorite book covers in order to throw off unwanted visuals of Jonathan and Bridget riding the hobbyhorse, but I did like the idea of unlimited sex with Nicholas.

The downs according to Bridget were dirty towels (and underwear) on the bathroom floor, the constant stench of marijuana, occasional snoring, stealing of covers in bed, and untimely farts (hers and his). Since Nicholas's faint snoring was adorbs, he didn't smoke pot, was extremely hygienic, and never farted (for real), I wasn't fazed. My earlier worries were a distant memory—except for one. Chewing on a fingernail, I asked, "Did you ever worry that moving in with Jonathan before getting engaged was a mistake?"

"Never even crossed my mind," Bridget said before taking a sip of her sangria. "Are you concerned?"

"I wasn't. Until Daneen said—"

"Why are you even listening to her? She's probably one of those women who thinks of marriage as a business proposition and cares more about the cut of the diamond than the identity of the groom." Increasing the volume of her voice as her face flushed with emotion, she added, "And by the way, getting married isn't the end all and be all. There are plenty of married couples that are miserable. Being in love is more important."

Not expecting such a heated reaction, my head swung back. In a soft voice, I said, "But what if I want both—marriage *and* love?"

Her cheeks returning to their normal fair hue, Bridget smiled at me. "Then you'll have both, whether or not you shack up with Nicholas before getting engaged. Daneen's jealous because no one, male or female, would ever want to live with her. She probably has to pay for a one-night stand."

I laughed, finally taking Daneen's jab for what it was—an attempt to make me doubt myself. I wouldn't let her. I knew living with Nicholas was going to be a grown-up and sexy version of playing house, and I couldn't wait.

Things in my personal life were at an all-time high. I couldn't say the same about my professional life yet, but like Bridget said, a lot could change in a year. With any luck, I'd be a published author, or least an agented author, by the time I turned thirty.

Chapter 4

I scanned through the emails Rob had forwarded me during one of his late-night work sessions the prior evening and tried to remain focused on what my younger sister Erin was saying to me. I was having trouble feigning interest in her search for the perfect dining room set—probably because she and her husband, Gerry, had been furnishing their four-bedroom colonial-style house in Sharon, Massachusetts, for over a year already. I smiled inwardly, envisioning my loveseat safely ensconced in my apartment (for now). I never shared my adoration of the couch with Erin because I knew if I let it slip, she'd have been on it like mosquitos in the tropics. And since her signed mortgage was likely more permanent (and grown-up) than my rental of a tiny one-bedroom apartment, she might have won any battle that ensued.

"So we nixed the five-piece Ashby for the seven-piece Ballard modern glass set."

"It sounds really pretty. Can you send me pictures or links to the website?" Nice job, Kim. Way to show sisterly support.

"It's not 'pretty,' Kim. It's elegant," Erin corrected.

"I'm sure it's very *elegant,* then. You'll have to host a dinner party at some point so we can see it for ourselves." At some point in the very distant future. I loved my sister but only *liked* her in small doses.

"Not if you host us first." Erin chuckled.

"Huh?"

"Of course, I wouldn't expect you to actually prepare dinner," Erin snorted. "Not one of your talents."

"Still lost." And a tad insulted even though she spoke the truth: the culinary arts were not my forte.

Erin sighed loudly into the phone. "We'll be in the city in March, remember?"

Then I recalled Erin's upcoming trip to the city. Gerry, a copartner for a media start-up company, was speaking at a tech conference, and Erin was tagging along for an all-expenses-paid trip to New York City. Since she'd been voluntarily unemployed for the better part of a year, she wouldn't even need to take any vacation days. "I didn't forget about our dinner," I confirmed.

"It won't be the same as standing in my dining room, but if by some miracle, the delivery goes off without a hitch, we'll be all set up by then, and I'll take pictures so you can see how the set looks with our ceramic wood tile floors and our driftwood gray walls. You can't get that from the store's website," she said knowingly. "Have you made the reservation yet?"

"Yes. We're all set for Peking Duck House."

Erin yelped, "Kim! You know I hate all Chinese food except for spare ribs. Why would I want to go to Peking Duck House?"

"You wouldn't. Which is why I plan to make a reservation for Artisanal like you asked me to do weeks ago. It's only December. We have plenty of time."

"I hate you," Erin said, but I could almost hear her relax into her chair. Or her bed if it was before noon.

"Ha. I love you too." Being the older sister was fun sometimes.

"So what's going on with you?"

Excited to share the news about Nicholas, I began, "Well, I—"

"I'm so excited for Hannah's new book."

A sudden coldness rushed through my core. "What new book?" Hannah Marshak was the queen bee in my high school, and there was no love lost between us until recently, when her debut novel, *Cut on the Bias*, was released, and her publicist asked me to review it. The prospect of actively promoting a book written by the girl who stole my diary and read excerpts to our tenth-grade class as part of her book report made my heart hurt. And although I'd never admitted it at the time (even to myself), writing was *my* passion. While I was stuck in a stilted job, my high-school nemesis was living my dream. The only possible upside to reviewing Hannah's book was to trash it (and her) to my loyal followers, and I almost did. A mouse click away from publishing a blog post outing some of Hannah's most deceitful activities in high school after reading some interviews where she feigned being humble and sweet instead of her true self—condescending and conceited—I came to my senses and chose to write an honest and positive review of *Cut on the Bias* instead.

"What new book?" I repeated. Rob's paralegal David walked past my desk and motioned toward Rob's office with a questioning look.

Trying to hide the quickening pace of my breathing in anticipation of Erin's next words, I smiled at him. Covering the phone with my hand, I whispered, "Go on in."

"It's the sequel to *Cut on the Bias*. The title is *Tearing at the Seams*. Isn't that clever?"

"Ingenious," I mumbled, while rubbing my temples. Hannah could have titled her book *Book* and my sister would still think it was, hands down, the best title in the history of the printed word. Even though Hannah called me Kim "Short" all through high school, tried to break up my relationship with Jonathan, and spread a rumor that Bridget was a lesbian, Erin had a lifelong girl crush on her and was now her biggest fan. All through high school, I worried that Erin wished Hannah was her sister instead of me, but then my mom showed me the essay Erin wrote for her college applications about the person she admired most—me. After that, I accepted Erin's worship of Hannah under the assumption if she had to rescue one of us from a burning building, she might have to think twice, but it would ultimately be me.

"It's releasing over the summer," Erin continued, completely oblivious to my lack of enthusiasm for the topic of conversation. "I thought you were friends with her on Facebook. Haven't you seen her posts?"

"No." I didn't bother to tell Erin I hid Hannah's newsfeeds. "But I'm on Facebook so infrequently." I swallowed hard. I was on Facebook and Twitter almost constantly to promote the reviews on *Pastel Is the New Black* and, most recently, to stalk literary agents. I felt beyond stupid lying to my younger sister about something so petty.

"Did you tell her about your book?"

"There's nothing to tell yet."

"You wrote a book. I'd say that's something," Erin argued.

Surprisingly touched by her show of support, I confessed, "I haven't gotten any bites from agents. Feeling kind of crummy about it."

"I have a great idea."

"What is it?" I held my breath, allowing myself to believe Erin could really help me.

"Why don't you ask Hannah for advice on getting an agent?"

I felt my face get hot. "No way."

"Why not? She'd probably be a good source of information since she's already experienced everything you're going through."

I wondered how many agent rejections Hannah got before Felicia Harrison of Harrison & Gold Literary took her on. I estimated less than ten. I hadn't queried her yet, even though she had a great reputation and, according to *Agent Inquiry*—a popular research website for authors seeking representation—she was accepting submissions in chick lit. I didn't trust how my fragile ego would handle being told by the agent who fell in love with Hannah that "my book didn't engage her as much as she would have liked" or, worse yet, getting a form rejection. "I'll think about it." When a monkey flies out of my ass.

"You do that. Okay, I'll let you get back to work. *Days of Our Lives* starts in five minutes, and I need to throw a load of laundry in the dryer. Gerry threw his boxers in with my delicates."

My happily unemployed and unencumbered baby sister led such a tortured life. "You'd better go then. I'll tell you about me and Nicholas next time."

I heard Erin suck in her breath. "Wait. What about you and Nicholas?"

"Next time. Kiss kiss." Before she could respond, I hung up with a satisfied smile. In the future, maybe she'd think twice before interrupting me right as I was about to tell her what was new in my life. But probably not.

Chapter 5

Nicholas plopped himself on my couch with an exaggerated sigh. "Whose idea was it to pack up your apartment on New Year's Eve?"

I stood in front of him and held out a fresh bottle of beer. "Some dumb chick."

Throwing me on his lap, Nicholas said, "Thank God she's cute."

"And has good taste in beer." Twisting my body so I was sitting sideways across his legs, I handed him the bottle of Westvleteren 12, a rare beer from Belgium that could only be obtained through a secret meeting with monks. My friend Caroline was in the midst of a year sabbatical from work to travel the world and had a six-pack specially delivered to me and Bridget. Neither of us were big beer drinkers, but Caroline accurately thought it would impress Nicholas and Jonathan. She refused to tell us the circumstances under which she was able to secure the beer—said it was "classified."

Joining us from the kitchen, Bridget sat down cross-legged on the floor with a bottle of Mike's Hard Lemonade and announced, "I think a break is in order." Her red hair was up in a bun, and she was wearing yoga pants the color of blue topaz, a yellow v-neck t-shirt, and pink and black zebra-printed flip-flops. Somehow, she made the unusual color combination work.

"I concur," Jonathan said from behind her. Then he clinked his beer bottle against Nicholas's. "Cheers."

Packing wasn't exactly a rockin' way to welcome the New Year, but when I mentioned it to Nicholas as a joke, he jumped on the idea and suggested we invite Bridget and Jonathan and make it a double date of sorts. I was positive Bridget and Jonathan would refuse the invitation outright and was pleasantly surprised when they were equally as enthused as Nicholas. Neither of them was interested in going to an expensive and overcrowded party in a bar and agreed to help me pack in exchange for free snacks and booze and access to my fire escape for smoking breaks. Nicholas was aware of my history with Jonathan, but understood it was squarely in the past, whereas Jonathan and Bridget's relationship was firmly rooted in the present and, with any luck, the future. I wouldn't place any bets on Nicholas and Jonathan becoming bosom buddies—if Nicholas was George Clooney, Jonathan was Sean Penn—but the four of us had a lot of laughs whenever we hung out.

Scanning the room, now filled with cardboard boxes and black Hefty bags, I said, "I think we're making good progress. Don't you agree?" I slid off of Nicholas's lap to give him room to breathe.

"We still have to decide what you're taking, what you're trashing, and what you're storing." Nicholas had offered to help me pay for a storage unit in Brooklyn for the items I wasn't going to take but didn't want to throw out, and we'd put up advertisements on eBay and Craigslist for pieces I wanted to sell, like my bed. I still had a couple of weeks before moving day to have them removed from the premises.

Bouncing on the loveseat, I said, "I want to take this."

Nicholas raised an eyebrow. "I was afraid you were going to say that."

Jabbing gently at his chest, I responded, "And I was afraid you were going to be afraid."

"It's pink," Nicholas said, as if the rest of us were color-blind.

I dropped my chin. "I like pink."

"But—"

I put a finger to his lips. "No buts. The loveseat and I are a package deal."

Nicholas stared me down for a few moments, but I wouldn't relent. Finally, with a loud exhalation, he said, "Fine. But how about we keep it in the bedroom? It can face the bed and be your special 'lady' couch. You can read all of your pastel books while sitting on it. This way, we can leave my gray leather couch in the living room since it's too big to fit in the bedroom."

A smile breaking out on my face, I said, "I like that idea."

Nicholas returned my smile and kissed me on the cheek. "See? I promised you we'd figure it out."

Jonathan snorted. "You're a much better man than me, Nicholas. A pink couch?"

Narrowing my eyes at him, I countered, "Need I remind you Bridget has a purple couch and matching purple chairs? I don't recall you insisting she refurnish before agreeing to move into her luxury apartment in the sky."

"Purple is psychedelic," Jonathan argued, scratching his shaved head. I was still getting used to his new hairstyle—or lack thereof. In his pre-Bridget days, Jonathan let his curly locks grow until they were unruly and tangled. This was a much better look.

Matter of factly, Nicholas said, "I'm a man who knows how to pick my battles. I can live with a pink couch, but I can't live without my Kimmie."

I released an appreciative sigh as my heart flip-flopped. "Thanks, sweets."

Leaning his back against my gray-stained wooden coffee table, which doubled as a storage chest and would probably be left behind in the move, Jonathan asked, "How do your parental figures feel about this move?" Since we dated in high school, he knew my father tended to be passive-aggressively overprotective compared to my more laid-back mother when it came to my relationships with the opposite sex.

"My mom was totally fine with it. My dad mumbled something about cows and milk into his newspaper." Daneen's comment about waiting for a ring before moving in pierced my brain space, but I quickly brushed it aside.

"You'll always be his little girl," Bridget said fondly.

"Once a parent, always a parent," Nicholas agreed, getting up to raise the volume on the Foo Fighters' song playing on his iPod.

"Precisely why I won't be having any daughters. I don't want to spend my middle-age years chasing away horny teenage boys," Jonathan said.

"How do you plan to avoid having daughters? As far as I know, it's still not possible to choose the gender of your children," I asked.

"I don't plan to have sons either," Jonathan said.

"What do you plan to have? Puppies? Or pussy cats?" Nicholas and I exchanged grins.

"I won't be having children. I never want to get married either," Jonathan said simply.

Widening my eyes in surprise, I turned to Bridget for her reaction, but she had gotten up and was headed to the kitchen with her back to me. I suspected Jonathan's stance on holy matrimony was the driving force behind Bridget's heated view of marriage during our one-on-one discussion a couple weeks earlier.

Nicholas nodded at Jonathan. "I respect that, man." Sitting back down next to me, he closed his eyes and tapped his fingers on my knee as he hummed along to the music.

The timing had never felt right to ask Nicholas about his own views on marriage, but Jonathan had now provided the perfect opening to do it in a casual manner. Feigning nonchalance, I asked him, "Do you never want to get married either?" I could almost picture Daneen wiggling her ring finger at me while chanting, "Never gonna get it."

Nicholas stopped humming and opened his eyes. "No, I want to get married, have kids, the whole shebang."

To myself, I said, *Thank God*. To Nicholas, I calmly responded, "Cool." Then I bent over and touched my toes to hide my smile.

Bridget returned to the living room with a container of the corn and tomato salad I had made and a bag of tortilla chips. After dipping a chip in the salad, she popped it in her mouth and looked pointedly at me. After swallowing, she asked, "Have you scoped out the coffee shops in the new hood?"

"I have. There's a place called Ground Support not too far from Nicholas's apartment where I intend to spend lots of evenings writing and maintaining the blog on the nights he works late, living the glamorous life of a lawyer."

"First of all, it won't be *my* apartment anymore. It's *our* place. And second of all, you should consider yourself lucky I didn't follow in my dad's footsteps and study medicine. I could be performing surgery at all hours of the day, even holidays. Although he would have preferred it that way," Nicholas said, mumbling the last part.

"I consider myself very lucky," I said, rubbing circles along his back. "And yes, it will be our place. And I can't wait."

Nicholas put his arm around me and kissed my cheek. "Me neither. It will be nice to have a little woman around to make me snacks and tidy up the place." In response to my mock glare, he loaded a tortilla chip with salad and brought it to my mouth.

"If your little woman is anything like my little woman, I wouldn't count on it," Jonathan said with a teasing glance at Bridget. When she pouted up at him, he bent down and embraced her from behind. She threw her head back, and he kissed her on the lips.

I observed Bridget and Jonathan from my spot on the couch. He was crazy about her—of that much I was certain. But I feared their relationship was headed for trouble if he was serious about never wanting to get married.

A few hours, several trash bags, thousands of calories, and one ball drop later, we said goodnight to Bridget and Jonathan. While Nicholas showed Jonathan a new music-streaming app on his phone, Bridget followed me to my hall closet where I removed their winter jackets. "Thanks so much for spending your New Year's Eve helping me pack."

"That's what best friends are for. BFFAEUDDUP, right?"

Best friends forever and ever until death do us part. The "secret" acronym we had devised in the seventh grade. "Speaking of 'until death do us part,' what's up with Jonathan not wanting to have kids?"

"What about it?" Crossing her arms over her chest, she said, "The house in the suburbs with the white picket fence and rugrats is not everyone's American dream."

Taken aback by her defensive stance, I backpedaled. "Of course not. I have no desire to live in the suburbs either. I, um, was just surprised to hear Jonathan didn't want to get married or have kids."

"Next time we talk about it, I'll conference you in." Bridget chuckled.

She joked, but I feared she was pushing aside her own desires for Jonathan's sake, and I didn't like it. As an only child, when we were younger, Bridget talked about having two daughters three years apart, like Erin and me. Leaning toward her, I said, "Any man who loves you will hold your dreams as tightly as his own."

Bridget rolled her eyes. "Like I told you before, marriage is not the end all be all. Love is what matters. I love Jonathan, and he loves me. End of story."

I knew better than to push, at least not yet, so when Nicholas and Jonathan joined us a few seconds later, I dropped the subject.

After hugging them goodbye, Nicholas and I traipsed to my bed where we collapsed on top of my peach duvet cover without uttering a word. I was tempted to take a shower to wipe the dust balls off of my body but was currently incapable of moving from my position flat on my back.

When I heard Nicholas say, "Happy New Year, Kimmie Long," I opened my eyes to find him lying sideways and smiling at me.

I turned on my side so we were facing each other. "Happy New Year, Nicholas Strong." Even after months of dating, I still got a kick out of the rhyming of our last names. I was positive it was kismet.

"Did you have fun?"

The obvious answer was "No." I did not have fun. Sorting through junk I hardly recalled purchasing was hard work. But when I opened my mouth, the answer I gave was, "Yes." And it was true. It was probably one of the best New Year's Eves I'd ever had, and I knew it was because I'd spent it with Nicholas. It was time. As my heart surged, I gazed into his eyes and reached out my hand to cup his chin. "I love you." Even though he'd said it first, I swallowed hard after hearing the phrase leave my lips.

His chocolate-brown eyes opened wide. "You don't have to say it just because I did."

A bit stung, I responded, "Do you really think that's the reason I told you I loved you? Because you said it to me?"

Nicholas moved toward me on the bed and placed his warm hand on my skin right where my shirt ended and my jeans started. "No. I know you really love me. But I also know it's not easy for you to let your guard down, and I don't want to pressure you. I know how you feel in here." He pointed at my heart.

Maybe it was from sheer exhaustion, or perhaps it was because no other guy I'd dated ever saw through me quite like Nicholas, but my eyes welled up. His intuition where I was concerned made my heart swell and palpitate in equal measure. "God, I love you." It was much easier to say the second time.

There was nothing like a mutual expression of love to bring on a second wind, and all need to play dead and recover from the hard work of the night was replaced by a desire to burn even more calories having my way with Nicholas. Packing was rewarding, but not nearly as satisfying as my sexy time with Nicholas. As he lay spent next to me afterward, I listened to the sound of his breathing gradually slow down until he fell asleep. I stayed up for a little while, unmoving and content to feel his body pressed against mine until my eyes closed too. When I opened them next, the sun was rising, and Nicholas was still asleep with a slight curl in his closed lips.

Chapter 6

After finishing my tuna sandwich, I pushed my tray to the side and pulled up the amended copy of my query letter on my phone. The version I used for my first twenty queries for *A Blogger's Life* began with a one-sentence teaser about the book, followed by a brief synopsis, and concluded with a bio listing my relevant publishing background. I knew an agent wouldn't care that I went to Syracuse University unless it was her alma mater (and probably not even then), but she might care about the ever-growing popularity of *Pastel Is the New Black* and the almost ten thousand likes on my Facebook page because it demonstrated my existing platform. One of my author friends suggested I send out a few queries with a distinct format to see if it made a difference in the type of response I received. Since fifteen agents rejected me outright, my track record could only improve. The new version began with a witty sentence about how my real-life role as a popular and sought-out book blogger lent itself to my ability to write a heartfelt, true-to-life, and humorous depiction of a blogger's life. I decided to send out five queries with this version to see if I got any bites.

Satisfied the letter was good to go, I glanced at my watch, confirmed I still had fifteen minutes left of my lunch hour, and checked Facebook. When I saw I had a new email—from Hannah Marshak—my pulse quickened. Biting my knuckles, I read it.

> *Hi Kimmie,*
> *Or is your man the only one allowed to call you that? He is*

still your man, right? I hope The Shitter hasn't gotten her claws into him. Must keep that one at arm's length. Although she's quite tall and you...(haha)

I hope all is well with you. Things are sensationnelle for me. As I'm sure you're aware, my second novel, the sequel to Cut on the Bias, *is being released on August 11th. No doubt hordes of romance-starved women will be devouring* Tearing at the Seams *poolside, along with their frozen cocktails, and I could not be more pleased.*

I wanted to give you and Pastel Is the New Black *the opportunity to participate in what will undoubtedly be the pre-publication tour of the year. You can do a cover reveal or perhaps an interview.*

I'm sure you're thrilled to be asked, so please let me know as soon as possible while space is still available.

Xoxo
Hannah Marshak
Bestselling author of Cut on the Bias

Here we go again. I let out a sigh and placed my head on the table. The cover reveal was only the first of many requests I expected to receive from Hannah regarding the release of *Tearing at the Seams* in the coming months. A request to read and review the book would undoubtedly follow, and I wouldn't be surprised if I were asked to host a giveaway for the upcoming one-year book birthday of *Cut on the Bias*. Yes, it was my job as a book blogger and, yes, I'd be insulted if she and Candace, her PR person, didn't consider exposure on *Pastel Is the New Black* an important part of the book's promotional campaign, but I didn't have to like it.

I sat up and contemplated the bright side—there had to be a bright side. At least this time, I received the request directly from Hannah instead of Candace, her publicist. And the way Hannah ragged on Daneen in her note as if we were allies made me question whether she still considered me "beneath" her. (The two of them went to the same college during freshman year, and it was Hannah who gave me the scoop on Daneen's drug-induced fecal incontinence while having sex.)

Another bright side: I'd read some lousy books lately between shoddy editing and storylines that just didn't pull me in. On the contrary, even with minor constructive criticism, I thoroughly enjoyed *Cut on the Bias*, thought it was a standout debut effort, and gave it four pink champagne flutes. If Hannah's storytelling skills were consistent in her sophomore novel, I was bound to enjoy *Tearing at the Seams* at least as much. And if her writing benefited even slightly from experience, it was possible I'd like it even more.

If I was being honest with myself—something I was attempting primarily as a means of self-improvement, and also because of Nicholas's frustrating ability to see right through me—I didn't consider a five-pink-champagne-flutes review of *Tearing at the Seams* to be much of a bright side. If *Tearing at the Seams* was as successful as *Cut on the Bias*, it would solidify Hannah as a true up-and-coming darling of chick lit. I no longer fantasized about Hannah's untimely weight gain, onset of acne, hair loss, gas emission (the list goes on), but the thought of her star shining as brightly as Sophie Kinsella's in the chick lit universe—one I worked tirelessly to keep alive—left me cold.

I figured Hannah was too busy chatting with her dream team of agent, editor, and publicist to expect an immediate response to her email, and because my lunch hour was now officially over, I returned my phone to my purse, tossed the remains of my lunch in the garbage can, and made my way back to my desk.

I stood in the center of Nicholas's apartment—now officially *our* apartment—and did a one-eighty. It had taken an entire weekend, but I was now completely moved in, and my clothes amassed half (more like three-quarters) of his closet space. My loveseat—or "lady couch" as Nicholas liked to call it—fit perfectly by the foot of his (our) queen-size bed. While looking on Etsy for the perfect housewarming gift for us to share, I hit the jackpot when I found a canvas painting with the words *Let It Be* drawn across a hot pink background. I knew Nicholas would be too enthused about adding to his already substantial collection of Beatles paraphernalia—a decorative light-switch plate cover, several watercolor paintings, and vintage painted plates and beer glasses—to refuse to hang it based on the color. At least it wasn't pastel.

"Kimmie," Nicholas called from behind me.

He was sitting on the couch with his legs stretched out in front of him and his feet crossed, grinning at me like he was holding in a secret.

I dipped my head down toward my toes and up the length of my body checking to see if I had packing tape hanging from my clothes before meeting his gaze again. "What?"

He chuckled. "Nothing. You're studying the place like you've never been here before."

I sat down next to him and planted my hand on his thigh. "It's different now. I live here." As the words came out of my mouth, I felt the pitter-patter of my heart.

Placing his hand on top of mine and squeezing it, Nicholas said, "Yup. With all of your stuff moved in and your old keys dropped off in your landlord's mailbox, there's no turning back. You okay with that?"

"I'm more than okay with it. Just a bit nerve-wracking." Bridget assured me it was completely normal to be anxious when making such a major life change. Nicholas had affirmed her comments by confessing to sharing my jitters before promising he'd make the best roommate ever. Leaning my head on his shoulder, I began to close my eyes, but right before they shut, I caught sight of something. Rising from the couch, I reached for Nicholas's hand. "Time to consummate."

Standing up and pulling me with him toward the bedroom, Nicholas said, "I like the way you think, Kimmie Long."

"I was referring to something else entirely." I giggled.

Nicholas scratched his jaw and furrowed his brow. "Okay…"

"Come with me," I said, dragging him to the far corner of his living room where a guitar and banjo were hung over a small brown upright piano, which leaned against the wall.

I'd had no idea Nicholas had taken piano and bass guitar lessons through most of his childhood and early teen years until he'd tried to impress me the morning following the first time we slept together by playing his harmonica and altering the chorus of "Penny Lane" to an R-rated ditty about our dalliance. Although he was a far better lawyer than musician, when I watched his long fingers play with the keys, I always wished he were playing me. I tapped one side of the wooden piano bench before placing my bum on the black velvet cushion on the other side. "Sit."

Looking sideways at me, Nicholas did as he was told. "I thought you wanted to consummate."

"That's exactly what we're doing," I said, hitting the second F key three times in a row. Tapping the F key again before hitting the E and D keys and back to F three times, I added, "We can't officially join our hearts and souls in cohabitation until we join our fingers in a duet of 'Heart and Soul' on your piano."

"Ah. You're the melody, and I'm the bass. Gotcha," Nicholas said as he caught the rhythm and joined in on his part.

When he one-upped me by playing with both hands while I remained a one-finger wonder, I muttered, "Show-off." Still, as we played together in harmony, laughing the entire time, the warmth in my belly assured me taking our relationship up a notch was the best decision ever.

We were on our sixth or seventh repeat of the song when Nicholas's phone rang. Still laughing, he placed the phone on speaker while I continued to play my part as softly as possible by barely pressing the keys. "Hi, Mom."

"It's not Mom," a deep masculine voice responded.

Nicholas picked up the phone. "Dad. Is Mom all right?"

I stopped playing and observed him walk to the couch while chewing on a knuckle. He must have felt me watching him because he looked up and shook his head. "Everything's fine," he mouthed.

I whispered, "Good," and flipped through some of his classical sheet music.

"No, I'm home. I took off to move Kim in."

I looked up and smiled at the sound of my name as Nicholas stood up and paced the living room.

"No, they didn't mind. I've only taken a couple of days since I started." He flopped himself onto the reclining chair. "I can't go in this weekend. We have plans, but I'll make up the time." He stood up again and leaned against the piano. "I'll think about it, okay?"

Resting my chin in my hand, I watched Nicholas with curiosity, wishing the phone was still on speaker so I could hear his father's end of the conversation. Whatever he was saying appeared to fluster Nicholas, and now his eyes were closed. "Good for Natalie. I'm proud of her too. Okay. Bye." He hung up the phone and gestured toward the sheet music on my lap. "Up for some Beethoven?"

Tilting my head to the side, I asked, "What did your dad want?"

"Nothing important." He shrugged.

"You sure? You seemed upset." Nicholas didn't talk about his parents much. All I knew was they lived in Vermont, and his dad was a doctor. I hadn't met them yet, but assumed I would be included in the next visit now that we lived together. Nicholas had already met my folks the August before when they escaped the heat and humidity of tropical Boca Raton—where they moved for an early retirement—to lavish in the heat and humidity of smelly New York City.

Nicholas smiled and closed the distance between us. "Nothing a little consummation can't fix." Pulling me toward the bedroom, he added, "And I mean that in the biblical sense this time."

Chapter 7

Tossing a stack of paper-clipped documents on my desk, Rob announced, "Squad drinks at five at Banc," before scurrying back to his office as if the hallway were on fire.

"Yes, sir," I said as enthusiastically as I could muster, even though the thought of spending the evening with my colleagues when I could be catching up on my reviews, sending out more query letters, or working on my next novel didn't thrill me. Rob's occasional department happy hours were so much more fun when Nicholas had been a member of the "squad" until the previous summer when he left to work for one of the firm's clients. In fact, it was at squad drinks, specifically at Banc Café, where Nicholas and I had our first real conversation. I suspected any discussion I engaged in tonight would not be nearly as arousing, but considering my paltry legal secretary salary, combined with my share of our pricey New York City rent, and my expensive taste in clothes, I couldn't justify turning down the opportunity for a free drink. Maybe I would text Nicholas to meet me somewhere else instead of going directly home. After even a single drink, I wouldn't trust myself to post a review or, God forbid, send out a query letter. If productivity was out of the question, I might as well make the most of it.

"Kim?"

I responded to Daneen's cold stare with a fake smile before offering a genuine one to David, who was standing next to her. "What's up?"

David grinned at me. "Cool umbrella," he said, referring to my new bubble umbrella, which I had laid open by my desk to dry after the morning rain shower. It was adorned with musical notes and the words "Singing in the Rain."

"Isn't it great? Nicholas bought it for me."

"Amy would love it," David said. "She—"

Daneen cleared her throat, interrupting him mid-sentence and wiping the smile off of my face in one fell swoop. I assumed she didn't share David's enthusiasm toward my umbrella or more likely, she resented that it was a gift from Nicholas.

"We're going for department drinks this evening. If anyone calls, please send them to my voicemail," Daneen said.

At least she said "please" this time. "I would...except I'm joining you guys," I responded with an apologetic shrug. Trying to be helpful, I added, "Do you want me to set your phone to go directly to voicemail?"

Waving her hand in dismissal she replied, "Never mind" before stomping away. I heard her mutter something about the firm wasting money buying drinks for the staff before she beckoned David to follow her.

With a sheepish grin, he said, "I'm glad you're coming tonight."

I smiled fondly at David. He lacked the "edge" I found attractive in men, but clean-cut and All-American, I could see what other girls, including his fiancée Amy, might find appealing. And he was such a pleasant guy. Even Daneen kept her abuse of him to a minimum, although Nicholas used to complain about how long it took him to complete assignments because he tended to tread as if under the influence of a muscle relaxer. "That makes one of you. Thank you."

It was no secret Daneen didn't consider my contribution to the department worthy of any distinction, much less Rob's loyalty to me. But while it came as no surprise she didn't think I earned my invitation to drinks, the ease with which she voiced her stuck-up opinion made my skin crawl. I was certain she'd find some way to cut me down and make me regret my attendance tonight. I released an audible sigh and reminded myself to accept the things I could not change. Inhale love. Exhale stress.

With the five minutes I had before it would be acceptable to gather my things and freshen up, I checked my Gmail account. My eyes immediately took notice of a new message from Ginny Webber, and I gasped in a combination of eagerness and dread. This was it. My dream agent. I'd memorized every blog she'd ever written on how to write the perfect query letter, how to attract an agent, and the top reasons an agent passed on a query. Had my research paid off? The answer was waiting for me at the click of a mouse. Partially covering my line of vision with my left hand, I opened the email and read the message between my fingers:

Dear Ms. Long,
Thanks for submitting your query for A Blogger's Life. *It's an interesting premise. Can you send me the first three chapters?*

Thanks,
Ginny

Bouncing in my chair, I yelped out loud and reached for my phone with shaky hands.

Bridget answered in one ring. "Hola, chica."

"Ginny Webber asked for a partial of *A Blogger's Life*!"

"Hip hip hooray," Bridget hooted. "And what exactly is a partial?"

"The first three chapters." I cradled the phone in my ear while I brought up the newest version of the document on my work computer. "This is huge, Bridge."

"I'm so happy for you. Celebrate tonight?"

"I wish I could, but I have squad drinks." After skimming the first page on the screen, I copied and pasted the first three chapters into a new Word document and printed them out to read one more time. I'd arrive late at Banc Café, but it would be worth it when I told Rob the reason behind my tardiness. "I need to call Nicholas."

Laughing, Bridget said, "I'm so flattered you told me first."

"It's a reflex after more than a decade of friendship."

"Whatever the reason, I'm so happy for you."

"Cross your fingers and toes she likes it enough to request the full."

"I'm guessing a 'full' means the entire book?"

"You're a quick study."

"There's hope for me yet. Consider my fingers, toes, and eyes crossed."

"Thanks." I ended the call as Rob walked out of his office with his jacket and briefcase. "Coming?"

"I'll be there in a few."

"Okay."

After he left, I removed the first three chapters from the printer and carefully read them out loud as quietly as possible. Once I was certain there were no typos, I drafted my response to Ginny.

Dear Ginny,

Thank you so much for your interest in A Blogger's Life. *As requested, I have attached the first three chapters.*

I look forward to hearing from you at your convenience and thank you very much for your consideration.

Best regards,
Kim

I debated telling her she was my dream agent, but what if she wasn't the warm-and-fuzzy type and didn't take well to ass-kissing? Deciding it was better to play it cool than gush, I kept it simple. After printing out a draft of the message, I reviewed it carefully to make sure I didn't leave out any words, use incorrect punctuation, or spell Ginny's name (or mine) wrong in my frenzy. When I was finally certain the message was flawless, I held my breath and released the email. After sending Nicholas a quick text with the news, I headed out to meet the others.

Arriving at Banc Café at five forty-five, I weaved through the crowd of patrons taking advantage of the restaurant's cheap happy-hour specials, and I found my group at the back. Along with several empty lipstick-stained martini glasses on the rectangular cherrywood table was a half-eaten platter of assorted appetizers.

Placing my coat across an empty chair, I said, "Sorry I'm late."

From her spot on the couch on the other side of the table, Daneen raised an eyebrow. "Working overtime, I presume?" She snorted as if positive that wasn't the reason.

I plastered on a fake smile. "Not this time, Daneen. Although I do need you to approve my OT for last month," I said to Rob, who was sitting in the chair next to me. Turning back toward Daneen, I went on to explain the cause of my delay. "An agent requested a partial of my manuscript, and I didn't want to keep her waiting."

"Sounds promising," Rob said, raising his glass. "Wait. You don't have a drink. What are you having?"

"A peach Bellini. Thanks."

As Rob excused himself to order my drink, I turned back to the others. I couldn't contain my smile. My first request for a partial, and it was from Ginny Webber. I allowed myself to imagine the possibilities of being her client. Maybe Olivia Geffen would agree to write a blurb for *A Blogger's Life.*

"It's insane what's passing for literature these days," Daneen said, before wincing as if she sucked on a lemon. "All you need is a brainless heroine and a controlling hero. Pepper it with some raunchy sex scenes, and you're guaranteed to hit the bestseller list."

I doubted Daneen could surrender enough control to engage in "raunchy sex," much less write about it and felt bile rise in my throat attempting a visual of the former. "My books have none of those things, so I guess I can kiss my chances of becoming a bestselling author goodbye." I frowned and raised my shoulders in a mock defeated shrug before accepting my drink from Rob and taking a large sip. While conversation turned to topics more lawyerly (a.k.a. less titillating), I discreetly sent Nicholas a text: "Daneen got me thinking about raunchy sex. I'd like to have some with you tonight if you're up for it."

Nicholas responded almost immediately. "I'm always 'up' for it if you know what I mean, Kimmie. Dare I ask how Daneen got you pondering X-rated thoughts?"

I texted back: "I could tell you, but I wouldn't want to ruin the mood." I placed the phone to the side and rejoined the conversation. David and Amy were nearing the end of their engagement and in the final planning stages of the wedding. They had narrowed down their honeymoon destinations to Barbados, Aruba, and the Cayman Islands, and Daneen and Rob were comparing notes on the Ritz Carlton in each location.

"There's no Ritz Carlton in Barbados yet, but Sandy Lane Hotel is a premier luxury resort worth considering," Rob said.

I resisted the urge to laugh. David was doing such a good job pretending to take it all in, but I knew he couldn't afford to stay at any of those hotels unless he could bill his honeymoon to a client.

Glancing at my phone, I saw a new text from Nicholas. "You needn't say more. When will you be home? I'm still at work."

Surmising it would take me about thirty minutes to finish my drink and twenty minutes to get home, I wrote back: "A little more than an hour," which gave me time to empty not only my glass, but also my bladder before I left the bar.

"I'll aim for the same. Long and Strong unite."

"Literally. See you soon, babe."

I smiled to myself at how nicely my life was taking shape since I got out of my own way and acknowledged I had dreams worth chasing. Not only did I have an amazing live-in boyfriend to show for it, but my novel had sparked the interest of a hotshot New York City literary agent.

About ten minutes later, Rob reached for his briefcase. "I should get back to the office. Anyone want anything else before I close out the tab?"

I knocked back the rest of my drink. "I'm out of here too.

Meeting Nicholas for dinner." It wasn't technically a lie depending on how narrowly you defined "dinner."

"I'll take one more beer," David said with a sheepish grin.

As predicted, Daneen said, "I'll come back to the office with you."

Once we exchanged our farewells, I walked around the bar to the bathroom. While washing my hands in the dimly lit restroom, my mind wandered to the three chapters of my book waiting in Ginny's inbox. According to QuerySpy, her response time to a partial request was anywhere from forty-eight hours to six weeks. It was unlikely she'd read my pages yet, but I knew I'd still check my email at least a dozen times between the bar and my apartment. At least I'd have Nicholas to occupy my time once I got home and for the remainder of the night.

"Honey, I'm home," I called out as I entered our apartment less than an hour later. "What are you listening to?" I didn't recognize the music playing out of the speakers in the living room, but every other word was "grind."

I dropped my keys on the kitchen counter as Nicholas's voice chimed in from behind me. "It's 'Grind With Me' by Pretty Ricky. I was setting the mood."

I turned around. "Setting the mood for what ex—" I stopped mid-sentence as my hand flew to my mouth.

Wearing nothing but a pair of black mesh briefs and holding a set of handcuffs in one hand and a fire-red silk blindfold in the other, Nicholas shrugged. "What? You said you wanted to engage in raunchy sex. Have at me."

I burst out laughing, all thoughts of Ginny Webber were temporarily forgotten as I wiggled my fingers in preparation to peel off Nicholas's cheesy underwear as soon as possible.

As I woke with the smell of hazelnut coffee teasing my nostrils, the first thing I did was let out a snort in remembrance of Nicholas's getup from the night before. The second thing I did was reach for my phone on the nightstand and confirm Ginny Webber had not yet responded to my partial. Dropping the phone on the bed next to me, I leaned back with a yawn as Nicholas joined me in the bedroom holding a cup of coffee. He had done such a thorough job distracting me with his risqué seduction, I never got around to showing him Ginny's email. No time like the present. Excitedly, I picked up my phone. "Can I show you Ginny's note? She said my book had an 'interesting premise.'"

With an apologetic frown, Nicholas said, "Can you show me later? I'm playing catch-up at work, so I should jet." Placing the coffee mug on the night table, he kissed me on the forehead. "Have a good day, Kimmie."

Running my fingers through my hair, I responded, "No worries. Enjoy your day too." As Nicholas left the room and then the apartment, I reached for my coffee. After a few sips, I was awake enough to get out of bed and take a shower. But first, I'd check my email one more time.

Not really expecting a response from Ginny for at least several days and merely resigned to be another obsessive-compulsive author who would likely refresh my email a hundred-odd times until she eventually did, my eyes bugged out at seeing a message from her delivered only four minutes earlier—around the time Nicholas kissed me goodbye. A rolling feeling in my stomach, I sat on the toilet with the lid closed to gain my bearings. If she responded this quickly with a request for a full, it would mean she really liked it. I closed my eyes and gave a silent prayer. Then, I opened my eyes and with a heavy exhalation, read the message.

Chapter 8

Dear Kim,

Thanks for submitting A Blogger's Life *to Webber Literary. You have an engaging writing style, and I enjoyed the read. However, after much consideration, I do not believe it is a novel I can sell in the current market.*

You are a talented author. Please feel free to query me in the future.

Best of luck.

Regards,
Ginny

I sniffed back my tears. After much consideration? It had been less than twenty-four hours since I sent her the pages. I couldn't even console myself with the possibility she had carefully deliberated the pros and cons of taking a chance on me, since she had made her decision faster than a junkie just said yes. And as much as I wanted to blame it on the publishing world's current disfavor of chick lit, other writers were succeeding where I was failing. Case in point: Hannah Marshak. If I were as talented as Hannah, Ginny might have at least asked for the full manuscript.

Deciding to take a sick day, I slunk back to the bed and crawled under the covers. I couldn't face my colleagues, especially not Daneen. I should have kept my big mouth shut, but no, I had to prematurely tell the entire squad my dream agent asked to read the first few chapters of my book. And now, I'd have to tell them she declined representation without even finding out how it ended.

Perhaps "author" was not meant to be on my resume. Maybe it was time I accepted my fate to be an uninspired legal secretary by day and sought-after book blogger by night. I had a supportive family, a loyal best friend, and a sexy live-in boyfriend who loved me. What else could I ask for?

I curled in the fetal position, pulled the blankets tighter over my head, and tried to fall back to sleep even as my heart wrenched.

Later that night, Nicholas climbed into bed next to me with his laptop, a stack of papers, and a bowl of chocolate-chip ice cream. "She said you were a talented author. That counts for something, right?"

"That and a bowl of ice cream will get me a bowl of ice cream," I replied dryly.

"She's only one agent," Nicholas said, taking a spoonful into his mouth before flipping through his documents.

Even as my stomach quaked in dread, my mouth salivated as I watched him eat. My hunger was not surprising considering I had hibernated within the confines of my bed the entire day, getting up only to use the bathroom and boil water for a single cup of soup. "She's more than an agent. She was *the* agent."

Nicholas frowned as he shuffled through his papers.

"My dream agent," I said, scooching closer to him on the bed.

Nicholas placed his documents in front of him and turned to me. "Kathryn Stockett got sixty rejections."

"Who else, besides Kathryn?" I held my breath, hoping for more evidence that many famous authors before me received the brush-off before finally landing an agent and reaching bestselling status.

Nicholas pursed his lips. "I don't know, but I'm sure there are hundreds of them."

I tried to shake off my disappointment. It was silly to expect Nicholas to possess encyclopedic knowledge of authors' histories with agent submissions. But man, how I wished for more proof that even the most successful writers didn't get there overnight. With each rejection I received, it became harder to take comfort in the statement, "She's only one agent." What if I ran out of agents to query?

Nicholas dipped his spoon into the ice cream dish once again, and my mouth opened in anticipation. If anyone could soothe my pain, even temporarily, it was Ben & Jerry.

Bringing the spoon to his own lips, Nicholas said with his mouth half-full, "Her loss, Kimmie."

This I knew to be false. "But—"

"Shrug it off and move on," he said, before returning his focus to his laptop.

Remembering something, panic rose in my throat, and I said, "Promise me you won't say anything to Daneen."

Nicholas glanced toward me only to roll his eyes. "Seriously?"

"Yes." I groaned. "Oh, the pleasure she'd derive from throwing it in my face."

"No comment," Nicholas mumbled, resuming his typing.

I placed my hand across his monitor to regain his attention. "What do you mean, 'no comment'?"

"You give her way too much power."

My eyes bugged out as I felt heat rise to my face. "She's been nasty since the first time we met without any provocation on my part. And you know it. I, on the other hand, have always taken the high road. I have dirt on her I've never shared with a soul." Not entirely true, as I had divulged the secret to Bridget, but she didn't count since Daneen had never met her. I turned on my side with my back to Nicholas.

Nicholas sighed. "Try to cut the girl some slack. She's had a tough life."

I pictured Daneen in her well-fitted Chanel suits with her chin upturned in confidence. "What's this about a tough life?" I asked, flipping over to face him.

"Her dad was a deadbeat, and her mom didn't make enough

money on her secretary's salary to afford more than the basics. Daneen had to pay her own way through college and law school with no encouragement from her mom, who saw no value in a woman's education despite her own poverty. To this day, she rarely comments on Daneen's successes."

Remembering her attempt the previous year to put down my alma mater, I sat up straighter in the bed. "Why did she say she wished her parents let her go to a party school when they clearly had no interest in her college education either way?"

Nicholas shrugged. "No clue. Trying to make you feel bad, probably."

"Aha. I'm sorry she had such a tough upbringing, but she seems to have come through it just fine. And it doesn't excuse her treatment of me."

"I don't know what her deal is, but she's not my concern—you are." He patted my back in a circular motion. "In any event, I'm sorry."

I flipped over. "I forgive you."

"Good." He smiled toward his computer monitor.

"Whatcha doin'?"

Continuing to type, he said, "Working. Still catching up on what I missed helping you move in."

Tickling his arm, I said, "I sure hope I'm worth the overtime."

"Uh-huh." Nicholas tousled my hair absently without turning around. "You're going in tomorrow, right?"

"Unfortunately."

"No one ever got promoted for taking the most personal days," he said with a wry grin. "One of my dad's 'isms.' Did I ever tell you he never called out during his entire time in medical school?"

With a crooked smile, I said, "I can see where you get your drive." By going to law school, Nicholas broke the Strong family tradition of studying medicine, and I suspected this decision was the force behind his ambition. If he wasn't in the medical field like the rest of his clan, at least he'd be at the top of the legal field.

"He's way more type A. You'll meet him soon enough."

"I can't wait," I said, even as butterflies danced in my belly. Nicholas's parents were coming in from Vermont the following month, and I was meeting them for the first time. What if they pictured their son with an attorney, medical professional, or at the very least, an agented author?

As if reading my mind, Nicholas said, "She was only one agent. One of many. You'll see."

I nodded at him, like an eager puppy, urging him to continue— to implore me not to give up.

"Atta girl, Kimmie," he said and gave me a peck on the nose. With the pep talk successfully concluded on his end, he fixated his attention back to his work while I rolled over on my stomach with more than a lingering of doubt.

Chapter 9

Glancing at the retro glitter wall clock above her entertainment center, I said to Bridget, "It's time."

Bridget took one more sip of prosecco before leaning over her laptop and clicking the icon to start a new video chat with Caroline. It was nine in the morning in China, the current stop on Caroline's world tour. I'd met Caroline years earlier in a book club and was thrilled when she hit it off so well with Bridget too. Caroline risked a coveted position as vice president of a Fortune 500 company, along with a salary in the high six figures, to chase her dream of traveling the world. She said it was now or never—before she got married and had kids and saw the fantasy disappear in her rearview mirror.

Even though she was currently romantically unattached, and a wedding didn't seem to be in her near future, I admired her courage. And I was touched when she said I inspired her by following my heart and completing my first novel despite my rampant fear of failing—a fear seemingly destined to become reality.

After a few moments of staring at the computer monitor and listening to the outgoing ringtone, there was a notification that Caroline was joining the chat, and then her radiant face appeared on the screen. Waving at us, she said, "Hi girls."

"Hi," Bridget and I said in chorus.

"You look so good," I gushed, immediately noticing the brightness in her blue eyes and the healthy color in her typically fair-skinned cheeks. Her blond locks were pulled back into a long ponytail. "Your hair is getting so long."

"Thank you." Caroline beamed. "Six months of not working does wonders for the skin and yes, I'm due for a trimming. I made an appointment to have my hair cut and styled at Christophe Robin when I get to Paris."

"I'm so jealous," Bridget said, even though I knew she was undesirous of a break from her budding career as a self-employed web designer—even more so now since Jonathan, a freelance graphic designer, shared the office located within the confines of their apartment.

"Me too," I said. "What's Shanghai like?"

"Times Square, except I can't read any of the billboards." Caroline laughed.

After we finished our initial greetings, Caroline filled us in about her trip, including some of the edible "delicacies" she'd had the guts to try. Her adventures in food sounded more like an episode of *The Amazing Race* than a vacation, and I was relieved the takeout Chinese food Bridget and I ate for dinner had already been digested or I might have needed a barf bag. Eventually, the conversation was steered toward my living arrangements. I told the girls about my fight with Nicholas over whether the toilet seat should be left up or down. Nicholas eventually conceded it should remain down at all times after I almost fell in when peeing in the middle of the night. At first, he tried to blame the near miss on my petite frame, but I argued my small behind was precisely why the lid on the toilet seat needed to be placed down. Then he said I should have been a lawyer.

"Sounds like things are going well," Caroline said with a chuckle. "How's the agent search?"

Through my peripheral vision, I caught Bridget slide her hand across her throat.

Caroline's eyes opened wide. "I'm sorry. I didn't mean to upset you."

Shrugging, I replied, "No worries. Nothing new to tell. More rejections, including one from my dream agent. I might as well give up." I turned away from the monitor momentarily to avoid seeing pity reflected in Caroline's eyes.

"And Hannah's second book is coming out in a few months," Bridget said.

"Way to rub it in, Bridge," I muttered, my eyes still cast downward.

"Sorry, K." Elbowing me gently, Bridget said, "Maybe book two will suck. What is it called, again? *Burning at the Stake*?"

Chuckling, I said, "*Tearing at the Seams.*"

Bridget rolled her eyes. "*Burning at the Stake* could be the title of her postmortem memoir. She *is* a witch." Although I had made a peace of sorts with Hannah, Bridget still held a mighty grudge from our high school days.

"She wants me to do a cover reveal and maybe an interview on my blog as part of the prerelease." I hadn't answered her yet, and my conscience was not pleased at my display of rudeness. I made a silent promise to check my blog schedule and respond with a few available dates when I got home later. Like it or not, featuring popular authors was part of the blogger gig, and like it or not, Hannah Marshak was a chick lit writer to watch. "And my sister thinks I should ask her for advice on getting an agent." I shook my head, bewildered as to why anyone would think that was a clever idea and hoping Caroline and Bridget would share my horror at the prospect.

From the other side of the computer—and the world—Caroline said, "Actually, Erin might be on to something."

I blinked in shock. "In what galaxy?"

"I'd like to hear this too. I can't imagine how Hannah could help Kim. And even if she had it in her power, Kim would probably have to sell her soul in exchange. Or at least her Louboutins," Bridget said, referring to my favorite pair of designer shoes. The ones I probably shouldn't have splurged on until I made bestseller status. Or at least snagged a publishing deal. Or an agent.

Caroline raised a finger in the air. Shaking her head softly, she smiled and said, "You guys..." She was very entertained by Bridget's disdain of Hannah and liked to play devil's advocate.

"You have the floor. We're listening." If Caroline hadn't urged me to fight for Nicholas the summer before, we wouldn't be sharing an apartment now, and I'd probably still be heartbroken. At the very least, I could hear her out.

Ignoring Bridget, who muttered, "This should be good," Caroline pled her case. "First of all, I don't want to hear any talk about 'giving up.' Judy Blume received rejections for two years, and Margaret Mitchell's *Gone with the Wind* was rejected thirty-eight times. You're in good company."

A glimmer of hope was ignited. I didn't know about Judy Blume.

Caroline continued, "Second of all, Hannah was once where you are. She had a completed manuscript and no agent."

"Exactly what Erin said." I wasn't convinced.

"The way you probably imagine it, Hannah's dream agent came to her and not the other way around."

Not true. I knew Hannah's agent didn't magically knock on her door. But I bet she didn't receive twenty rejections. "Not exactly—"

Dismissing me with a wave of her hand, Caroline said, "Let me finish."

"Fine."

"I bet you can't imagine Hannah's email inbox flooded with rejections though. Am I right?"

Nodding, I said, "You're right."

Caroline pursed her lips. "I'm willing to bet Hannah's agent search was not as effortless as you imagine."

"Maybe," I acquiesced.

"But that's not even my point."

Downing the rest of her wine and walking into the kitchen, Bridget called out, "So what *is* your point?"

Raising her voice so Bridget could hear her from a distance, Caroline said, "My point is Hannah has no qualms about asking Kim to help her out despite their rocky past. What would be so odd about Kim asking her for advice in return?" Staring me down, she added, "And the timing is perfect since, if I know you at all, you're procrastinating getting back to her on this latest request."

"Call me Captain Predictable." I wasn't swayed yet, but my logical side was headed there. My emotional side was stubborn.

"Why don't you ping her back and tell her you'll try to make room in your blog schedule to reveal her cover? Then you can subtly mention you have a favor to ask too, if she has time. If you don't offer her a specific spot on your blog outright, hopefully she'll treat it like an exchange and eagerly offer her services."

"Lightning might strike after I say this, but Caroline's idea is kind of brilliant. As long as you keep it all business," Bridget said, returning to the couch with Jonathan at her side. He'd been directed to stay out of the living room so we could have a proper girls' night like old times.

Angling his head toward the laptop, he said, "Hey, Caroline. What morsel of genius are you sharing with us today?"

Caroline opened her mouth to respond as Jonathan added, "Never mind. I don't care." With a wry grin, he added, "No offense." Then he removed a cigarette from Bridget's pack and walked over to the windowsill as Caroline laughed.

"None taken."

It was no use attempting to dispute Caroline's no-nonsense thought process. So much for Nicholas's claim I should have been a lawyer. In desperate need of a subject change, I said, "Okay. I'll do it. Thanks, Caroline."

Caroline directed her gaze at Bridget. "And what about you, missy? Anything new in your world?"

Shaking her head, Bridget responded, "Nada." She smiled. "But I'm totally fine with the status quo."

As Jonathan finished his cigarette and retreated to the bedroom, I muttered, "Very convenient for Jonathan."

Bridget's eyebrows squished together. "You lost me."

"Jonathan is happy with the status quo too, right?"

Bridget flinched but didn't respond.

Caroline chuckled. "You guys seem to be speaking in code."

"It's nothing." Presenting Caroline with a sheepish grin, Bridget said, "Anyway, the Belgian beer was a huge hit with the boys, but I'm hoping the next care package will be for us."

"Yes," I agreed. "Preferably in the nature of a visit from you."

"I miss you guys too," Caroline said.

A few minutes later, we concluded our chat session with Caroline, and Bridget walked me to her front door. "Thanks for hosting the girls' night, Bridge," I said, reaching up to give her a hug. She was only five foot three herself but seemed to tower over me in her hot pink platform Vans.

"My pleasure. Glad Jonathan kept his distance for most of it. Although I may or may not have promised something in return, if you know what I mean." Bridget waggled her eyebrows suggestively.

I held up my hand. "TMI."

Folding her arms across her chest, Bridget said, "Speaking of Jonathan, what was with your passive-aggressive dig before?"

I dipped my chin to my chest for a beat before meeting her eyes. "I shouldn't have mentioned it in front of Caroline. I'm sorry."

With a hard smile, Bridget said, "I don't get why you mentioned it at all."

Reaching out to touch a leaf of the mass cane plant by Bridget's door, I said, "We've shared our fantasy wedding stories more times than I can count. Remember flipping through pages of *Bride Magazine*—flagging our favorite dresses?"

Spots of color entered Bridget's cheeks. "We were sixteen, Kim. It was fun to play pretend. We're almost thirty now. My priorities have changed." She yawned. Bringing a hand to her mouth, she said, "Sorry. I'm so tired, K. Can we talk about this another time?"

Releasing a heavy sigh, I replied, "Of course. I'll let you go. I'm exhausted too."

After another hug goodbye, I headed to the subway and back to my apartment.

As the almost empty 6 train pushed its way through the darkness, I set aside my concern for Bridget temporarily. Fixating my stare on a spot through the dirty glass windows, I revisited the possibility of asking Hannah for help.

My stomach was tangled in knots as I tried to visualize how the conversation with Hannah would go. To the outside observer, I gave as good as I got back in junior high and high school. Hannah tried to knock me down with her petty accusations and rumors, but just like Chumbawamba said, "I got back up again." As far as Hannah was concerned, I was a tough little bitch. The only time I let her see me sweat was when she caught me crying at Starbucks over my breakup with Nicholas and my growing paranoia he was dating Daneen. Over a couple of vodka martinis, she gave me the lowdown on Daneen, and I discovered Hannah had moments of humanity. Despite a lousy bedside manner, Hannah helped me that day. Was it possible her experience and wisdom could also assist in my quest to become a published author? And was it worth risking my bold—albeit tiny—exterior to find out?

Like Caroline, Nicholas was very results-oriented, and so I knew without asking he would tell me to tuck away my pride and ask Hannah for help. I would have preferred to double-check, but he was working late, and it was too complicated to discuss via text. My choices were either to take a calculated risk and write her now—without awaiting positive reinforcement from Nicholas—or sleep on it and ask him in the morning. But my brain was too wired to sleep, certainly not without the aid of Tylenol PM or something similar. Even Bridget was able to see past her bias against Hannah to acknowledge the upshot of reaching out to her under the circumstances.

My decision made, I sent the email before I could change my mind and got ready for bed. After a few minutes of tossing and turning, it became clear a sleeping pill would have been helpful regardless of which decision I had made.

Chapter 10

After a rather productive lunch hour—I tore through the last two chapters of *Baby or Bust,* the first in a series of British chick lit novels I was reading for my blog, and scheduled tweets of my most recent reviews—I returned to my desk, hopeful the afternoon would fly by. And then I checked my email.

From: DBarnett@EmanQuinn.com
To: KLong@EmanQuinn.com
Subject: Urgent: Orange Essence Exhibits

Kim,
We'll need four collated copies of Exhibits A-K in the conference room on 24 by 2:15. Each set should be fastened together with a butterfly clip. (No paper clips. No binder clips. NO staples.)

Daneen

No "thank you" either, huh, Daneen?

I whistled through my teeth in annoyance as my fingers moved rapidly over the keys to access the exhibits in the W drive. Daneen wrote me at 1:49 p.m., and it was now 2:02 p.m. She knew I took lunch at one o'clock and wasn't expected to check my Blackberry on my breaks. In fact, on the rare occasions I needed access to work email on off-hours, I had to dump the contents of my entire bag to find the antiquated device at the bottom, hiding under my makeup case, hairbrush, bank receipts, chewing-gum wrappers, and a slew of other more frequently utilized items.

After printing out four sets of the eleven exhibits, I sprung out of my chair, grabbed them from the printer, and placed them on the carpet of Rob's office to organize. The office was empty since Rob was presumably waiting for me in the conference room with Daneen. Carefully collating the documents using butterfly clips (since Daneen's aversion to binder clips rivaled Mommy Dearest's hatred of wire hangers), I walked slowly and assuredly to the conference room. It was already 2:23 p.m., but it was the best I could do without Olympic secretarial skills or, at the very least, a faster printer.

The door was closed, and I didn't want to drop the copies, so I knocked with my elbow, immediately receiving a muffled "Come in" from Rob. My first instinct was to snottily announce I could use some assistance opening the door, but I kept my mouth shut. Instead, I bent down and carefully placed the copies on the floor. When I lifted myself to a standing position, I came face to face with the sexiest man alive. Not Adam Levine. And not Channing Tatum either. Nicholas. My Nicholas—who I lived with. Or, as Daneen would obnoxiously correct, with whom I lived.

I bit back the urge to jump into his arms, wrap my legs around his waist, and stick my tongue down his throat, but I couldn't withhold the giant grin that appeared on my face. "I didn't know you'd be here today." Now that Nicholas was a client, it wasn't unusual for him to meet with Rob at our office, but he hadn't mentioned he'd be here today. Between Nicholas leaving for work before I even woke up and staying well past sundown most days, it felt like ages since we'd been in the same room for more than a few minutes. Sleeping didn't count.

Removing the papers from my hands, he smiled back and said, "I wanted to surprise you. Let me help you with these." Then he flashed me a wink before walking toward the conference table and placing a set in front of Rob, Daneen, and David.

"Do you need anything else from me?" I asked, directing the

question to Rob who already had his head buried in the papers.

"Not right now, Kim. But don't go too far," Daneen said.

"I promise not to go farther than the bathroom," I replied. I tried to keep it together when Nicholas made a funny face behind Daneen's back.

"That will do," Daneen said.

Motioning toward Nicholas, I said, "Don't forget to say goodbye before you leave."

"I thought we could head out together," Nicholas said.

Nicholas was as aware of my five thirty clock-out time as I was of his tendency to work until eight or later, so my mouth dropped open in surprise. Recovering quickly, I beamed at him and said, "*Magnifique*," before gleefully exiting the conference room.

Unfortunately, my use of the French language served as a reminder of the email I had sent to Hannah the night before. My mood took a nosedive as I swallowed back the unease in my gut, which had been building ever since. I had taken Caroline's advice and told Hannah I would attempt to fit a cover reveal for *Tearing at the Seams* and a possible interview into my blog schedule but wanted to pick her brain on an unrelated topic if she had the time. I chose to leave my request vague. I didn't want rumors flying around about my writing a novel and begging Hannah for her advice on getting it published. Even if it was less rumor and more truth.

Because Daneen seemed to have an uncanny ability for finding the most inconvenient times to ask for immediate assistance, for the course of the afternoon, I held my breath each time I returned to my desk after using the restroom, fearing what was waiting for me. I wouldn't have been shocked to learn Daneen had installed a secret camera at my cubicle to keep tabs on me at all times, but I didn't receive a single email or phone call from the conference room all day. It was close to five thirty when Nicholas and Rob walked by my cubicle on the way to Rob's office. While Nicholas concluded his meeting with Rob, I gathered up my belongings and went to log out of my computer. I would read more of my book while I waited for him. I closed out all of my open tabs and was about to exit Facebook when I noticed an unread private message. My heart skipped a beat when I saw it was from Hannah.

Greetings, Kim.

I'm so glad to hear from you. My tour dates are filling up fast and furious, but if I double up, I can make room for Pastel Is the New Black. *No such thing as too much exposure, right?*

You have piqued my interest, my little friend. I'm lunching with some girls from our graduating class a week from Saturday—Plum and Marla—and have early evening drinks with my agent, but I can give you some time in between. How's Forcella on Park and 27th? They have tasty cocktails and the best-looking bartenders in town. Say, 4:30 p.m.?

À Bientôt,
Hannah

As a wave of dread washed over me, I realized I subconsciously hoped Hannah would flat-out deny my request. It would validate my low opinion of her as well as let me off the hook. But even as I swallowed down the anxiety, I chuckled at how fluidly she managed to turn it around to make it seem like promoting *Tearing at the Seams* on *Pastel Is the New Black* was a favor she was doing for me and not the other way around.

Before I could chicken out, I wrote her back and said I'd see her then. It was good timing since Nicholas's parents were visiting this coming weekend. Lucky me had two items at the top of her "things to freak out about" list.

I shut down my computer as Nicholas exited Rob's office. With a smile, he said, "Ready?"

I stood up and tossed my purse over my shoulder. "You know it. Is it a national holiday for lawyers or something?"

Putting an arm around me as we walked toward the elevator bank, Nicholas laughed. "I don't think there's such a thing."

"I'm not used to seeing you before sunset these days." I pressed the down button on the elevator.

"You exaggerate."

The only time in the last month Nicholas beat me home from work was the night I sent the first three chapters of my novel to Ginny Webber, and it was only because I went out for department drinks first. But I didn't want to fight about it. And I certainly didn't want to think about Ginny Webber. I stood up and kissed him on the lips. "Homeward bound?"

"I thought we'd grab dinner at Hillstone. Unless you want to head home now."

"I'm starving. And in desperate need of a generously poured glass of wine. Hillstone sounds perfect."

Cocking an eyebrow, Nicholas asked, "Any particular reason for your thirst?"

We squeezed into the elevator, crowded due to rush-hour traffic. I whispered, "I'll tell you over a liquid refreshment."

A few minutes later, we were seated at a high-top table on the outskirts of the dimly lit bar area of Hillstone, an upscale New American restaurant located on the bottom floor of my office building. As always, the bar was overflowing with business professionals in their late twenties through fifties, and a wait for a table in the dining area was forty-five minutes long.

Nicholas tilted his head toward the speaker above our heads where "Tonight, Tonight" by The Smashing Pumpkins was playing. "Little known trivia about The Smashing Pumpkins. Although front man Billy Corgan was not, as rumored, the boy in the eighties sitcom *A Small Wonder*, he did publish a book of poetry that hit number one on the *New York Times* bestseller list." He smiled and squeezed my hand across the table. "So, what's behind this thirst for alcohol?"

Over a glass of wine and a bowl of spinach and artichoke dip, I told him about my plan to meet with Hannah the following weekend and hoped he'd support the decision. "Do you think it was a huge mistake?" My heart was beating wildly, especially since regardless of what Nicholas thought, the deed was done, and I'd already set a date to meet with her. If he was vehemently opposed, I'd come up with a believable excuse to bow out.

When his cell phone pinged, Nicholas picked it up with a furrowed brow. I waited for him to finish typing a response and absently swung my legs up and down under the table.

Nicholas put his phone down and looked at me. "What were you saying? You're going to let Hannah read your book?"

Recoiling, I said, "God, no." Realizing I had practically shouted my answer, I lowered my voice. "Caroline suggested I ask her for advice about getting an agent. The possibility of her reading my book never came up, but the answer would be no." I bit the inside of my cheek. "You don't think it will come to that, do you?"

Nicholas gave me an amused smile before popping a chip in his mouth. He swallowed. "I don't have a clue what it will come to, but I guess you'll find out soon."

"Have you started it?" I held my breath.

Nicholas frowned. "I haven't had time yet."

I swallowed down my disappointment. "Okay."

Nicholas tossed his napkin across his plate. "I hope you're not worried about my opinion. I'm sure it's fantastic."

I raised an eyebrow. "Easy to say having not read it."

"I know. I promise to read it soon. Bear with—" He exhaled loudly before glancing at his vibrating phone. "This will be one second."

I gave a grateful smile to the waitress who had placed our entrées on the table. While Nicholas read his latest text, I sipped my wine and pondered the possibility of Hannah asking to read *A Blogger's Life*. Asking Hannah for advice on getting an agent's attention was one thing. Letting her read the novel was quite another.

What if she stole my idea? More worrisome: what if she hated my book?

Nicholas tapped me on the hand, interrupting my mini panic attack. "I'm sorry. Work is nuts," he said.

Nicholas's schedule was wearing on him, and noting the red in his eyes, I pushed the Hannah stuff to the side. "How are *you*? Get a lot accomplished at your meeting?"

He nodded. "It was productive. Sometimes, I forget the squad works *for* me now. When we're all together brainstorming, it's like we're still part of the same team. Only this time, I can tell Rob what to do instead of the other way around." Giving me a sheepish grin, he said, "I much prefer it this way."

I chuckled. "I wonder why. What's the game plan with the case?"

Scrunching his eyebrows together, he questioned, "Since when do you care about work stuff?"

"If it's important to you, it's important to me." In all honesty, I found legal jargon endlessly boring, but Nicholas could make a bowl of plastic fruit compelling, and I wanted to show my support. I considered it my job to be his biggest cheerleader.

"You're sweet, but I won't bore you with the details. It's not like I'm saving lives." When his phone rang, he shook his head and muttered, "Speaking of which," before picking it up. "Hi, Dad."

Whenever Nicholas spoke to his dad, his entire demeanor changed. He tapped his legs repeatedly and even chewed on his cuticles. The confident—dare I say cocky?—man I fell in love with reverted to what I imagined he was like as a child: a doe-eyed little boy seeking the approval of his daddy.

"I'm having dinner with Kim." Nicholas locked his brown eyes on mine. Tugging on his tie, he said, "I did work today. I was at a meeting in her office. She's Rob's secretary, remember?"

My heart skipped a beat, and I glanced around the restaurant to avoid seeing Dr. Strong's reaction written all over Nicholas's face.

"It went well. Yes. We made a one o'clock reservation. Got it. You too. Bye." Nicholas hung up the phone and took a breath. "That was my dad."

I smiled. "I figured."

"We're all set for Saturday."

I inwardly shuddered in anticipation of meeting Dr. Strong. If a juris doctorate couldn't compare with a medical degree, I could only imagine his thoughts on a measly bachelor's degree. I doubted writing a book would hold much weight unless I could brag about having an interested agent or publisher. "Great."

Nicholas took a bite of his burger. "Where were we?"

"I asked about your work."

As his phone vibrated again, Nicholas rolled his eyes and muttered, "Dammit," before picking it up.

I watched him with amusement until he placed his hand over his face and shook his head. After he hung up, I asked whether everything was all right.

"Would you be terribly disappointed if I put you in a cab and went back to the office?"

Tapping a finger over my bottom lip, I said, "Do you want the supportive-girlfriend answer or the truth?"

Waving down the waitress for our bill, Nicholas frowned. "I'm sorry, Kimmie."

Shrugging, I said, "At least we had dinner together." Not a lie: Nicholas, his work, and I had a lovely meal together—one big happy family.

Nicholas glanced at the check and threw several bills on the table. "This will cover it." Guiding me to the exit, he said, "I'll make it up to you. I promise."

Chapter 11

"I'm sure they'll love you," my mom said with certainty.

I placed the phone in the crook of my neck while studying my reflection in the full-length mirror I had insisted Nicholas affix to the bathroom door. "I'm wearing a gray-and-black-striped scoop-neck sweater dress with gray suede boots. Should I change into jeans? I don't want them to think I'm trying too hard."

"If you wear jeans, you'll worry they'll think you aren't trying enough."

"You know me so well."

"I wouldn't be a good mother if I didn't, now would I? Where are you meeting them?"

I put the phone on speaker and placed it on the countertop while I added a bit more blush to the apples of my cheeks. "A French brasserie in the neighborhood. Nicholas thought it would be less awkward if we met at the restaurant, but we'll come back here for coffee and cake. I made cookies too." When my mom didn't respond, I took the phone off speaker and said, "You still there?"

"Sorry, Kim. I thought you said you made cookies."

"Hardy har har. Bridget made them, which is pretty much the same thing, right?"

My mom chuckled. "If you say so."

"You sure I shouldn't rethink the outfit? Do thigh-high suede boots scream 'lovely future-daughter-in-law material' or 'gold-digging whore'?"

"Just be your sassy, spunky self, and the rest will follow."

I inhaled deeply through my nose and out of my mouth. "I'll

try." I had planned to take a yoga class earlier, but Nicholas convinced me to use my poses in other ways. Forward fold had been especially pleasant.

"Have you reached out to Hannah yet?"

"About what?" I said, suddenly in defensive mode.

"Erin told me you were going to ask Hannah for advice on getting an agent."

"Since you're such a good mother, you should be aware your youngest daughter is prone to exaggeration. Erin merely suggested I seek Hannah's help. I never said I would." Even though I did.

"It's not a bad idea."

"I know!" Lowering my voice, I said, "I'm sorry, Mom. Don't tell Erin, but Caroline and Bridget agreed it was a great idea. I'm meeting with Hannah next weekend. I can't even think about it right now though. I need to tackle one hurdle at a time. Let me charm the Strongs first."

"I'm not sure I heard you correctly. Did you say Bridget agreed?"

Giggling, I said, "Reluctantly. But, yes."

Nicholas popped his head into the bathroom. "You almost ready?"

I nodded. "I gotta run, Mom. I'll call you later."

"Good luck, honey. If they don't fall in love with you, they're not as intelligent as their son."

"Thanks, Mom. Love you."

"Love you too."

From across our cramped table in the populous brasserie, Nicholas's mom smiled at us. "Have you two eaten here before?"

I shook my head as Nicholas said, "I have, Mom. You have to try a popover. They're mouth-wateringly delicious." He pushed the basket of assorted rolls to his mother.

Looking tentatively at her husband, she said, "Split one with me, Warren? I don't want to ruin my appetite."

Nicholas's dad waved her away. "Then just eat half."

"I'll split it with you," I offered.

"Thank you, Kim," she said, handing me half of the popover. "How do you manage to stay so slim living in New York City with so many amazing restaurant choices practically outside your door?"

"I do a lot of yoga and spin classes. But mostly it's just good genes." I took a small bite of the popover. Nicholas was right—it tasted heavenly.

"Kimmie here loves to exercise," Nicholas said, rubbing my knee under the table.

I felt my face get warm and gave him a discreet kick. I'd be mortified if our behavior gave the Strongs the impression we were sex addicts who couldn't go a meal without groping each other. "I don't think you have anything to worry about, Mrs. Strong. You're so petite." And it was true. Mrs. Strong was maybe two inches taller than me, and we could probably share clothes. With dark brown hair, eyes the color of milk chocolate, and a warm smile, she was Nicholas in female form, thankfully minus the stubble. On the other hand, Nicholas bore no resemblance to his father, who had to be at least six feet tall and was broad with silver hair and emerald-green eyes.

"Please call me Jeanine. I'm so happy to finally meet the girl who convinced Nicholas to give love another try. After what Amanda did to my poor boy, I wasn't so sure he'd ever commit again." She made a sour face. "I could strangle that girl." Amanda was Nicholas's girlfriend before me. She cheated on him the entire length of their relationship with her high-school sweetheart. According to his friends, and now his mother, Nicholas carried serious trust issues until I came along.

"This isn't the time, Mom. Besides, if I hadn't broken up with Amanda, I wouldn't be here with Kim."

This time, it was me who massaged his knee under the table. Okay, maybe we *were* sex addicts who couldn't go a meal without groping each other.

Nicholas's dad cleared his throat. "Can you stop smothering

him, Jeanine? The umbilical cord was cut thirty-one years ago."

"I don't care. He'll always be my baby boy."

While Nicholas winked at his mother, Warren scowled, and I sat lower in my chair and nibbled on my popover. If one were to compare Nicholas's folks to breeds of dog, Jeanine would be a pug—snuggly and cute. Whereas Warren would be a bull terrier—known for preying on the small and meek.

Turning to Nicholas, Warren asked, "How's the new job?"

Nicholas pushed his shoulders back. "I've been there over six months now, so it's not that new. But it's going very well."

Warren's green eyes lit up. "Atta boy. Make sure the higher-ups know your name and recognize your face. I can't emphasize how important this is. When I was a resident, my attending physician—"

"I know, Dad." Nicholas interrupted in a quiet voice before darting his eyes toward his mom.

As the waitress placed our salads on the table, Warren continued, "Have they talked about promoting you from Assistant General Counsel to General Counsel?"

Nicholas paused as if taken aback by the question. "The company already has a General Counsel. But I'm also the Director of Legal Affairs. It comes with a lot of responsibility."

"I'm not sure going the corporate route was the best move for your career."

"I got a significant pay raise, Dad," Nicholas said while cutting into a piece of buffalo mozzarella.

Even though Nicholas argued his father's statement, I noticed his shoulders droop an inch and wanted to gag Warren with a dirty sock.

"Your brother began his oncology fellowship," his dad announced proudly before stabbing a cherry tomato with a fork and bringing it to his mouth.

"Which brother is that?" I asked. Nicholas had two older brothers, and both were doctors like his dad. His younger sister was in medical school.

"Neil," Nicholas said.

"Nathan already heads up pediatrics at Mercy," Warren added.

I stifled the urge to chuckle at his sons' similar-sounding names. And his sister's name was Natalie. Nicholas no longer found it amusing after thirty years. When he first told me, I tried unsuccessfully to get a rise out of him. The only thing that worked was when I called him Nathan in bed. Unfortunately, what had risen quickly deflated, and neither of us were laughing after that.

"What about your family, Kim? Nicholas told us your parents retired to Florida, and your sister lives in Massachusetts with her husband. Do you see them often?" Jeanine asked, blessedly taking the conversation in a different direction.

"Aren't they a bit young for retirement?" Warren asked.

"Really, Dad?" Nicholas said, shaking his head.

"It's okay," I said, wanting to avoid more tension. "Yes, they're a bit young, but after they sold their store, they decided to get a head start on their golden years."

"Good for them." Jeanine smiled warmly at me. "By the time this one retires," she said, elbowing her husband, "he'll be ready for the old-age home."

"Work is keeping me young." Wiggling his fingers, he said, "I use the muscles so I don't lose the muscles."

"Can we let Kim answer Mom's question about how often she sees her family now?" Nicholas asked. He winked at me. "Go on."

I grabbed hold of his hand under the table. "I try to get to Florida at least a couple of times a year. Preferably in the winter to escape the cold. I don't see my sister much, but she and her husband have a trip planned very soon, and Nicholas will finally meet them. Right?" I smiled up at Nicholas.

He returned my grin. "I'm looking forward to it. Mostly to see if she's as annoying as Kim says."

I felt myself blush. "I don't think she's annoying. She's just..." I didn't want Nicholas's parents to think I was a bitch. "She's my younger sister," I mumbled. "You have one too," I said to Nicholas. "It comes with the role, right?"

"Natalie is irritating. Younger sister or not," Nicholas said with a straight face before relaxing into a laugh.

"She might be irritating, but she's top of her class in medical school. I'm proud of my little girl," Warren said, smiling broadly.

Nicholas bounced his knees under the table. His discomfort was palpable, and I hated being powerless to ease it.

While absently shifting her food around her plate with her fork, Jeanine said, "We're proud of all four of our wonderful and successful children. Aren't we, Warren?"

"Of course we are," Warren agreed. "I'm just sorry Nicholas will never know the satisfaction of saving someone's life."

Nicholas released a heavy sigh and flicked his gaze upward.

"I've played Operation with Nicholas. It isn't pretty," I joked.

Warren and Jeanine blinked at me while Nicholas cocked his head in obvious confusion.

"The board game," I clarified.

"Oh." Jeanine laughed.

I gave a timid smile. "On the other hand, he's amazing in front of the judge—well-prepared, quick on his feet, eloquent." I'd never actually witnessed Nicholas in the courtroom, but what his parents didn't know couldn't hurt them.

"Kim's just given me a great idea," Warren belted out.

"What is it, honey?" Jeanine asked cautiously.

Warren beamed at Nicholas and paused dramatically.

Like his son, Warren's smile could light up a starless midnight sky, and I was pleased to be responsible for the first one of the evening.

"Maybe you should consider running for office. My son, the senator."

Or not.

Jeanine pressed her lips together in a grimace while Nicholas slumped into his chair.

In desperate need for a subject change, I blurted out, "Don't forget to leave room for dessert. I made cookies. And we're christening our new Nespresso machine."

"Sounds wonderful, Kim. I can't wait," Jeanine said in the same rushed tone. Then she winked at me across the table and mouthed, "Thank you."

A few hours later, after we had reconvened at our apartment for dessert and coffee, I walked Mrs. Strong to the front door to say goodbye.

She extended her arms and pulled me into a hug. I immediately recognized the subtle floral scent of her perfume as one from Nicholas's company. I wondered if it was a coincidence or a show of support to her son. "It was so nice to finally meet you," she murmured in my ear before releasing me.

I smiled at her. "Same here. I hope you enjoy the rest of your stay and your time with Neil and Clarissa." The next stop on the trip was two nights at their eldest son's McMansion in Scarsdale, New York, about thirty-five minutes outside of the city.

"We will. But I wish we had more time to spend with you. Thank you for a wonderful afternoon. Those cookies were delicious."

I blushed, embarrassed at taking credit for Bridget's creation. "My pleasure." I glanced over her shoulder where Warren was speaking in a muffled tone to Nicholas, whose facial expression had morphed into a deep frown.

Noticing her husband and Nicholas in an intense and seemingly one-sided conversation, Mrs. Strong mimicked her youngest son's downturned mouth. "I'm so proud of Nicholas for marching to his own beat. He always has," she said fondly.

I nodded. "He's a special guy."

"He's lucky to have you," she said, patting me gently on the arm as the men joined us to conclude our goodbyes.

When we finally closed the door behind us, we exhaled a collective sigh of relief. "Thank God that's over," I said, leaning against the door.

Nicholas stood in front of me with his eyes narrowed.

"Whatever do you mean?"

I swallowed. "I, uh...your parents are great, but..." Was Nicholas so accustomed to his father's behavior he could shrug it off within a minute?

Nicholas closed the distance between us and kissed my lips. "I'm teasing you, Kim. I'm not sure you took a breath all afternoon. You turned green there for a minute."

"It's not me I was worried about. You told me your dad was intense but...wow." I faked a shiver.

Nicholas shrugged. "Nothing a little Beatles can't fix. I promise by the time we get to the fifth track of *A Hard Day's Night*, the pink will return to your cheeks. What's the fifth track of *A Hard Day's Night*?"

Knowing Nicholas wouldn't open up until I played along, I trailed him to the stereo system. "Unlike you, I don't have every Beatles album memorized, remember?"

"Take a gander." He dared me with his eyes.

"'Can't Buy Me Love'?"

Nicholas smiled brightly, and for a moment, I wondered if I nailed it. "No. But 'Can't Buy Me Love' is the seventh track. Nice, Kimmie. The fifth track is 'And I Love Her.' Amazing song."

"Yes, it is," I agreed. "Not to change the subject or anything, but does your dad always ride you so hard about not being a doctor?"

Nicholas took my hand and walked me over to the couch where we sat down side by side and stretched our feet across the coffee table. "First of all, only you're allowed to ride me hard," he said, smiling in response to my eye roll. "But, yeah, I'm afraid I was his biggest disappointment."

My jaw dropped. "Wow. If my biggest disappointment is raising a son who grows up to be a successful, hard-working, honest attorney, I will consider myself the best parent ever." My heart ached for Nicholas and pounded in anger toward Dr. Strong for belittling his son's decisions solely because they differed from his own.

"In and of itself, seeking a career in law is not the worst thing in the world, but when your first-born child devotes his life to treating and ultimately curing cancer, and your second-born brings babies into the world, how can protecting the trademark rights of a cosmetics company measure up?"

"I think protecting trademark rights is unbelievably sexy." At least it was when Nicholas did it. "What was he saying to you when he pulled you aside before they left?"

Nicholas leaned against the couch with his eyes closed. "We were discussing my plans to become the next senator."

As my breath caught in my throat, I said, "Oh no. When I touted your legal prowess, I hoped your dad would lay off the medical talk. I didn't mean to give him ideas about you running for public office."

Nicholas opened his eyes and gave me a weak smile. "I'm kidding. He wants me to consider going back to a law firm where I can get on a partner track and possibly make the management committee. He thinks the corporate world is a dead end unless I can become General Counsel or something more prestigious than one of many vice presidents."

"But you're so much happier in the corporate environment. No billable hours, for one."

"Apparently, happiness is overrated according to the gospel of Warren Strong. Although I do think my brothers are happy with their chosen professions. Maybe I'm the milkman's kid. Would explain a lot."

I chuckled. "Well, you're way hotter than your brothers, and *I* like you best. So there," I said while rubbing his thigh.

"Then it's a good thing I'm dating you instead of my dad now, isn't it?" Nicholas said with a crooked grin.

I maneuvered my body so I was sitting across his lap facing him. "That's the understatement of the century. Now kiss me so I can get the vision of you and Warren dating out of my head. And if you're lucky, I might even ride you hard."

*   *   *

I woke up tangled in my covers with my pillow dangling off the side of the bed. When I saw I was alone, I worried I had kept Nicholas up with my restless sleeping. I'd had at least one wild dream during the night—Hannah was pregnant with triplets, and Jonathan was the father. Riddle me that.

I stepped out of bed and walked to the living room, where Nicholas was sitting in the reclining chair. His back was to me, but I could see the top of his head peeking out. Not wanting to startle him, I tiptoed toward him and leaned over the chair. He had his computer on his lap opened to the website of Thompson, Rosenberg, and Sheehan, LLP.

"What's that?"

Nicholas's back jutted forward, and he quickly closed his laptop. "Jesus, Kim. You scared me."

"Sorry."

I squeezed myself onto the chair with him and placed a hand on this thigh. "What are you doing up so late? What is Thompson, Rosenberg, and Sheehan, LLP?"

"Nothing." He rubbed the back of his neck. "It's a law firm."

"What do you need a lawyer for at almost three in the morning?" I asked with a yawn.

"I don't need a lawyer. I was thinking about what my dad said—about going back to a firm."

"Oh, sweetie. Don't listen to him," I said while stroking his hair.

"You love your job. And besides, Rob might put a hit on you if you went back to a law firm and it wasn't his. He'd take you back in a drum beat."

"True." Nicholas yawned. Waving his hand in front of his mouth, he said, "It's contagious."

"It's also the middle of the night." I kissed him softly on the lips and stood up. Reaching for his hand, I said, "Come to bed. Wait till I tell you about my dream."

Nicholas placed his laptop on the coffee table and followed me to the bedroom. "Was it dirty?"

"No. But it was kind of foul."

Chapter 12

Hannah was already at the mostly empty restaurant sitting at the bar when I arrived. Naturally, she was flirting with the bartender, who appeared enchanted. As he read something on her phone, he smiled so wide, I could spot his dimples all the way from the restaurant's entrance. It felt like déjà vu, as the bartender was a captive audience to Hannah the last time I was in a bar with her too.

I sat down at the stool next to her, not wanting to interrupt the moment, but the bartender turned to me immediately with a grin before placing a glass of water in front of my chair. Handing me a cocktail menu, he said, "You must be Hannah's little friend Long. What can I get you?"

Humored by his use of my last name, and surprised Hannah referred to me as "Long" instead of "Short," I chuckled. Glancing at Hannah's drink, I said, "Hi there. I'll have what she's having, please." I didn't know what it was except it was pink and in a champagne flute—good enough for me. I turned to Hannah. "Hey. I hope I'm not too late." It was 4:40, but Hannah wisely used the ten minutes to become chummy with the bartender.

Twirling a strand of long, straight ebony hair around her perfectly manicured finger, Hannah said, "Rafael here kept me company." Then she turned toward Rafael and flashed her pearly smile in his direction. He looked up from preparing my drink and winked at her. Hannah glanced at her diamond-encrusted Movado. "You're not *that* late. Plum and Marla failed to mention they had to get to the Island early to prepare for their weekly date night with the hubsters," she said, rolling her almond-shaped hazel eyes. "Remind me not to reserve a full afternoon for those ungrateful girls again." Waving her hand, she said, "But never mind me, what's the big secret? You know, I was *this* close to making you spill over email. But then I realized it couldn't possibly be that interesting, and I needed a way to pass the time before meeting with Felicia anyway."

I opened my mouth to respond, but clamped it shut after her insulting comment sunk in.

"Well?" Hannah regarded me with wide innocent eyes as if completely oblivious. Pushing my drink closer to me, she said, "Drink."

As I did what she said—not because she told me to but because I needed alcohol to get through this meeting—I silently cursed Caroline's "brilliant plan." Reminding myself the sooner I got it over with, the quicker I could go home and distract Nicholas from his boring work, I took a deep breath and told Hannah I wrote a book. I barely heard the words leave my mouth, but was vaguely aware of the occasional blinking of Hannah's eyes as she listened to me in what appeared to be rapt interest. I finished speaking and held my breath awaiting her reaction. Would she express how *cute* she thought it was that little Kim wrote a little book? Would she outwardly wish me luck while not so subtly implying it couldn't possibly be as well-written or interesting as *Cut on the Bias* and *Tearing at the Seams*? Would I have the courage to ask for advice in snagging an agent? To avoid eye contact temporarily, I swallowed some of what turned out to be a delicious fizzy cocktail. When I faced Hannah again, her cheeks were flushed pink, and she had a slender hand clamped against her flawlessly painted mouth.

"I *knew* you wanted to be a writer, but you..." she said, pointing to me with her bright red nails and laughing. "You always denied, denied, denied." Motioning toward Rafael, she yelped, "Rafey, Kimmie here wrote a book."

I choked on my drink. Rafey? How early *was* Hannah?

A crease forming in Rafael's chiseled face, he glanced from Hannah to me and questioned, "Kimmie?"

Flipping her hair and pointing at me, Hannah said, "Long."

His facial muscles relaxing, Rafael said, "Ohhh, Long. How nice. Hannah here is a writer too."

I narrowed my eyes at Hannah. "You never asked if I wanted to be a writer." Given, it wasn't the first time she'd *accused* me of wanting to be a writer, but she'd never actually asked before. However, if she had asked, I would have absolutely denied, denied, denied.

Scrutinizing me from head to toe as if she only just noticed I was there, Hannah said, "Great pants." With a very deliberate gaze at my face, she asked, "Since when have you had freckles?"

I instinctively went to scratch my nose, the only part of my face decorated with freckles. "Since always."

Hannah nodded and removed her phone from her Dooney & Bourke satchel while I stared at her incredulously, thinking what the hell?

After typing a few words, she dropped the phone back in the bag and turned to me. "Did you need to ask me something? I don't have much time."

I licked my dry lips. "Like I said, I wrote a novel. Unfortunately, the only bite I got from an agent resulted in a rejection because she couldn't sell it in this market..." I swallowed hard as I pushed a hair out of my face. "I wondered if you could give me some advice." I took a huge gulp of my drink and with a shaky hand placed the glass back on the bar.

Hannah cocked her head to the side. "This book you wrote. It's good?"

Nodding, I said, "Yeah. I think it is. Everyone who's read it really liked it."

"And you're not related to, codependent on, or screwing these people?"

I laughed, despite myself. "No. I'm not related to, codependent on, or screwing any of them, actually." The one person I was sleeping with would have to read it in order to like it. "Although my mom and Bridget both read it, I was referring to the three authors who beta read for me and one blogger friend. Even Ginny Webber liked the first three chapters." Just not enough. Realizing I was babbling, I silenced myself.

Hannah looked pensive as she chewed her lower lip—of course not smudging her lipstick—and contemplated me. We engaged in a staring contest for a moment until I couldn't take it any longer and broke eye contact. While Hannah paid the bill, insisting it was a tax-deductible business expense, I cursed Caroline's brilliant idea once more.

Facing me again, she asked, "Do you have a copy of the manuscript with you?"

"Not on me, no. But I was hoping you could simply give me advice on my query letter and a way to get past the chick-lit-doesn't-sell curse. I don't need you to read the novel."

Exhaling loudly, Hannah said, "I have no desire to read your novel, Long. Although I'm sure it's as cute as a bug."

I rolled my eyes as discreetly as possible.

Hannah continued, "The reason I asked is because I'm meeting with my agent after this. I'm sure she'd agree to read some of it as a favor to me. I *am* one of her more profitable clients."

"You would? She would?" My heart rate increased exponentially. Keep it together, Kim.

Keep. It. Together.

With a bored expression, Hannah said, "Yes." Then she leaned over the bar as Rafael came scurrying over.

With only a short window of opportunity available to me, my brain worked double time until an idea sprung to my mind. I tapped Hannah on her toned arm.

"Yeah?"

"There's a Staples around the corner. I can access my manuscript from the Cloud and print out as many pages as you think Felicia would want to read, along with the synopsis."

Without taking her eyes off Rafael, she said, "You might as

well print out the whole thing. You have twenty minutes." Pointing at the door she said, "Go."

And like my little black dress the first time I hooked up with Nicholas, I was off.

Chapter 13

I miraculously managed to walk (okay, run) to Staples, print out my manuscript and synopsis, and walk (okay, jog, as by then, I was too tired to run) back to Forcella in twenty-five minutes. Even more miraculous, Hannah was still there. She credited Rafael's charming company for keeping her around the extra five minutes. I was both grateful to Hannah for offering to pass along the book to her agent and paranoid she would dump the papers in the closest trash can as soon as I was out of eyesight, and Felicia Harrison would never actually see them. Nicholas thought I was being silly.

"What would be the point in that?" he asked the next morning as we sat at our breakfast nook drinking coffee.

"When it comes to Hannah, I'm not sure there needs to be a point."

I wanted to believe Hannah was capable of committing a random act of kindness with no expectation of any personal gain. There was no evidence to suggest the twenty-first-century Hannah possessed the streak of evil held by her fourteen-year-old self.

The "old" Hannah felt no remorse after surreptitiously staining the back of another girl's white pants with a red Sharpie while she was in gym and then pointing it out to other students in the crowded hallway when the girl, completely unaware, walked to her next class. The modern version of Hannah, although full of herself and more than a little condescending, didn't seem interested in reviving her former vicious ways. But I was hesitant to let my guard down. What if she altered the book and made it completely unreadable?

"That's ridiculous," Nicholas said, bending over to lace his Converse sneakers.

Not realizing I had spoken out loud, my face heated up. "I know," I mumbled. "You don't understand how important this is to me."

Nicholas rolled his eyes. "Considering you've talked about nothing else since coming home last night, I think I do. And besides, she's only one agent."

"You said the same thing about Ginny Webber and the fifteen agents who rejected me before her," I muttered. And as I had received yet another rejection earlier in the week, the rejection count was now at sixteen.

Pouring his leftover coffee into a to-go cup, he said, "Just relax. It could be a long time before you hear anything. Try not to think about it."

"A much easier task with you here to distract me," I said with an exaggerated pout.

"Sorry, Kimmie. I have a ton of work to do."

"What time will you be home? Should I wait for you to eat dinner?"

As his phone rang, he said, "Hold that thought," and walked into the living room.

My mind continued to conjure up various ways in which Hannah could use my book against me. What if she posted some of the more risqué scenes on our high school's Facebook page out of context to humiliate me? I would rate the novel PG-13 due to language and mature themes, but the two brief sex scenes were arguably R-rated.

Returning to the kitchen, Nicholas said, "I will. Bye," before placing his phone in the back pocket of his jeans.

"Who was that?"

Nicholas looked at me with dull eyes. "My dad."

"What did he want?"

Nicholas walked to the kitchen sink. With his back to me, he said, "You know my dad."

I knew I didn't like him very much but didn't dare say it out loud. "Not really," I mumbled. "Did you tell him about the award you're getting?" Nicholas had recently found out he was named one of *Law360*'s top intellectual property lawyers under the age of forty for that year. He was one of a hundred or so attorneys chosen from over one thousand nominees.

"Uh huh."

I stood up from the table and brought my coffee cup to the sink. "What did he say?"

"He said congratulations before telling me Neil was recognized with a Giants of Cancer Care award for his continuing contribution to the cause."

"Wow."

"Can't compete with cancer research." Nicholas shrugged.

"Who said it was a competition?"

Nicholas didn't respond.

I wrapped my arms around his waist. "I have an idea. Let's go to Brinkley's for dinner. You've been touting their wings since I moved in."

Stiffening against my embrace, he said, "Better not wait for me for dinner. I'm not sure what time I'll be home."

Leaning into him, I said, "Okay. How about tomorrow night?"

Extricating himself from me, he said, "I don't know, Kim. It depends on how late I work." He removed his wallet from the kitchen table and placed it in his jacket pocket. "I gotta run. I'll see you later."

As he walked to our front door, I called out, "No kiss goodbye?"

"I gotta go. Smooches," he said as the door closed behind him.

Chapter 14

As fond as I was of my pink loveseat, I quickly discovered Nicholas's suede gray couch in the living room was significantly more conducive for both engaging in X-rated activities and binge-watching television. Since Nicholas wasn't available for the former, I settled for the latter, hoping to distract myself from the way he had bolted out the door earlier. I had several books in my queue for review, and the time would have been wiser spent reading or working on a blog post, but I was jonesing big time for bad reality TV. I threw a blanket over my legs and got cozy for an afternoon of back-to-back episodes of *The Real Housewives of New York* on Bravo. I was especially interested in Carole's story line since she was a published author long before she entered the world of "unscripted" television. When Bethany had two meltdowns within the first ten minutes of my viewing session, I dialed Bridget's number to see if she was watching too.

Bridget answered after one ring with an enthusiastic "Hi!"

"I'm bored," I said in response while examining the ends of my hair. I was in desperate need of a haircut.

"Come over. Jonathan's not here. We can watch *Housewives*."

"The thought of getting on the subway right now does not thrill me."

"Your fault for moving downtown. This time a couple of months ago, you could be here in five minutes."

I heard her take a drag of a cigarette. I opened my mouth to nag her, but decided to save my breath. Jonathan smoked too, and I had a feeling they enabled each other's nasty habit. "Hey now. I like downtown. I'm finally an expert outside the grid." The majority of Manhattan was easy to navigate because the streets were numbered, but once you got below First Street, it became tricky because the streets had real names, like Broome (where I lived with Nicholas), Spring, and Bowery. There was no rhyme or reason to where the named streets were situated. Until I started dating Nicholas, when I ventured to his neighborhood, I either needed the aid of a map or friends who were more directionally inclined, like Bridget.

Bridget snickered. "About time you stopped relying on Citymapper." Citymapper was my handy go-to website when I needed directions off the grid. "So what's new?"

"I gave Hannah a copy of *A Blogger's Life* to give to her agent."

Bridget gasped. "What possessed you to do such a stupid thing?"

"She offered."

"This conversation requires face-to-face contact. Come uptown. We can order from Uva later. My treat."

Uva was one of my favorite Italian restaurants and the venue of my first real date with Nicholas. I pushed the blanket off my legs and stood up. "Be there in half an hour."

Forty-five minutes later, I was curled in the corner of Bridget's purple couch, telling her about my meeting with Hannah. Bridget was on the other side of the sofa with her feet resting on the coffee table. After cracking a peanut and tossing the shell in the ceramic bowl on her lap, she turned to me, her eyes narrowed in doubt. "What's in it for Hannah?"

Twirling a strand of hair around my finger, I said, "Dunno. Maybe she did it out of the kindness of her heart?"

"Unless Hannah met with the Great and Powerful Wizard of Oz, she doesn't have a heart. What if she tossed it in the closest garbage can?" Her face draining of color, she said, "Or worse, what if she took your book and changed it so it reads like a sixth-grader wrote it?"

I reached over to scoop up a handful of peanuts. "Exactly what

I said to Nicholas. Great minds." I giggled, although the thought of Hannah manipulating the novel I put so much time and effort into made me want to cry, not laugh. Back in middle school, Hannah was the mastermind behind a "harmless" prank resulting in her friend Jax unknowingly reciting a sex scene from *Lady Chatterley's Lover* out loud in class rather than a scene from the designated reading assignment, *Of Mice and Men*. I didn't want to underestimate her evil prowess.

"What was Nicholas's response?"

"He told me I was being ridiculous," I mumbled.

With a shake of her head, Bridget said, "I never did like that Nicholas fellow." The twinkle in her shamrock-green eyes showed me she was teasing.

"I'm worried about him, to be honest."

With a crease in her forehead, Bridget asked, "Trouble in paradise?"

I shrugged. "I don't think so, but he's been preoccupied lately."

"How so?"

"With work stuff. He's been putting in crazy hours at the office—even more than normal. And he's on call twenty-four seven even when he's home. He hoofed it out of the apartment this morning after a phone call with his domineering dad without so much as a kiss goodbye."

"His dad probably stressed him out. He's something else, huh?"

"You don't know the half of it."

"Sounds like Jonathan's mom. She's constantly packing on the guilt about how much more often his sister visits even though she lives much farther away than a twenty-minute ride on the Long Island Railroad."

"Does Jonathan ever take it out on you?" Cocking my head to the side, I added, "For instance, by leaving the apartment without kissing you goodbye?"

"Never," Bridget said assuredly. Blushing, she added, "But as the only son, Jonathan can get away with almost anything when it comes to his mother and he knows it, which makes shrugging off her comments easier. It seems like Nicholas's issues with his father run much deeper." She frowned. "I'm sure his brushing you off was a one-off occurrence and has nothing to do with you. He's crazy about you."

I dropped my chin toward the floor unable to shake the paranoia. "And I've been talking nonstop about the agent stuff and whining about my rejections. My annoying him probably isn't helping things."

"I doubt he's annoyed, but if you're concerned, just lay off of the book talk a little. When you're freaking out, text me instead. I'll never get irked with you. And I'll always kiss you goodbye. I'm a great kisser too."

"But Daddy says I'm the best at it," I joked, quoting a line from *National Lampoon's Vacation.*

Bridget smiled. "But seriously, I'd stop wasting time worrying about your imagined problems with Nicholas and devise a plan for getting even with Hannah when she posts your book all over the internet."

"I'm going to give her the benefit of the doubt." I bit my cheek, not entirely believing my own statement.

"You aren't going to be friends with her now or anything, are you?" Bridget picked at an invisible loose thread on her t-shirt.

I patted her leg. "Friends is a stretch. This is merely a business transaction."

Bridget gave me a slow smile. "Okay. Let's put a wager on it—although it pains me to bet on something that will cause you sorrow. If...*When* Hannah proves herself to be the same ole Hannah, dinner at Gina's on you."

"And if I win?"

"Anything you want."

I pondered my options for a moment. "Okay. If Hannah pulls through, we can have a real heart-to-heart about Jonathan's aversion to marriage and kids."

Bridget grimaced. "This again?"

Raising an eyebrow, I said, "You got to choose dinner at Gina's. I choose this."

"Fine," Bridget said with an exaggerated sigh. "But it's not much of a gamble, considering I already told you I'm fine with it. Seems like a win-win for me."

"We'll see," I said, shaking her hand firmly.

I really wanted to win, but since doing so meant putting my trust in Hannah, I suspected there would be a dinner at Gina's—my treat—in the near future.

For the umpteenth night in a row, Nicholas was working late, leaving very little to distract me from obsessing over what Felicia Harrison thought of my manuscript. For all I knew, the minute she removed it from Hannah's expensively moisturized hands, she passed it off to her assistant who then buried it at the bottom of her slush pile. But I was in no worse a position than if I queried her directly.

Putting my preoccupation with Felicia to good use, I made it my mission to learn everything I could about her. With my laptop in front of me—a glass of water on one side and a notepad with a list of websites on the other—I sat on my couch and got to work. The first page on my list was the Harrison & Gold website, where I discovered Felicia represented not only Hannah, but Lizzy Pelk, another powerhouse in the chick lit genre, and Christine Bannah, a popular writer of romantic comedy, whose latest novel was recently optioned for film rights. Based on her client list, Felicia believed chick lit was a viable market and she had bestselling clients who helped pay her rent (or mortgage) and feed her faith in the genre. I pictured my name and photo on the page alongside those other authors, and I allowed myself a moment of confidence. According to the second website on my list, *Publisher's Forum*, Felicia had sold an impressive twelve novels to the major publishing houses in the last year. Why not mine?

But even with a "dream" agent in their corner, only a small

population of the authors with books being pitched to editors at any given time would be on the receiving end of the words, "I sold your book." So why mine? I sat back and sunk farther onto the couch, a sick feeling rotting at the pit of my stomach. I needed to be realistic. The likelihood of a debut author obtaining an agent was meager, and the chances of securing a big publishing deal, even with an agent, was even more miniscule. Sure, it could happen to me, but the odds were not in my favor—with or without a referral from Hannah Marshak.

Reaching once again for my laptop, I opened up a new document and got lost in my still-untitled next novel. I might never be a published author, but I was forever a writer.

Chapter 15

"Nicholas should be here soon. He was coming straight from work," I said to my sister and her husband Gerry as we stood in the buzzing bar area of Artisanal Fromagerie Bistro. We had planned to meet at the restaurant at seven for our seven thirty reservation so we'd have time for a quick drink before dinner.

"Is he always late?" my sister asked with a note of disapproval.

"It's only 7:05, Erin. Don't get your curls in a knot," I said, referring to my sister's head of tight spiral curls, the color of coffee with only a hint of cream.

"Should I get us a round of drinks? It will make the wait go by faster," Gerry asked while scratching his goatee.

I took in my brother-in-law, who perfected the part of a young hipster, wearing a plaid beanie atop his ruffled ginger locks, a buffalo checkered shirt, skinny jeans, and weathered sneakers with mismatched shoelaces. I wondered, not for the first time, how he came to fall in love with my perfectly tailored sister—who coordinated her lipstick with her nail polish—and vice versa. "Sounds like a great plan."

Aggressively flipping her head toward the fully occupied cherrywood bar and nearly slapping another patron in the face with her hair, Erin said, "There's nowhere to sit." She frowned.

I rolled my eyes toward the *Great Gatsby*-esque lights on the high ceiling.

"Stop acting like a geriatric. You're only twenty-six. I think you can stand for a few minutes." I glanced at my watch and then toward the entrance of the crowded restaurant. Hurry up, Nicholas.

"Would you mind ordering me a glass of prosecco, Ger? My sister could use a shot of Jagermeister."

"Ugh," Erin said, shuddering. "A whisky sour for me, honey." Gerry retreated his slender frame to the bar, and Erin turned back to me. "I haven't put an ounce of Jager into my body since I almost died from it. You were a horrible babysitter."

My eyes bugged out. "Babysitter? You weren't five. You were visiting me in college and if I recall, very anxious to be independent. And you didn't almost die. Although the smell of your stale puke wafting through our dorm room for the next forty-eight hours almost killed me and my roommate."

Erin examined her maroon-painted fingernails. "You have your version, and I have mine."

"Seriously? But for me, you would have lost your virginity to some sleazy frat boy while you were passed out drunk. I protected you."

"Protected her from what?" Gerry asked with a curious arch of his brow as he returned with our drinks. "What did I miss?"

"Nothing," Erin said before taking a sip of her drink. "Where is Nicholas?"

"I'm sure he's on his way, but I'll text him if you're so concerned." I sent Nicholas a quick text asking how long he would be and turned back to Gerry, who was still looking at us expectantly. "Erin never told you how I swooped in and saved her from an overzealous and completely shit-faced college sophomore who had no idea she was only fifteen?"

"Unlike my sister, I developed very young," Erin said, her eyes dropping to her significant cleavage with a smirk.

"I'm not going to argue with you, but I got my boobs pretty early too," I said. Erin had several inches on me both in height and general frame, and although we didn't share many physical attributes, our large bra size ran in the family.

"I thought you weren't going to argue with me," Erin said, rolling her doe eyes.

"Anyway…" I said to a bemused Gerry. "I let Erin flirt

shamelessly with the guy, Zeke, but maintained a hawkeye watch on her the entire night because I knew she wasn't used to drinking. When I saw Zeke lead a swaying and half-awake Erin into a bedroom, I followed them, pulled him off of her with strength I didn't know I had, and told him to get the hell off of my fifteen-year-old sister before I called the cops." Turning to Erin, I said, "I was never invited to one of their parties again, by the way."

Ruffling Erin's hair, Gerry said, "Thank you for protecting my wife's virtue."

"I'm glad someone appreciates me," I said, nudging my sister.

Smoothing down her hair, Erin said, "I appreciate you."

After we finished our drinks and Erin showed me pictures of their newly furnished house, she looked at her watch and made a sour face. "Where's your man? It's seven thirty."

"I don't know," I said, reaching for my phone and seeing Nicholas had returned my text. I read his message and looked up at Erin and Gerry with a frown. "He's running late. He said we should sit down and order drinks and appetizers."

"Are you okay with that, sis?" Erin asked hopefully.

"I don't mind waiting as long as we keep drinking," Gerry said, raising his empty glass.

I was about to agree with Gerry when Erin piped in. "We'll lose our table."

"Technically, they need to wait fifteen minutes before giving away our table. Do you mind stalling a bit? He should be here soon."

"Fine," Erin said, leaning against Gerry as if she were too exhausted to hold herself up. "Have you heard from Hannah lately?"

"No," I lied. I wasn't ready to tell Erin I took her advice and asked Hannah for help and that her agent was now reading my book. I'd never hear the end of it. "I'll buy the next round of drinks," I said, scurrying to the bar.

When Nicholas still hadn't shown up ten minutes later, and I didn't think I could take one more inquiry from my sister regarding his arrival time, the hostess led us to our table where we ordered another round of drinks and a couple of appetizers to share.

"I should pick Nicholas's brain about our new phone app. I'm not sure I trust our intellectual property lawyer," Gerry said, tossing the pit from a marinated olive onto his plate.

I glanced at my phone again. "Assuming he ever gets here, I'm sure he'd be happy to help you." I sat up straighter, hoping to spot Nicholas walking through the restaurant toward our table. Where the hell was he?

Echoing my inner thoughts, Erin asked, "Where is he?"

"I don't know," I said, sinking lower into my chair as my stomach churned with anxiety. He hadn't responded to my last text, which I hoped meant he was on the subway.

"Would he mind if we ordered our main courses?" Gesturing toward the empty plates on the table, Erin said, "I'm starving, and oysters and olives aren't going to cut it."

I was famished too. "Fine. Let's order." I caught the eye of our waiter and waved him over. I sent another text to Nicholas telling him if he didn't get here soon, we were eating all of the fondue.

Forty-five minutes later, I poked a fingerling potato into the four-cheese fondue and brought it to my mouth with a sigh. "I'm out." I raised my palms up in defeat.

"Me too," Gerry said, tossing his napkin on his plate. "I'm stuffed."

Erin yawned. "I'm sleepy. It's almost my bed time."

"You really are an old lady," I said with a chuckle until it dawned on me it was eight thirty, and Nicholas was still nowhere to be seen.

"I'm so sorry we didn't get to meet Nicholas," Erin said.

"He could still be on his..." I cut myself off as my heart sank in realization. Nicholas wasn't going to make it. "He's been so busy at work lately. But next time, I promise," I said, with a meek smile in my sister's direction. We had saved dinner for the tail end of their trip, and they were headed home in the morning.

In a show of unexpected kindness, Erin patted my hand across the table. "Maybe his boss cornered him, and he couldn't get out of it. Or maybe he was working against a crazy deadline. Maybe the electricity went out, and he got stuck in the elevator."

I bit my lip. The last one was highly unlikely, but I appreciated my sister's imaginative attempt to let Nicholas off the hook.

"I'm sure there's a perfectly reasonable explanation, and he'll make it up to you," she said confidently.

Gerry smiled kindly. "When I mess up, Erin likes to drag me shopping with her as punishment. I'm sure you'll come up with comparable retribution for Nicholas."

"Not meeting us, not to mention missing an amazing dinner, is punishment enough," Erin said, only half-joking.

"Damn straight," I agreed in a tone suggesting a lighter mood than I was in. I checked my phone again to see if Nicholas had returned my text. The answer was no.

"Dinner's on me," Gerry said, calling over the waiter.

"Thank you," I said, too resigned to insist on paying my share.

Outside the restaurant, we exchanged hugs, and I offered another embarrassed apology on Nicholas's behalf before hailing two cabs—one for them and another for me. As my taxi driver mumbled nonstop into his cell phone in a language I couldn't pinpoint, I leaned my head back against the seat and attempted to ignore the tight knots in my stomach resulting from Nicholas skipping out on the entire dinner.

Back at home, I was about to slip under my covers when I heard the jiggle of a lock followed by Nicholas's entrance into the apartment. About thirty seconds later, he leaned against the door of our bedroom.

"I'm so sorry I missed dinner, Kimmie."

Tilting my head down and frowning, I said, "You and me both. What happened?"

He sat on the edge of our bed. "I was finishing up something and completely lost track of time."

My stomach sank. Despite Nicholas's workaholic tendencies of late, I fully expected him to make an exception to meet my sister and hoped for a better excuse than "I lost track of the time." It wasn't even on Erin's list of possibilities.

"I texted you. More than once," I said in a low voice, in an attempt to disguise my annoyance.

"I got so wrapped up in what I was doing, I didn't even notice the phone vibrating. I hoped I'd get there for dessert, but then I saw your last text about meeting me at home." With a wry smile, he said, "On a bright note, I was saved from the wrath of the infamous Erin."

Wincing, I said, "So not funny, Nicholas." As much as I enjoyed complaining about my sister, she was the only person in the world who shared my history—only we made silly faces behind our dad's back when he slurped his cold cereal, and only we, along with my father, were victims of my mom's absentminded habit of turning off the light whenever she left a room even if we were still in there—I really wanted her to meet the first man I'd ever truly loved. "It's not like I sprung these plans on you at the last minute."

Nicholas to his dresser, and with his back to me said, "I didn't realize it was so important to you. It's not as if you're super close."

I weaved my fingers through my hair and pulled. "She's my only sister, Nicholas." Blinking back the onset of tears at his nonchalance, I said, "It's bad enough you stood us up. Please don't try to downplay it too."

"You're right," he said, turning around. When his eyes met mine, his face dropped. "Shit, Kimmie. I really *am* sorry." He sat back down on the bed and took my hand in his. "I screwed up royally, didn't I?"

I shrugged, unable to communicate my conflicting emotions. As disappointed as I was with Nicholas for working through dinner and angered by his casual dismissal of the situation, I also didn't want to be the needy girlfriend who got in the way of his career advancement.

Handing me a tissue, he said, "I promise to make it up to you."

Wiping a tear from my eye, I said, "What do you have in mind?"

Nicholas appeared to contemplate for a moment before responding. "How about we take a road trip to Massachusetts as soon as things slow down a bit?"

"Yeah?" We had never taken a trip together.

Nicholas nodded. "We can make it a long weekend. A night or two with Erin and Gerry and then a couple of nights in a hotel in downtown Boston just the two of us. We can go to Faneuil Hall and do all the fun touristy stuff."

"Sounds fun." I was still mad but bending.

"Please don't hate me, Kimmie Long."

"I don't hate you," I muttered.

He cupped my face with his hands. "Maybe not, but your brown eyes are blue, and it's my fault."

My mouth quivered. "It *is* your fault."

Nicholas lowered his forehead toward mine. "I take full responsibility."

"Okay," I conceded with a small smile. At least he was trying.

"Does this mean you forgive me?"

"Yes." I could never stay angry with him for too long.

Nicholas joined me under the covers and pulled me to him. "Thank you," he said with a squeeze.

"You're welcome," I said, melting into his embrace.

Chapter 16

Constance Dash has just turned thirty-four, but she's already counting down the days until her thirty-fifth birthday with dread. Although she lives with her boyfriend of several years, she has a nagging fear he might not be The One. Should she toss her concerns aside and settle down like most women her age, or should she be honest with her boyfriend and risk being single on the dark side of thirty-five?

My phone rang, interrupting the drafting of my five-pink-champagne-flutes review of *Thriving at Thirty (Five)*. Not used to my cell phone ringing during work hours, I jolted out of the chair where I was eating lunch in my law firm's cafeteria. I didn't recognize the number, but it was a local call. With trepidation, I answered, "Hello?" I was afraid something might have happened to Nicholas, like a heart attack from too much stress. His schedule had not slowed down at all, and I was beginning to worry it was more permanent than a temporary result of a rough patch at work.

A female voice asked, "Is this Kimberly Long?"

"Yes, this is she. Who's calling, please?" I put a finger in my ear in an attempt to drown out the noise from the conversations taking place around me.

"Hi Kimberly. This is Felicia Harrison from Harrison & Gold Literary."

My mouth instantly dried up, and I took a sip of water before responding "Hi" as calmly as I could. My heart beat rapidly beneath my v-neck cashmere poncho, and I breathed deeply through my nose to calm down.

"Your friend Hannah Marshak asked me to read your novel, *A Blogger's Life*, as a favor to her. I just finished it."

My first reaction was the realization I shockingly won my bet with Bridget, and I smiled to myself, but amusement quickly morphed into terror. Did she like it? The silence was deafening, and I took it as my cue to say something. "Thank you so much for taking the time." I took another deep breath.

"I loved it."

Leaning forward in my chair, I blurted out, "Say what?" Mortified, I corrected myself. "I mean, you did?"

Chuckling, Felicia said, "Yes, I did. I think with some rewrites, it could be a winner. I'd like to run my ideas by you and find out more about you and your publishing goals if you're interested."

"Of course I'm interested."

"I'm so glad. How about Thursday evening? Five o'clock?"

Without hesitation, I responded, "That would be great," only afterward remembering I worked until five thirty and would have to leave early. I hoped Rob wouldn't mind, considering the circumstances.

"Where's your office?"

"Twenty-seventh and Park, but I can come to you, if it's more convenient." I would travel by train, plane, or automobile.

"How about we meet at the lobby bar at the Ace Hotel?"

"Perfect." The Ace was only a few blocks from my office. I could leave at 4:50 and still be on time.

"Terrific. I'll see you then. I saw your picture on *Pastel Is the New Black,* and Hannah mentioned you were very petite. I should be able to spot you, but if you see a woman with straight brown hair down her back with her nose in a manuscript, it's probably me."

Even though I knew exactly what she looked like from her website and additional internet stalking on Google Images, I responded cheerfully, "Good to know."

"See you Thursday, Kim."

"See you Thursday," I repeated before hanging up the phone. I immediately called Nicholas.

He picked up after the second ring. "Hey."

Drumming my feet against the floor, I asked, "Guess who just called me?" in a raised voice, unable to contain my excitement.

After a brief silence, during which I bounced up and down in my chair, dying to do a victory dance, Nicholas said, "Um, Felicia Harrison?"

I pouted. "How did you know?"

"Lucky guess?"

"Thanks for stealing my thunder, smarty pants," I said. "But, yes, Felicia freakin' Harrison called me. She loved my book. Can you believe it?"

"Of course I can believe it, Kimmie. It's a great book."

"You started it?" If my smile got any wider, I'd need a bigger face.

"Well...no. But I know it's terrific. And I'll read it soon."

Undaunted, I continued, "She wants to get together to discuss it. We're meeting on Thursday after work."

"Hooray, Kimmie! Congratulations."

My elation morphed into anxiety as I took a virtual tour of my book, wondering what parts she didn't like. "What if she wants me to rewrite the whole thing?"

I heard Nicholas blow air out of his cheeks. "Don't let your mind wander, Kim. Just hear what she has to say."

I bit my fingernail. "You're right."

"Listen, I'm so happy for you, but I have to get back to work. We'll talk more at home later, okay? I'll probably be late."

"Okay." The words "I love you" were spilling out of my mouth, but he disconnected the call before I could finish. Too keyed up to let it get to me, I vaulted from my chair and hoofed it out of the cafeteria to the elevator bank. When I reached my floor, I barreled through Rob's office door. "Guess what?"

From Rob's visitor chair, Daneen turned around and eyeballed me. "Let me take a stab. You reached ten thousand fans on your blog?"

I smirked at her. "That was so last month."

Rob glanced from Daneen to me and rolled his eyes. He was familiar with our hate-hate relationship. "What's the big news, Kim?"

Glancing at Daneen, I said, "I can tell you later if it's a bad time."

Daneen shrugged halfheartedly. "We're all friends here, Kim. Besides, the chances of you being the slightest bit productive until you dish the hair-raising developments in the blogosphere are nil."

Rob chuckled. "Daneen has a point. What's up?"

I hated when Rob made jabs about my work ethic in front of Daneen. Even though I knew he was playing, she didn't, but I let it slide to get on with my announcement. "A New York literary agent is interested in my book."

Rob beamed at me. "Fantastic, Kim. Next stop, *New York Times* bestseller list."

I crossed my fingers. "She hasn't signed me yet, so let's not get carried away." Nevertheless, I couldn't contain my grin.

"Yes, let's not get carried away," Daneen mumbled.

I turned to face her, my face heating up. "What did you say?"

Daneen smiled sweetly. "I think it's terrific an agent liked your book..."

"Thank you—"

"But like you said, she hasn't signed you yet. Remember that other agent? The one you were so revved up about at squad drinks? I wouldn't want you to get your hopes up too high again."

Even though I was privately afraid Daneen was right, I opened my mouth to tell her she could shove my hopes up her bony ass. I closed my mouth when it dawned on me the only way Daneen would have known Ginny rejected me was if Nicholas had told her. What was wrong with him?

"What's the next step?" Rob asked.

"We're meeting on Thursday at the lobby bar at the Ace Hotel." I bit my lip. "I'll need to leave early. I hope you don't mind. I was so thrilled, I agreed to meet her at five o'clock without thinking. I can come in a half hour early or work through lunch."

Rob smiled. "That won't be necessary. I think we can hold down the fort for thirty minutes."

"Thank you." Needling me in front of the enemy notwithstanding, I had every reason to love my boss. And being pessimistic would not protect me from an eventual rejection, so I might as well embrace being optimistic while it lasted.

"Kind of weird she wants to meet at a bar instead of her office, no?" Daneen asked.

I glared at her.

Daneen shrugged. "I'm just saying. It doesn't sound very official, and I would hate to see you disappointed."

"Sure you would," I muttered.

Rob cleared his throat. "Great job, Long. Keep us posted. And get back to work."

I chuckled. "On my way." Without a backward glance at Daneen, I turned on my heel and walked out of his office to my desk. I had several more calls to make.

Later that night, I lay in bed binge-watching *Orange Is the New Black*. I was in no danger of falling asleep—too charged with adrenaline due to the day's events and stoked for Nicholas to get home from work so we could celebrate. When I heard the key in the door, I abruptly sat up, eager to greet him. I wondered if he picked up flowers or bubbly on the way home. I smoothed out my hair, positioned myself casually on the bed, and turned off the television set. The sound of him dropping his keys on the kitchen table was followed by the opening and closing of the refrigerator door, and I waited impatiently for him to make his way into our bedroom. When he finally did, his head was down.

"Hi, baby," I said in a low voice. My stomach dropped in disappointment when I glanced at his empty hands.

Nicholas appeared startled as he whipped his head in my direction and smiled. "Hey. I thought you'd be asleep."

I stretched my arms over my head. "Too wired to sleep."

Nicholas sat on the edge of the bed. Kissing me on the forehead, he said, "What's going on?"

"Felicia Harrison wants to meet with me. Remember?"

Nicholas's mouth opened, but no sound came out.

"I take it your silence means you forgot." I forced a smile.

Nicholas frowned. "I'm sorry, Kimmie. Work was crazy today. It slipped my mind." He scratched his scruffy chin.

Maybe Daneen was right and I was getting riled up over nothing. "No worries. Like Daneen said, there's no need to get carried away. She hasn't signed me or anything. Speaking of Daneen—"

"She will," Nicholas interrupted before I could complete my sentence.

"You think?" I held my breath.

"I don't think," he said, brushing a hair away from my face. "I know. And when she does, we'll celebrate in style."

"Promise?"

"I promise. But I've got just the activity to keep your mind off of it for now," he said, planting soft kisses on my neck.

As a rush of warmth coursed through my body, all thoughts of confronting him about spilling my private business to Daneen were forgotten. I ran a hand over his rough jaw. No one wore scruff as well as Nicholas. "Yeah? What were you thinking?"

Lifting my nightshirt over my head, he flashed me a devilish grin. "To borrow a phrase I've heard you use many times, better to show than tell."

Chapter 17

Although, regretfully, I didn't connect with any of the characters enough to enjoy this book as much as I'd hoped, I think many fans of chick lit, especially those in the music industry, would adore the solid writing and spicy romance of Radio Nights *by Missy Spencer.*

"Kim."

I lifted my head from my laptop and locked eyes with Bridget, who was sitting next to me on her couch. "Huh?"

"Are you almost finished? We're starving here." She glanced over at Jonathan, who was standing by the windowsill smoking a cigarette. "Aren't we?"

Jonathan nodded in agreement.

Rather than go directly home after work, I had made plans with Bridget and Jonathan for dinner to distract me from obsessing over my meeting with Felicia Harrison the following night. Of course, I had every intention of analyzing it ad nauseum during our meal. "Okay, I need five more minutes to proofread this review, post it, and then share it on Facebook, Twitter, and Google Plus." Rob had me running around like crazy all day, and I didn't have time to post a review for a blog tour I was coordinating. The author had already sent me a gentle email asking what time it would be up. Thankfully, she lived in California where it was three hours earlier, but I knew she was anxiously awaiting my review, and I prided myself on keeping my authors happy. Although I suspected she wouldn't be too pleased with the three-pink-champagne-flutes review.

"Five minutes," Bridget repeated with a nod of her head.

I chewed the inside of my cheek. "Actually, make it ten. I also want to post the review on Goodreads, Barnes & Noble, and Amazon."

Bridget sighed. "Can't you do those things later?"

"I have my process down to a science, Bridge. I need to follow protocol, or my system will be all messed up."

Jonathan rolled his eyes. "If we don't eat soon, I'm going to order the entire menu, and then guess whose system will be messed up? It won't be pretty."

Bridget wrinkled her nose. "I can vouch for that. Please, K?"

I chuckled. "You've convinced me. Besides, it will give me something to do when I get home later besides imagine all of the ways I'm going to embarrass myself in front of Felicia."

Twenty minutes later, we were feasting on edamame, shumai, four special rolls, and one salmon and avocado roll at Poke, a BYOB sushi restaurant around the corner from Bridget and Jonathan's apartment. On the way, we stopped at a liquor store, and Jonathan bought a bottle of sake to share with Bridget. Rather than risk a hangover, I was sticking to water, but my arm was twisted to nurse one small glass of sake to take the edge off of my anxiety.

"Why are you so nervous, Long?" Jonathan asked.

I tossed an empty edamame shell in the plate set in the middle of our table. "Because she's a big New York City agent. I want to impress her."

"You've already crossed the most important threshold," he said before sliding a shot of sake down his throat and refilling his glass.

"And what threshold is that?" I asked.

He looked at me incredulously. "Uh, she liked the book and wants to meet you?"

I slouched in my chair. "Yeah, there's that."

Bridget giggled. "Leave it to Kim to take something potentially great and rewrite it into something ominous."

"I'm a writer. It's what I do." I chuckled as I grabbed a piece of spicy tuna and jalapeño roll with my chopsticks and dipped it into soy sauce.

Looking at me fondly, Bridget said, "It's so Kim of you."

"I'm PMSing too," I confided.

Rolling his eyes, Jonathan said, "And that's my cue." He glanced at his watch. "I need to step out early for my weekly Risk night, but here's my advice, for what's it worth. Go in there with quiet confidence. She already told you she loved your book. I know you're worried about the changes she mentioned, but be open to them, and don't get defensive. Don't forget to breathe and, if necessary, excuse yourself to the bathroom to gather your thoughts before you respond. I firmly believe in the twenty-second rule."

"What's the twenty-second rule?" Bridget and I asked at the same time.

Jonathan placed his chopsticks on the table. "It's human nature to defend ourselves against criticism, or any behavior we think of as unfair or insulting. If we follow our first instinct to lash out in response, we can set ourselves up for getting in deep trouble, but if we wait twenty seconds, we're more likely to act rationally. Imagine receiving an email from your boss asking you to stay late on a night he knows you have major plans."

"I do not miss the days of having a boss," Bridget said.

Jonathan scooted his chair closer to Bridget's. "Neither do I."

I waited patiently for Bridget and Jonathan to finish rubbing noses like Inuit while basking in their self-employed status.

Focusing his attention back on me, Jonathan continued. "After reading an email like that, you might mutter 'screw you' under your breath, but if you take it one step further and send a scathing response to your boss, you can kiss your job goodbye. Better to take a deep breath, walk a lap around the floor, or go to the bathroom before reacting. In your case, listen to what this agent has to say and take your time responding. Initially, you might think 'There is no way I'm making these changes to my book,' but after some thought, you might realize she has a point. Don't burn bridges."

My mouth fell open, unaccustomed to receiving such sage

advice from Jonathan—the same guy who spent most of our senior prom smoking pot in the parking lot and still maintained a weekly night in with the boys to play Risk. It was obvious Bridget was equally wowed by the way she was beaming at him. "I don't even know how to respond, Jonathan. Great advice. Thank you."

Jonathan waved me away. "You're welcome. It was nothing."

Bridget kissed a blushing Jonathan on the cheek. "It was something. Don't sell yourself short, sweetie."

Jonathan tossed two twenties on the table and stood up. "Sorry to run. Good luck tomorrow. I'm sure Bridget will let me know how it went." After a quick peck on Bridget's lips, he threw on his coat and exited the restaurant.

"Color me impressed," I said to Bridget.

Bridget watched through the window as Jonathan walked down the street. "The love of a good woman has the power to open up a man's potential." A film of pink creeping up her cheeks, she said, "Not that you weren't a good woman back in high school."

I laughed. "No offense taken. I wasn't a woman; I was a girl. And I didn't really love Jonathan. Not the way you do."

With a faraway look in her eyes, Bridget smiled.

"I won the bet, you know." In response to her confused expression, I clarified. "You bet me Hannah wouldn't deliver my book to Felicia as promised. You lost."

Bridget shrugged. "There must be something in it for her. Maybe she gets some sort of referral fee."

Whatever motivated Hannah to come through for me, I was grateful and not interested in fighting about it with Bridget. "In any event, it's payback time."

Bridget raised an eyebrow. "Remind me of the conditions of this bet."

"If you won, I owed you dinner at Gina's. If *I* won..." I smiled wickedly. "You promised me your honest take on Jonathan's wacko refusal to ever get married."

"Just because you don't agree with something doesn't make it 'wacko.'"

Bridget tossed her napkin on the plate. "I already told you I'm cool with it. Several times."

"Since when? We've had countless discussions on this topic over the course of our friendship, and you were always pro-marriage."

Bridget shook her head. "We never shared our thoughts on being in a committed relationship without actually tying the knot."

"But—"

"And the reason I never mentioned the latter possibility is because I didn't even know it was an option. We were raised accepting marriage as a given. I wasn't aware of any alternatives because I wasn't exposed to them. I love Jonathan. I'm *in* love for the first time in my life, and I'm certain beyond debate he feels the same way about me. Making it 'legal' is inconsequential."

"How can you say that? Do you know how hard LBGT people worked to get same-sex marriages legalized?"

Bridget threw her head back and sighed impatiently. "And I vehemently support those rights, Kim. But it doesn't mean I want to get married. Just because I'm legally entitled to do something doesn't mean I have to do it. Just because prostitution is legal in some states doesn't mean I'm going to whore myself out." Narrowing her eyes at me, she asked, "Why is this so important to you? Is it because of Nicholas?"

I frowned into my plate at the sound of his name. Despite amazing sex the night before, I couldn't kick my disappointment with his lackluster response to Felicia's interest in my novel and his failure to keep my personal business from Daneen, something I still hadn't confronted him about. "It has nothing to do with him. I'm worried you're giving up on something important to you without a fight, but I'll let it go."

She smiled at me. "Thank you. If I change my mind, you'll be the second to know. Right after Jonathan."

"Swear?" Even though I was tempted to accuse her of merely repeating Jonathan's arguments, I knew my continued pursuit of the subject would seriously piss her off.

She extended her pinky toward me. "On Hannah Marshak's life."

I narrowed my eyes at her. "If you're attempting to reassure me, you might want to choose a person you don't hate."

"I don't hate her. Any friend of yours is a friend of mine," Bridget said unconvincingly.

"She's not my friend," I corrected.

"Could've fooled me," Bridget mumbled into her plate.

"What's that supposed to mean?"

Not looking me in the eyes, Bridget said, "You've had drinks with her twice now."

My head jerked back. "Yes, two times in the course of almost a year. And the first time, she dragged me out of Starbucks insisting the dirt she had on Daneen required a seedier environment than a chain coffee shop. And if you recall, you and Caroline encouraged me to meet her the second time so I could ask for help getting an agent."

Bridget's face turned red.

Knowing I had her cornered, I pressed on. "Using that logic, you can blame yourself for my budding *friendship* with Hannah."

Bridget covered her ears with her hands. "I don't hear you. La la la la."

Smirking, I shook my head at her until we broke out into simultaneous laughter.

Chapter 18

The following afternoon, David hovered over my desk while waiting for Rob to give him the heads-up to enter. He was in a closed-door meeting with another partner. "We decided on Barbados. Amy's fantasy is to honeymoon in Fiji or Bora Bora, but we just can't afford the airfare."

I frowned. "I can only imagine. But at least this way, you can use the money you saved on airfare on fancy restaurants or exciting excursions. My sister said the seafood in Barbados is amazing, and she's difficult to please. I can ask her for restaurant recommendations." Even though it would mean an extended phone call with my sister so soon after her visit, during which she would no doubt rehash the details of the weeklong vacation she and Gerry had taken the year before and probably drill me about Hannah, David was one of my favorite colleagues.

David beamed at me, his blue eyes bright. "I'd appreciate it. Thanks."

"Anytime. Besides, I'm sure marrying you is Amy's fantasy come true."

Thrusting his chest out, David said, "I certainly hope so. Her becoming my wife is definitely a dream come true for me."

I wasn't planning to tell anyone about my meeting with Felicia, but was afraid I'd burst if I kept silent any longer. "Between you and me, one of my dreams might come true tonight as well."

David leaned toward me. "Do tell."

"A literary agent read my book and we're meeting after work to discuss it. I'm praying she'll want to represent me."

My breathing quickened just saying the words.

When Rob bellowed, "You there, David?" from his office, I noticed his door was now open and Daneen had come out.

David shrugged. "I guess it's my turn now. If I don't see you before you leave, good luck tonight."

When the door closed behind him, I glanced at the bottom of my computer, praying it was significantly closer to four forty than the last time I checked. I wanted ten minutes of prep time to brush my teeth and freshen up my makeup before leaving to meet Felicia. It was only a few minutes past three.

"So your meeting with that literary agent is tonight?"

I looked up at Daneen and nodded softly. I wouldn't dare brag to her, especially since my overconfidence with Ginny Webber had blown up in my face.

"What time?"

"Five. Rob said I could leave a little early." I braced myself for her less than supportive response. In typical Daneen fashion, she would probably remind me not to get my hopes up and to think twice about taking advantage of my boss's good nature over a pipe dream.

"I remember. Good luck," she said before walking away.

I swiveled in my chair and watched her retreating back in shock. Maybe she'd mellowed.

Unable to concentrate, I headed to the bathroom, running into Lucy on her way out. Although very bookish during the day, Lucy was a work-hard play-hard gal who knew how to let her thin blond hair down from its usual bun at sunset. I first experienced this at the farewell party the firm threw for Nicholas at a karaoke bar when, after downing several apple martinis, a tipsy Lucy belted out an enthusiastic, albeit off-key, rendition of "It's Raining Men." Since getting serious with Nicholas, I had enjoyed the company of what he called "Bad Lucy" many times.

"I love your outfit, Kim."

"Thank you," I said, looking down at my current uniform: a pink wool skirt paired with a gingham top and black pumps.

Lucy glanced down at her stodgy brown skirt and white button-down. "I really need to upgrade my daytime style."

I agreed she was overdue for a shopping spree, but I reserved brutal honesty for my close friends. "When you're on a budget like mine, the key is to keep the distinction between daytime and nighttime style to a minimum, and make sure all outfits can easily transfer from work to play."

"Good point. Thanks, Kim," Lucy said, before removing the pen from her bun and scribbling on her legal pad.

In the same day, I had dished helpful advice to both David and Lucy. I hoped karma in the nature of an offer for agent representation was in my near future.

After using the bathroom, I returned to my desk, happy for the validation provided by Lucy that I was aptly dressed. I wondered what Hannah wore on her first meeting with Felicia. As if reading my mind, my phone pinged the arrival of a message on Facebook from Hannah.

Felicia told me about your little meet and greet this evening. Bonne Chance. Don't make me sorry I referred you.

I chuckled. Coming from Hannah, this was the sincerest expression of good luck I could expect, and I wasn't expecting any. I would tell Bridget about it, but she would roll her eyes and rattle off all of the ways Hannah was brainwashing me.

I had now received good-luck messages from my parents, Bridget, Hannah, and even Jonathan—all of the important people in my life except Caroline and Nicholas. But I couldn't blame Caroline. She was on a different continent, unlike Nicholas, who slept next to me in bed last night. I tried to find the humor in receiving encouragement from Hannah—the girl who used every trick in the Mean Girl manual to trash my self-esteem back in high school—but not Nicholas—the man who professed to love me. But instead of making me laugh, the thought threatened to make my eyes tear. Despite anger quietly brewing deep in my belly, I would forgive his lack of forethought on the assumption he was slammed at work again. Giving him an opportunity to provide positive reinforcement, I sent him a text: "T-1:30 before I meet with Felicia. Wish me luck!" I placed my cell phone back in my purse as my office phone rang—Daneen. I answered it with a tentative, "Hello."

"Can you please meet me in the conference room on this floor?"

"Um..." What if she concocted some evil plan to make me work overtime? I was not above doing overtime on occasion—it was par for the course in the law-firm environment—but I would sooner pay a temp out of my own pocket than miss my appointment with the first agent to take genuine interest in *A Blogger's Life*.

As if reading my mind, Daneen said, "It won't take long."

"Be right there." With shaky legs, I walked around the corner and knocked on the closed door of the conference room.

"Come in."

When I opened the door, I was met with Daneen standing at the foot of the table with three stacks of documents. "I need your help with something." She pointed at the papers. "These documents were sent by the other side as part of discovery on a case. Unfortunately, the pagination is all off and it's impossible to make sense of them out of order." She shook her head in disgust. "I'm not entirely sure opposing counsel didn't do it on purpose. I need your help getting them in page order."

I glanced down at the documents. I figured there had to be anywhere between 150 and 300 pages in total. "You're going to help me?" Between the two of us, it might not take that long.

Daneen cackled. "I can't possibly bill for this at my four hundred dollar an hour rate."

My voice trembled as I asked, "Do you think David might be able to assist? Or one of the other secretaries?" I licked my lips. "It's not that I don't want to help you, but I—" What if I couldn't finish before I was supposed to leave to meet Felicia?

"Don't worry. I know you have your appointment. It shouldn't take long." She smiled at me. "I really appreciate your help." Then she closed the door behind her.

I breathed in and out through my nose and regarded the

documents from a distance again. The sooner I got started, the quicker I'd be finished. I'd left my phone in my purse and wasn't wearing my watch but it couldn't be later than three thirty. Maybe only portions of the pages were out of order and it wouldn't take me long. How bad could it be?

It only took a few minutes to discover the answer to that question was very, very bad. From what I could tell, there were no two consecutive pages in any of the three stacks—page two was right before page ninety-six which was right before page one hundred and twenty-three—which meant I had to start from scratch. My plan was to make piles for every twenty pages—one through twenty, twenty through forty, and so on—and put them all together at the end. I only hoped the conference table was large enough to fit all of the piles because I was afraid changing my number system would be too complicated for my math-challenged brain.

After a rough start, I got into a nice rhythm and the piles were coming along nicely. At first, I pulled one paper at a time, but I was now grabbing three at once and circling the table to insert them in their rightful piles before going back for three more. I thought I was making good progress, but I really wished I knew what time it was. I'd only gone through one pile and worried it was almost five o'clock. Worst case scenario, I wouldn't have time to freshen up first. Felicia was judging my writing skills, not whether my makeup application was stale. On the flip side, presentation spoke volumes as to how serious I was about my writing career. What if I was a sweaty mess from running around the table and my lipstick cakey from lack of hydration and Felicia assumed I didn't care enough to make a good impression?

My stomach quaked in anxiety and I made an impulsive decision to quicken my pace by filing more pages at a time. I grabbed a thicker stack from the second pile and yelped in pain from a stinging sensation in my right index finger. It felt like a paper cut, but there was no blood. Thank God. I stared down at my finger and chanted, "Please don't bleed. Please don't bleed" until a tiny dot of blood formed that, within two seconds, grew bigger. I held my finger away from my body to avoid staining my outfit and darted my eyes around the room in a panic. I needed a bandage. The receptionist kept a stash in her desk, but there was no time. A piece of paper would work for applying pressure to the cut, but Daneen would kill me if I used one of the documents.

I pressed my thumb hard against the cut hoping to stop the bleeding while I searched the room for something I could use. What would MacGyver do? When I saw the stack of yellow notepads, I jumped up and down in glee. I grabbed a couple and wrapped them around my finger using the adhesive strips to keep them in place. Once I was confident the bleeding had stopped, I wiped my thumb on the table, vowing to clean the blood off later, continued my filing and prayed I hadn't wasted too much time.

The door opened and Daneen said, "How's it going in here, Kimberly?"

I winced. When Daneen first started at the firm, she insisted on calling me Kimberly after I told her I preferred Kim. She'd smirk each time she went against my request and didn't stop until I hinted about knowing her embarrassing secret from her college days. She must have realized I didn't have it in me to actually use the dirt against her and was back to her old tricks. It was annoying, but I had bigger problems right now.

I motioned toward the many piles on the table. "I'm making progress. Do you know what time it is?"

Daneen glanced at her watch. "It's four o'clock. You're very efficient when you put your mind to it." She walked out and closed the door behind her again.

Too busy to respond to her condescending "compliment," I resumed my steady pace, careful not to cut myself again. When I was down to one more stack of pages, I felt a burst of pride. Almost finished.

The next time Daneen came in, instead of asking me how things were going, she circled the table and silently studied my progress. "Interesting system," she said.

"It gets the job done," I said with more energy than I felt. "What time is it now?"

"Four fifteen."

I beamed. "Great. I should be able to finish with plenty of time to get to my meeting." I might even have a few minutes to replenish my lip gloss and run a brush through my hair. Maybe spritz some perfume. If paper had a scent, I'd be drenched in it by now.

"You can take your sweet time at this point." She chuckled, turned on her heel, and walked out.

Even though it wasn't taking as long to complete the assignment as I'd feared, I didn't think it was wise to dilly dally. I would continue at the same frantic speed so I could head to the Ace Hotel at a leisurely pace. A moment later, the door creaked back open. I assumed it was Daneen, but it was Rob.

His eyes bugged out and he looked at his watch. "Shouldn't you have left for your meeting?"

"I'm almost finished," I said, pointing to the remaining very short stack of unsorted documents. "It's only four fifteen and I don't have to leave until ten minutes of five."

Rob's mouth dropped open. "You need to reset your watch, kiddo. It's ten after five."

The paper I was holding fell out of my shaking hand. "What?" I could feel the color drain from my face. I was already ten minutes late.

"Leave this. Just go."

My breath was ragged as I jogged uptown, zigzagging through the crowd of commuters, toward 29th Street where Ace Hotel was located between Broadway and Fifth Avenue. My heavy purse banged against my side with each step, but the only pain I experienced was the ache of watching my publishing dream fray like paper through a shredder. Thank God Rob had come in when he did or I'd still be on Daneen's time under the false assumption I was early enough to make myself pretty and still arrive five minutes early. Instead, after Rob set me straight, I sprinted to my cubicle, where I grabbed my purse and my jacket and bolted out the door without bothering to shut down my computer. I didn't even have a chance to warn Rob about the blood stain I'd left on the table. While the elevator made its descent to the lobby, I searched through my emails to find Felicia's phone number, but I couldn't locate it fast enough and decided it was better to go directly to the hotel than waste more time searching.

What if I'd blown my one chance at the big time? At the next stoplight, I reached into my bag and called Nicholas. When his voicemail picked up, I choked back a sob. "It's me. I'm so scared. I'm on my way to meet Felicia, but I'm really late. Daneen gave me an assignment and told me it was only a little after four when it was really five so I'm racing to the hotel now." I stared at the street light, willing it to turn red so pedestrians would have the right of way. I was tempted to run through the traffic, but death from being hit by a car would guarantee I missed my meeting with Felicia even if Daneen's evil plan didn't. "Light changed," I shouted into the phone while racing across the street. "Please cross your fingers she's still there. I don't know what I'll do if I screwed this up. Oh, God, Nicholas, I'm terrified. Okay, bye." I hung up and tossed the phone back in my bag, and speed walked across the street to the hotel.

I barreled right past the dimly lit lobby, ignoring the many people sitting on wrap-around leather couches and working on laptops, and headed directly to the bar in the back where I was supposed to meet Felicia. I scanned the room, praying I'd see her sitting on one of the black upholstered couches, but she wasn't there. My search of the bar yielded the same results and my chin quivered uncontrollably in the knowledge I was too late.

A torrent of tears threatening to be shed within seconds, I hurried to the ladies' room. The sink area was empty and I kneeled on the ground and cried with my head between my legs. I heard the sound of someone using the bathroom and opened my eyes to see a pair of brown leather boots in one of the stalls. Sighing loudly, I raised myself to a standing position, leaned against the sink, and called Nicholas again, although I doubted he'd be able to understand my message through my tears. "She left, Nicholas. What am I going to do? Felicia only agreed to read my book because of Hannah and I blew it. Why did Daneen do this to me? Why didn't I wear my watch to work today? Why is this happening to me? Where are you? Please call me. I need you." I placed the phone on the edge of the sink and gazed at my reflection in the mirror. My cheeks were red, my eyes swollen from crying, and my hair was wet from perspiration and matted to my face.

The door to the occupied bathroom opened slowly and I grimaced wondering how much the woman had heard. When she emerged from the stall and I saw who it was, my mouth dropped open.

Chapter 19

I rubbed my eyes to make sure I wasn't seeing things. "Felicia?"

She took a step forward and nodded. "Kim, I presume?"

My throat was dry, and I swallowed hard, praying my voice wouldn't crack or worse fail me completely. I nodded. "I'm so sorry I'm late. I thought it was only four fifteen and when my boss told me it was after five, I literally ran here from Twenty-seventh and Park. When I didn't see you at the bar, I assumed you left. And you heard the rest. I'm so sorry." Gesturing to my disheveled reflection in the mirror, I said, "I'm not usually a train wreck."

Felicia patted my shoulder comfortingly. "I'd like to hear the whole story, but first let's get you out of the bathroom." She opened the door and held it for me to walk out.

"Thanks," I said, my voice shaking. I followed her to an empty couch.

"Have a seat. Do you want a drink?"

The answer to her question was an unequivocal "hell yes," but I didn't know the proper protocol. Was it a trick question?

As if reading my mind, Felicia said, "You look like you need one."

I smiled. "I kind of do."

Felicia laughed. "I'll get a glass of champagne for both of us. You catch your breath."

Nodding like an obedient child, I said, "Okay."

Even though I had seen pictures of Felicia during various stages of agent stalking, I discreetly checked her out as she ordered our drinks at the bar. With fifteen years' experience, she was probably about forty, although she could easily pass for thirty-five. She was tall—at least compared to me—and thin with killer legs and warm brown eyes. Her chestnut brown hair was styled all one length except for bangs. She was pretty and so far seemed as kind as her appearance suggested. The fact that she didn't chastise me for wasting her time and, instead, offered to buy me a drink made me kind of love her.

Returning from the bar, Felicia handed me a glass of champagne before sitting down next to me. Then she clinked her glass against mine. "Better?"

I took a small sip, determined to pace myself. "Much better," I confessed.

Felicia placed her glass on the finished wood table in front of us. "Before we get down to business, I need to know why you thought it was only four fifteen."

I shook my head in dismay. "Because one of the attorneys gave me an assignment knowing I had to leave early and then she lied to me about what time it was. Twice."

Felicia pulled a face. "Why would she lie about the time?"

"Because she hates me and wants my boyfriend." I gulped. Too much formation.

"Classic chick lit material right there," Felicia said with a laugh.

"Tell me about it," I muttered before apologizing again.

"I did assume you were a no show and was going to head out after I used the facilities, but you're here now. Do you still want to talk about *A Blogger's Life*?"

Tears welled up behind my eyelids, but this time in relief. "Definitely. Thank you so much for reading it." Anticipating the conversation about to take place, I felt a pulsing in my throat. I had made it to the meeting, but I still had to get through it.

Felicia picked up her glass and took a sip. "It was my pleasure. It's a great story, Kim. You should be proud."

Lifting my chin, I said, "Thank you." So far so good.

"Although the market is flooded with bloggers-turned-authors, a novel from the perspective of a book blogger is fresh." Tipping her head, she queried, "It is fiction, right?"

"Yes. I mean, I relied on my own experiences as a book blogger for authenticity, but the story itself, as well as the characters, are completely fictitious."

Felicia nodded. "You've got talent, Kim, and I think the novel has a wide appeal for younger readers of chick lit, romantic comedy, and humorous women's fiction. But…"

But. I held my breath, praying she wouldn't say she couldn't sell *A Blogger's Life* in this market unless I was an established author. I didn't think I could take hearing it again.

"I'm concerned with one angle of the story."

Drawing on Jonathan's advice, I kept my urge to be defensive at bay and took a deep breath. "Which angle?"

Felicia sighed. "Readers of chick lit forgive their heroines for many things from poor judgment to lack of backbone to downright stupidity. Part of the fun is rooting for them to come into their own and earn their happy endings. You know?"

I nodded. "Definitely."

Felicia gave me a closed-lip smile. "But some mistakes are easier to forgive than others. I think readers will pull for Laurel through her uncertainty over her relationship with Henry and even her flirtation with other guys, but if she crosses the line and cheats on him, I think you'll lose them."

I exhaled. "Oh."

"Do you feel strongly about this subplot?"

I silently counted to three to collect my thoughts. "Not really. The truth is, I was afraid writing a novel about a book blogger would naturally lend itself to telling my own life story, and I was trying to avoid it. Laurel does things I'd never consider—like cheating on my boyfriend."

Felicia nodded in understanding. "Fair enough. But my advice is to avoid infidelity by Laurel. And if you want her to end up with Henry, I would choose something besides cheating on either of their parts as the major conflict. You want the reader to pull for the couple getting their happily ever after, but if Henry cheats, they might turn against him too." She shrugged. "That's my free advice, even if you don't choose to work with me."

Oh. My. God. My voice barely a whisper, I said, "Are you saying you want to be my agent?" I crossed my fingers.

Felicia grinned. "I love your voice, and if you're open to rewrites, yes, I'd like to represent you. I'd be happy to brainstorm some ideas with you."

My mind was already churning. "I have some thoughts."

Giving me an amused smile, Felicia said, "You don't have to decide this minute. Think about it. It's your baby, and you need to trust your instincts."

I debated playing it cool. "I've thought about it, and I'm in. All in."

Raising her palms in the air, Felicia pouted. "I didn't even get to my hard sell."

With a crooked smile, I said, "Yeah, I suppose I should ask you more questions, find out where you see my future as an author, right? I'm clearly playing this all wrong, aren't I?"

Felicia gave me a reassuring pat on the arm. "You're doing fine. I'm excited to work with you and already have some editors in mind. Chick lit is not the easiest genre to sell, but contrary to public opinion, it's not dead. Although I might be selling it as humorous women's fiction or romantic comedy depending on the house, chick lit by any other name is still chick lit. What else are you working on?"

Buoyed by her confidence in the genre, I was thrilled to provide details on my work in progress. "I've started another chick lit novel about a country girl who takes a summer internship in New York City and rents an apartment on Stone Street not realizing it's one of the liveliest streets in the city. The story revolves around the constant drama playing out in the half a dozen cafes and bars lining the cobblestone street." I came up with the idea one night when Bridget, Jonathan, Nicholas, and I sat outside drinking beers at Bavaria Bier House on the street. We got dizzy watching people, mostly tourists, walk back and forth past our table, and it was so loud, we could barely hear ourselves speak. I wondered out loud what it must be like to live in an apartment on top of one of the cafes and inspiration struck.

Felicia's face lit up. "I love it. You can call it *Love on Stone Street.*"

"You're brilliant!" I lifted my hand to give her a high five, but blessedly got my wits about me before it was too late. I placed my glass of champagne on the table and pushed it out of arm's length.

Tilting her head to the side, Felicia asked, "So, what are these ideas you have for revising *A Blogger's Life?*"

I shared my thoughts with Felicia, and as we bounced possibilities back and forth, I became more and more convinced she was the perfect agent for me. Besides having a confidence-inspiring track record—she helped turn Hannah Marshak into a bestselling chick lit author—she loved my voice, my writing style, and my story, was impressed with my existing social media platform and ideas for promotion, and it sounded like she might go after a two-book deal. And, let's not forget how forgiving she was of my tardiness.

"The popularity of *Pastel Is the New Black* and the volume of your Facebook and Twitter followers will be a powerful tool to reach potential readers, but it's never too early to build an author platform separate from the blog. I did a quick search and saw that www.kimberlylong.com is available. You should get on that."

I removed my pink silk-screen journal from my bag and jotted down: Talk to Bridget about buying author website. Facing Felicia again, I said, "Got it."

She pointed to her own black leather-bound journal. Smiling, she said, "With modern technology, printed journals are a dying breed."

I glanced at my journal and grinned. When Nicholas bought it for me before we even started dating, he said he hoped it would inspire me to write great things. "I never leave home without it."

"Glad to see I'm not the only holdout," she said before tapping her chin and appearing to contemplate. "Have you considered getting associate reviewers for *Pastel Is the New Black*?"

Nodding, I said, "I have. I'm inundated with reviews and coordinating blog tours on top of a day job, writing, and trying to maintain a personal life, but I've always found a reason not to do it." I gave her a sheepish grin. "I'm kind of a control freak about my blog."

Chuckling, Felicia said, "I understand. I just think as an author, you'll need to be careful about reviewing other books. I've read your reviews. They're well thought out and thorough. And sometimes brutal."

I remembered Nicholas saying the same thing when he first read my blog. "I'm very frank in my reviews, yes."

"Honesty is a great characteristic in a book reviewer." Laughing, she added, "Although I'm sure some authors would disagree with me. But when you're one of them, it gets tricky."

I bit my lip. "So you don't think I should review books anymore?"

I'd defined myself as a book blogger for years. Giving it up would leave a gaping hole in my identity I wasn't sure even writing my own novels would fill.

Felicia shook her head. "Definitely don't do away with *Pastel Is the New Black*. Besides posting book reviews, you can cross-promote with other successful and up-and-coming authors. But maybe consider getting an assistant so you can pick and choose the books you want to review. Perhaps the ones you're more certain you'll review positively. That way, you can be honest without calling attention to yourself or possibly asking for bitter authors to slam your books in retaliation. Anonymously, of course," she said, rolling her eyes.

Felicia had a point. There were many trolls who left one- and two-star ratings on Goodreads, and I often wondered if they were other authors doing it to keep the competition at bay. There wasn't much I could do to prevent it, but I didn't have to invite it by posting negative reviews on my blog.

"Anyway, you don't need to decide anything right now. Just something to consider," Felicia said.

I exhaled deeply. "It's a lot to think about. I'm not complaining, mind you."

"I'll send you a contract in the next few days. It's a standard contract, but you should review it with an attorney."

I smirked. It was about time my association with so many lawyers worked in my favor. "I'm pretty sure finding legal counsel won't be a problem. My boyfriend is a lawyer and so is my boss. And my best friend is a website designer who can help me with Kimberlylong.com."

Felicia stood up. "Aren't you lucky to have friends in such important places? And let's not forget Hannah." She smiled.

I raised myself to a standing position and nodded. "Definitely. Hannah's a great friend," I said, my voice catching. The words sounded so odd rolling off my tongue. "Thanks so much for the champagne and for...well...everything. I'm so excited." We walked side by side toward the front of the hotel.

"My pleasure, Kim. I'm eager to see the changes you make. How much time do you think you'll need?"

"I'll get started right away. Is two weeks, give or take a few days, okay?"

"Sounds perfect to me."

I feared "give" was more likely than "take," but hoped for the best. I'd buckle down and write every evening after work and part of the weekends, devoting lunch hours to my blog to avoid falling desperately behind. Nicholas would understand. He was an expert at putting work before our relationship lately. My mind wandered to the text I sent him before I left and the two panicked voicemails I'd left him, but I brushed it aside. I refused to let anything diminish the awesomeness of this conversation—not even the possibility my boyfriend was too busy to support me on one of the most important days of my life so far.

When we got outside, we stopped momentarily on the sidewalk. Felicia pointed east. "I'm heading this way."

I pointed south. "I'm grabbing the train on 23rd."

"Have a great night, Kim, and I'll be in touch." She extended her hand to me.

Shaking it, I said, "Great."

For an instant, I worried it was all a dream and pinched myself to confirm I was awake. If it were a sleep-induced hallucination, it topped even my most erotic dream to date. I walked to the subway station with an extra bounce in my step and a huge smile on my face, tempted to announce my news to every passing pedestrian. When I arrived on the platform, I checked my phone. I assumed Nicholas would have called me back by now, but there were no voice messages or missed calls, just a quick text. "Breathe, Kimmie. Just give Felicia a call if she's not there. I'm sure she'll understand. It's not life or death. Good luck and keep me posted."

I chewed at my lip, disappointed that Nicholas was so nonchalant over a situation that could have been a major disaster and roadblock to my dreams of publication. Choosing to focus on the fact that despite the rocky start, the evening ended with an offer for representation, I wrote him back: "I found her in the bathroom of all places. She heard me crying to you on the phone. I told her what happened and she was totally cool. Even better, she wants to be my agent! Celebrate tonight?"

I made a conscious effort to keep my mouth closed on the train, but my lips had a mind of their own and insisted on grinning shamelessly from 23rd Street to Spring Street. My legs bounced up and down as I sat, impatient for the doors of the train to open so I could hurry home to Nicholas. Over a bottle of wine, I would tell him everything. Then I would lavish in his admiration and pride. Finally, we would undress in a frenzy and make love late into the night.

At last, the train arrived at my stop, and I plowed through the crowd, jogging up the subway stairs and out onto the street as quickly as my three-inch heels would take me. I whipped out my phone and smiled when I saw a text from Nicholas.

"Awesome! I'm so proud of you. Unfortunately, I have an

insane deadline at work. I promise to make it up to you. How about tomorrow?"

Feeling like a tire diminished of air, I slowed my steps. Nicholas liked to joke about "the glamorous life of an attorney," but as the suffering girlfriend, I wasn't laughing.

In no rush to go home to a celebration of one, I switched directions and walked toward the coffee shop. There was no time like the present to start my rewrites—right after I dished the big news to Bridget and my parents who, unlike Nicholas, wouldn't be too busy to celebrate with me, albeit telephonically.

Chapter 20

I woke the next morning to the sound of the shower running and stretched my body across the empty bed. I hadn't heard Nicholas get home the night before and slept through his alarm clock too. Either he was being especially stealthy or I had slept hard. Slowly, the events of the prior night came to me. After Nicholas's work ethic stuck a pin in my happiness balloon, I had called my folks and Bridget, whose reaction to my news lifted me back up. Besides being thrilled for me, they encouraged me to put my disappointment with Nicholas into perspective. He was a lawyer and working late came with the initials "J.D." I was well aware of this when we started dating and had no expectations of his career obligations changing once we moved in together. And besides, he was delaying our celebration by twenty-four hours, not blowing it off completely. Rather than mope around our apartment all by myself, I'd headed to Ground Support Café, where I made a nice dent in my edits over a decaf latte and a grilled cheese sandwich. By the time I got into bed at eleven, my eyes were heavy, and my bones weary and ready for sleep. I had dreamed about movie deals and Nicholas devouring me until the sun came up. I hoped at least one half of the dream would come true that night.

Nicholas stepped out of the bathroom with a towel around his hips and approached the bed with a smile. "Sleeping Beauty wakes."

I lifted my arms over my head and yawned, not bothering to cover my mouth.

"What time did you get home last night?" I scooted closer to the center of the bed to give him room to sit next to me.

"It was about twelve thirty. I would have woken you, but you were dead to the world."

"I'm surprised I was able to fall asleep. I was so psyched up."

"With good reason. I'm so happy for you, Kimmie." He leaned down and nuzzled my neck.

I patted the bed. "Can you snuggle for a minute?"

Nicholas glanced at the digital clock on the nightstand before joining me on the bed. "Just for a minute."

We lay facing each other—me under the covers and him on top. "It was close there for a while," I said.

Nicholas's brow furrowed. "What do you mean?"

I pinched my lips together. "Did you even listen to my voicemails?"

"Of course I did, but by the time I heard them, it was later in the evening. I assumed if Felicia hadn't been there, you would have left another message."

"Daneen almost messed things up for me big-time."

Nicholas frowned. "Do you really think she would sink that low? What was in it for her if you missed the appointment?"

I shrugged. "Seeing me miserable?"

Nicholas smiled softly and ruffled my hair. "I say, all's well that ends well."

My gut told me Daneen purposely tried to sabotage my meeting, but Nicholas was around so infrequently lately and I didn't want to spend the precious time we had together arguing over her. I missed him too much for that.

Nicholas placed his forehead against mine and whispered, "What's with the sad face, Kimmie?"

I hadn't realized I'd made an unhappy face, but since he'd brought it up, I asked, "Are we okay?" Confrontation was not my favorite hobby, and I braced myself for his response.

Pulling away, Nicholas gazed at me with his eyebrows drawn together. "Of course we are. Why would you ask?"

"I don't know. We barely see each other anymore. Is your dad pressuring you to put in all these extra hours at the office?"

Nicholas stared down toward his feet. "He only wants to guide me in the right direction. He means well, and he's right. I need to up my game."

I didn't consider Warren's mode of tutelage "guiding" as much as "coercing," but I held my tongue. "I miss you madly."

"I know I've been around less than usual, but work is insanely busy right now. Bear with me, okay?"

I nodded. "I will. But can you say it back?"

"Say what back?"

"That you miss me too, buster. Do I have to beat it out of you?"

Nicholas chuckled. "I'm not sure I can defend myself against someone of your stature."

I shifted closer to him. "So, do you?"

Nicholas cocked his head to the side. "Do I what?"

I didn't buy the innocent act. "Miss me," I said, playfully kicking him from under the covers.

His eyes widening, he said, "Oh, that. Yes, I miss you, Kimmie Long. But I will have my way with you tonight." He got out of bed, leaving the towel behind.

I gazed at him longingly. "You promise?"

"I swear on my left testicle." Nicholas winked as he pulled his boxers over his hips. Glancing at the clock again, he asked, "Shouldn't you get up?"

"Oh yeah, work." I reluctantly lifted myself off the bed. "But the sooner I get to the office, the sooner I can leave and celebrate with you." I walked over to where Nicholas was standing and placed my hands on his hips. Lifting my chin to meet his eyes, I said, "Right?"

"Right." Nicholas nodded.

Chapter 21

"To Kim," Rob said, raising his glass of water.

David and Lucy repeated an enthusiastic, "To Kim."

Rob took a bite of his Oriental chicken salad. "I'm sorry we have to rush the celebration, but with the Judge's Dinner tonight, I need to be as productive as possible this afternoon."

In honor of Felicia's offer for representation, Rob took the squad out for a quick celebratory lunch at California Pizza Kitchen a few blocks from our office. Rob, a health nut in his mid-fifties with the energy and workout ethic of a thirty-year-old and a wife twenty years his junior, opted to eat salad instead of pizza. So did Daneen and Lucy. Only David and I shared a pizza. Then again, we were the only two who didn't need to save our appetites for the dinner to honor the Federal Judiciary that evening at the Waldorf Astoria.

"Thanks, guys. You have no idea how thrilled I am. I'm just glad it all worked out. I was this close to missing the meeting." After I said it, I made eye contact with everyone at the table, including Daneen. She didn't even flinch.

"What happened?" Lucy asked before taking a forkful of salad.

"I lost track of time and didn't leave the office until a quarter past five. Unfortunately for me, the meeting was scheduled for five at a bar ten minutes away." Both Daneen and I (and even Rob), knew whose fault it really was, but I didn't want to give Daneen the satisfaction of stooping to her level by telling everyone else what she'd done.

"Oh, no," Lucy said with wide eyes.

I waved my hand in the air. "It's all good. She was so understanding. We even shared a Champagne toast." I beamed at Lucy and then Daneen.

Daneen pouted at me. "It might be a tiny bit my fault too. As soon as I realized my watch was broken, I thought of you and worried I'd messed you up. But it was after hours by then. My bad. Forgive me?"

I smiled sweetly even as I seethed on the inside. "All's well that ends well."

"And as it turns out, those documents were useless anyway so it was all for nothing." Daneen snorted as if what she said was actually humorous.

Rob cleared his throat. "When the book comes out, we'll go someplace fancier. I promise."

"Your agent needs to sell the book to a publisher first. Isn't that correct?" Daneen asked before demurely wiping her mouth with a napkin.

"That's the way it usually works," I responded dryly.

Daneen nodded. "I was just checking. This is uncharted territory for me."

I narrowed my eyes at her but didn't respond. From the multitude of tidbits she had disclosed about the publishing process under the transparent guise of being helpful and supportive, one would assume she was an expert in the field. I took a bite of my California veggie slice, hoping someone would change the subject by the time I chewed and swallowed.

Daneen smiled at me without showing any teeth. "It could be a long process though, right?"

My stomach sank. I was acutely aware securing an agent was only the first step toward becoming a published author. "Yes. I don't know how long it will take Felicia to sell my book. Could be a very long time." If ever.

"Good thing for me you're not ready to quit the day job yet," Rob piped in, clearly trying to lighten the mood.

Pretending not to hear Daneen mumble, "And we all know

how vital secretaries are" under her breath, I smiled at Rob. "Yes, because I'm obviously the best assistant you've ever had."

Rob shrugged. "Eh. You might not be the most enthusiastic sometimes, but you've got good skills. And no one multitasks like you."

I gave myself a pat on the back. "I do what I can."

"Well, congratulations. I can't wait to tell Amy. She loves chick lit." David beamed at me.

"Good to know I have a guaranteed sale from someone not related to me."

"I'll buy it too," Lucy chimed in.

"As will I," Rob said. "Although I probably won't actually read it."

I rolled my eyes at him.

He winked at me. "It's all about the sale, kiddo. *Ca-ching*."

It did not escape my attention that Daneen was the only one at the table who didn't express her intention to purchase my book, but I would rather her not buy it than read it and give me her unsolicited opinion after the fact. Or worse, leave a three-paragraph review critiquing my writing style, technical skills, and character development.

"I'm sure Nicholas will buy it too," David said.

"He'd better," I said.

"I'll corner him tonight and threaten him bodily damage if he doesn't," Lucy said.

I chuckled as I imagined skinny Lucy beating on Nicholas. And then I felt the color drain from my face. "What do you mean tonight?"

"At the Judges' Dinner," Lucy said.

My mouth fell open in surprise.

"He didn't tell you he was going?" Daneen asked me, her eyes shining in unabashed delight.

"No, of course he did," I lied. "It's been such a crazy twenty-four hours. I completely forgot." I planted on a fake smile. "I need to use the restroom."

I walked calmly to the bathroom, entered a stall, and placed paper on the toilet seat before sitting down. Then I reached into my pocketbook and grabbed my phone. Not surprisingly, I had a text from Nicholas. I took a calming breath and slowly exhaled before reading it. "Don't kill me. The Patent Prom is tonight at the Waldorf, and I completely forgot about it. I need to be there, although, trust me, I'd much rather spend the night with you. Weekend festivities are much better, anyway. Saturday? Pick a place. Any place. I'm so sorry."

The Judges' Dinner, also known as the Patent Prom, was an annual black-tie event attended by anyone who was anyone in intellectual property law. Nicholas had attended the year before as well. We were broken up at the time, but still friends on Facebook, and when I saw Nicholas tagged in Daneen's picture, I thought the two of them were on a date and cried into my coffee. This was before Nicholas resigned, and it never occurred to me he would still attend, especially since he never told me. Playing the role of the understanding girlfriend, I texted him back: "No worries. I hope you won't miss your left testicle too much."

I placed my palm on my forehead and closed my eyes trying to regain my composure before returning to the table. Stopping at the mirror on the way out, I peered at my dejected reflection. My "celebration" had taken an unexpectedly uncelebratory turn. Afraid Lucy—or worse, Daneen—would come after me if I didn't go back soon, I pinched my cheeks for some color and took a deep breath through my nose. Wishing I were dating a bike messenger, an unemployed trust-fund kid, or a schoolteacher instead of a motivated and ambitious attorney, I headed back to my colleagues as if I hadn't a trouble in the world.

Chapter 22

I went to Ground Support directly from the office to work on the edits of *A Blogger's Life*. One advantage of not having a boyfriend to come home to—I could count on my nostrils how many times Nicholas beat me home from work since we moved in together—was I had nothing competing for my precious writing time. At the rate I was going, I would hand over the revised manuscript to Felicia days in advance of my estimated two-week turnaround.

Comfortably ahead of schedule on my edits, I took a break to update *Pastel Is the New Black* with an announcement.

Do you have an unhealthy addiction to reading? When you pass a bookstore, is the urge to go inside overwhelming? Are you drawn to the women's fiction section, and in particular, to books with pretty eye-catching covers? After you read one of these delicious books, do you want to tell the world what you thought?

If you answered yes to all of these questions, keep reading to see if Pastel Is the New Black *is looking for* you!

For the first time ever, Pastel Is the New Black *is seeking an associate reviewer. If your fondness for reading comes with a good command of the English language, an ability to meet deadlines, and a willingness to provide honest feedback (including criticism if warranted), in a kind and fair manner, please email three sample book reviews to the address located in the "Contact Me" section of my website.*

I will review all entries over the course of the next month and will contact all candidates who have been selected for the next round via return email. Note: This is an unpaid position. However, it does come with its perks (free books!). Also, you must be comfortable reading an ebook.

Good luck and happy reading!

With my mouse hovering over the "publish" button, I chewed on my lip. I liked being a one-man show, but Felicia was right: between working a full-time job and nurturing my writing career, *Pastel Is the New Black* was bound to suffer. My choices were either to enlist an assistant or decrease the activity on the blog. Felicia's concern about my posting unfavorable reviews once I joined the author ranks was also valid.

Taking on an assistant was the solution, and the first step was the selection process. I would carefully vet all of the candidates in terms of their writing skills, enthusiasm meter, and diplomacy. Phone interviews or video chats in the second round would hopefully weed out potential crazies. It could be fun. Confident I was doing the right thing, I published the post.

With one more item crossed off my to-do list, I checked my email. Caroline had sent a message to Bridget and me asking if we were available for a video chat at ten o'clock our time to catch up. She apologized for the last-minute scheduling, but said her itinerary was going to be hectic in the next couple of weeks, and she missed us. Bridget had already responded with an enthusiastic, "Count me in. K?"

I glanced at the time on my computer. It was past nine, but more than enough time to close up shop and head home. I messaged back: "Sorry for the late response. I'll see you guys at ten."

Forty-five minutes later, I was perched at my kitchen table in front of my laptop, whooping at Bridget and Jonathan's matching blue velour hooded pajamas. We were still waiting for Caroline to join the session. "Where in heaven did you pick those up? And why?" I snorted, and a drop of the ginger ale I was drinking leaked out of my nose.

Tightening the hood's drawstring around her neck, Bridget drew closer to the computer and cocked her head to the side. "No likey?"

"This writer has no words. No. Words. Who bought them for you?"

"They were a gag gift from my sister for Hanukkah. We thought we'd whip them out for this momentous occasion," Jonathan said.

"The occasion being?" I questioned.

"Meeting with my peeps, of course," Bridget said, rolling her eyes. "And I'm not one hundred percent convinced Rebecca meant it as a gag gift. Do you see the way she dresses your niece and nephew?"

Elbowing her, Jonathan said, "Watch yourself. That's my sister you're ranking on" just as Caroline joined the call. Her hand immediately went to her mouth, presumably in response to Bridget and Jonathan's PJs.

Elbowing him back, Bridget replied, "You've said worse about your sister. Anyhoo...time for you to skedaddle. Girls only. Buh-bye. Love you."

After waving his hand in front of the computer, Jonathan did as he was told and skedaddled.

Once Caroline wrapped up the requisite chuckle at Bridget's getup, and Bridget quit her half-assed attempt to convince us velour was the new silk in sexy sleepwear, we got down to business. "Guess who just booked a flight to New York City?" Caroline asked, smiling wide.

"You're coming home?" Bridget asked excitedly.

"Don't you still have several months of leave accumulated?" I missed Caroline like crazy and was stoked at the thought of having her back in town for in-person get-togethers. But aside from the trip to Iceland her father paid for the year before in an attempt to buy her forgiveness for marrying a woman her age, Caroline went several years without more than a few long weekends off from work before insisting on this sabbatical. I suspected once she returned to her job, it would be another decade before she treated herself to well-deserved time off again.

"Yes and yes," Caroline said.

"Elaborate, *por favor*," Bridget said.

Giggling, I said, "Don't you mean *s'il vous plaît*? She's in France."

Caroline chuckled. "In English, you're both right. I am coming home. And I do have several more months remaining of my vacation. My trip to New York is only a pit stop before I leave again. I have some exciting news, and I want to share it in person."

"What news?" Bridget and I asked at the same time.

Caroline shook her head. "It's hush-hush until I see you."

"This sounds serious," Bridget said.

I frowned. What could Caroline have to say that had to be shared face to face? The possibilities were endless. Was she sick? Moving abroad for good? Obviously, the latter was preferable to the former, but I didn't want our friendship to be long-distance permanently. "Is everything all right?"

"I'm not dying, girls, I promise. But you'll have to be patient because these lips are sealed." Caroline pressed her thumb and pointer finger together and ran them across her lips for emphasis. "I'll be here two Fridays from now. Save the date. Invite Jonathan and Nicholas too. I'll make reservations somewhere cool."

"Consider the date saved. Jonathan and I will be there," Bridget exclaimed gleefully.

"I'll be there too," I said.

"With Nicholas, right?" Caroline asked.

Chewing on my lower lip, I shrugged.

Bridget furrowed her brow. "What's up with Nicholas, K?"

"Nothing's up with Nicholas. It's just...he's not very reliable these days. We haven't even celebrated my snagging an agent yet."

Caroline's mouth dropped open. "Whoa...what? Snagged an agent? Spill."

I couldn't help but smile. "I haven't signed the contract yet, but yes, Felicia Harrison wants to represent me."

"Hannah Marshak's agent," Bridget added with a snort. "But we'll forgive her for that lapse in judgment."

I told Caroline about Felicia's interest in *A Blogger's Life* on the condition I make some major plot changes.

I left out Daneen's attempt at sabotage choosing to focus on the positive.

"I'm designing Kim's new author website. It will be among my best work, obviously," Bridget said, smiling.

"I'm thrilled for you, Kim," Caroline yelped.

I nodded. "It's a dream come true."

Tilting her head to the side, Caroline said, "But?"

"But...Nicholas has been so distracted by work lately. I rushed home after my meeting with Felicia last night prepared to toast with him, but he stayed late at the office. This morning, he promised we'd celebrate tonight." I glanced around the empty apartment. "Clearly that didn't happen."

"Working late again?" Caroline asked.

"More like schmoozing late." In response to the confused expression on Caroline and Bridget's faces, I clarified. "He's at a lawyer event at the Waldorf Astoria. He'd forgotten all about it. I'm hesitant to rely on his latest assurance to take me out on Saturday instead." I swallowed down the lump in my stomach as it hit me how much I missed my boyfriend. If it were only the last couple of nights, it would be one thing. I knew his attendance at the Patent Prom was important to his career and would never expect him to skip it on my account, but it seemed I was forever coming in second to his employer lately.

"I'm positive he won't cancel on you for Saturday," Bridget said encouragingly,

Caroline nodded. "Me too. But maybe you should show him what he's been missing while working late instead of getting cuddly with his sexy girlfriend."

"What's the plan this time, Ace?" I asked.

Smiling wickedly, Caroline said, "Buy some sexy lingerie and wear it under your outfit. During your celebratory dinner, tease

Nicholas with what's waiting for him at home. And then make good on your teasing later."

I closed my eyes, recalling how easy it used to be to obtain and keep Nicholas's attention focused on me simply by donning a low-cut shirt and showcasing my cleavage in all its glory. I opened my eyes. Maybe it was time to sex things up a bit. "I can do that."

"Of course you can," Caroline said confidently.

My mind wandering, I said, "Maybe we can recreate the piano sex scene from *Pretty Woman*. I've been wanting to do that since I moved in."

"Let me know if you do. I'll wipe down the piano keys with antibacterial spray before playing 'Chopsticks' next time I come over," Bridget said.

"Ha ha. Anyway, I feel better now. Thank you both," I said.

Caroline smiled. "What are friends for?"

After I told the girls about my plan to hire an associate reviewer, Bridget described her ideas for my new website, and Caroline remained firm on her decision to keep her big news under wraps until we saw her face to face, we ended the chat. I briefly perused the Victoria's Secret website before deciding to visit La Petite Coquette, a smaller lingerie shop in Union Square, during lunch the next day. If I didn't find the perfect prop for my night of seduction, I would stop by Victoria's Secret in the evening before heading home.

Sex with Nicholas was always mind-blowing, but since I moved in, I hadn't bothered with flirty undergarments, choosing to get naked as quickly as possible instead. I reveled at the thought of Nicholas's jaw dropping when he saw me in a sexy chemise or babydoll, and I imagined him peeling it off of me with soft, yet firm, hands. Naughty thoughts lulled me to sleep, and although I had a vague recollection of Nicholas slipping into the bed at some point, I didn't wake up.

Chapter 23

I reached across our candlelit table in the romantic West Village Italian restaurant and squeezed Nicholas's hand. He had come through on his promise to make Saturday night all about me. And since I convinced him to go an extra day without shaving, his stubbly jaw looked yummier than any of the appetizers currently on our table. I thought about the blue silk chiffon babydoll I was wearing underneath my outfit, and my mind raced in anticipation of Nicholas's reaction to seeing everything through the sheer material. I had definitely splurged on the piece but justified it as a necessary expense to save my relationship. Hopefully, luxuries like this wouldn't crack my piggy bank for much longer once Felicia negotiated a nice author advance from the sale of my novel to a huge publisher.

"What are you grinning at?" Nicholas asked.

"That's for me to know and you to find out," I teased, before biting into a stuffed mushroom.

"Fair enough." He took a slow sip of his red wine and smiled at me over his glass.

"Tell me about the Patent Prom. Any gossip?" The ramifications of the event's open-bar post-party in the firm's hospitality suite were legendary. Rumor had it one year, one of the more attractive male paralegals sucked face in plain sight with one of the much older married female associates, although the episode was never spoken of again. The after-party was open to employees of the firm deemed important enough to snag invitations to the main event as well as clients, and I was sure Nicholas wouldn't want to miss hanging out with his old colleagues. As long as the gossip didn't involve him and one Daneen Barnett (or him and anyone else, for that matter), I was on a need-to-know basis—meaning, I needed to know.

Nicholas shook his head. "It was a disappointing showing all in all. Although Bad Lucy made an appearance. She bet Mary she could hold a full glass of wine in the palm of each of her hands for twenty seconds."

My eyes bugged out. "Holy crap. What happened?"

Nicholas gave me a half smile. "What do you think happened?" He pushed the platter of fried calamari toward me. "Take some more."

Happily scooping a few pieces of the squid onto my plate, I said, "Mary won the bet?"

Nodding, Nicholas said, "And Bad Lucy went home with red wine stains all over her cute yellow dress."

I shook my head. "Poor Lucy."

"And rich Mary. Lucy owes her a hundred bucks."

I giggled. "How is Mary? Aside from being a hundred dollars wealthier?" A friend of Nicholas's from way back, Mary Jones was in her third year at law school but had worked as a summer associate at the firm the year before and would be returning in September as a first-year associate. With her blond locks, golden skin, and toned physique, she was Beach Barbie in the urban jungle. When I spied her eating lunch with Nicholas one day before we started dating, I assumed the two of them were an item and hated her. Naturally. But then another one of Nicholas's friends told me Mary was a lesbian, and now I loved her—not because she wasn't into men—because she was a sweetheart. Of course, her lack of sexual interest in my man didn't hurt her position.

"She's already freaking out about taking the bar exam. I told her to pass all her courses first, graduate law school, and then worry about the bar."

"Good advice."

Gazing at me fondly, Nicholas said, "But enough about Mary. This is your celebration. Let's talk about you."

"You won't get any arguments from me, Counselor." I smiled at him.

"Did Felicia send you the contract?"

"It landed in my inbox this morning, in fact."

"Hand me your phone, I'll take a quick look at it now."

I waved him away. "I'll have Rob review it at work on Monday."

Nicholas raised his palms upward and shrugged. "What? You don't trust me to give you good legal advice?"

Cocking my head to the side, I said, "Don't be silly. Of course I trust you, and if you have time, I'll print it out and show you tomorrow. But not during my celebration dinner. It's not exactly sexy."

"You don't find indemnity, termination, and royalty clauses provocative? You don't know what you're missing, Kimmie." He winked.

Angling my body so the sleeve of my white boatneck sweater hung off my shoulder to reveal the blue silk strap of my negligee, I leaned closer to him over the table and whispered, "Neither do you."

Nicholas glanced at my shoulder and back to my face, his dark eyes piercing mine. "I propose we skip dessert."

I shook my head. "I can never be a proponent of skipping dessert." I paused dramatically. "But if you're suggesting we move elsewhere...say to our place...for that course, I support your plan wholeheartedly."

Nicholas looked down at the main courses the waitress had brought to our table only moments ago. "First one to finish their plate goes first, if you know what I mean." He raised his eyebrows.

I knew exactly what he meant. As I twirled as much linguini onto my spoon and into my mouth as possible, I silently thanked Caroline for devising yet another genius plan. I was beginning to think she was my guardian angel of love.

*   *   *

Without a word, Nicholas shut the door of our apartment behind us and in one swift motion, turned me around so my back was against the entryway. I arched my body against the steel as his fingers deftly lifted the bottom of my sweater. Breathing in my ear, he whispered, "What are you hiding under this heavy sweater, Kimmie?"

Summoning all of the self-control I could muster, I pushed him away. "Patience. Meet me in the bedroom in five minutes." Peeking past him toward the piano at the back of the living room, I said, "Scratch that. Wait in the bedroom until I call your name. Then come out and find me."

Nicholas gave me a pained expression. "Five minutes is an eternity," he said before bending down and nipping at my lip. I pressed my lips against his and buried my tongue in his mouth until I found the strength to untangle myself from his embrace. I held up my hand and wiggled my fingers at him. "Five minutes."

Nicholas stroked his jaw in his fail-proof "drive Kim crazy" move. "Hurry," he said.

I ran to the bathroom, kicked off my white patent leather platform shoes, and slid out of my stretch blue velvet leggings until I was wearing nothing but my baggy boatneck wool sweater and thong panties. I stood in front of the full-length mirror and contemplated whether to keep the sweater on *Flashdance* style and make Nicholas work to get to the sexy garment underneath. But I wanted to watch his eyes as he scanned the length of my naked body, fully visible underneath the translucent material. I removed the sweater and, in only the lingerie, took a deep breath. This was hardly the first time I'd been intimate with Nicholas, but I was as nervous as a virgin. I giggled at the absurdity. After flipping my hair upside down for added volume, I gave a final glance at myself in the mirror and breathed in. Ready or not, here I come. I walked out of the bathroom and straight to the piano bench, where I sat down with my ankles crossed and my knees facing opposite directions. I called out, "Come out, come out wherever you are" in a high-pitched voice and felt my heart slam against my chest while I waited.

And waited.

And waited.

"Nicholas?"

The silence was deafening, and I wondered in annoyance if he was trying to take control of the seduction. Tonight was meant to be a utopia of my creation, not his, and I wouldn't let him win. I ran a hand through my hair, adjusted my teddy, and stared at the bedroom door willing Nicholas to walk out. "Don't you want your surprise?"

When a minute passed and he still didn't come out, I reconsidered my position. So what if Alpha Nicholas came out to play? Would the end result not be exactly the same—earth-shattering violent endings for both of us? In fact, in most of the books I read, the main character lusted over a guy who would probably do precisely what my real-life red-blooded boyfriend was doing right now. With the confidence of a book heroine who already got the guy, I made my way to the bedroom, twisted the doorknob open, and walked in. "You win," I said, before posing seductively at the entrance.

"Nicholas?" I stepped closer to the bed, where my boyfriend was fast asleep, naked aside from his record-emblazoned boxer shorts. If my nipples were hard in anticipation of Nicholas's touch, they withered like raisins at the sight of him passed out in a slumber, along with my celebratory mood.

Rather than try to wake Nicholas up from his repose, I wiped away the tear that lodged in my eye and crawled under the covers next to him. Unable to slow my breathing, I studied Nicholas in his peaceful sleep, his eyelids fluttering rhythmically. After a few minutes, I got up, removed my coral-colored fleece blanket from the closet, and relocated to the living room.

Chapter 24

When my eyes opened for the first time the next morning, rather than sigh contentedly in the knowledge it was Sunday and I didn't have to get up early, I bolted off of the couch and into the shower. The cascading hot water did nothing to scrub away my embarrassment at putting Nicholas to sleep last night with my attempted seduction—what should have been a no-brainer. Rationally, I knew it was not my lack of appeal that led Nicholas to lose consciousness before he could even manage a "quickie," as he'd been very eager before I banished him to the bedroom for the five-minute break. But it had only been five minutes—three hundred seconds. He was so exhausted that he couldn't keep his eyes open for three hundred seconds—enough time to behold my see-through negligee? I knew *why* he was tired—working eighteen-hour days will do that to you—but I doubted he fell asleep in the middle of the Patent Prom. Couldn't he have tried to stay awake for me too? Didn't he want to?

I couldn't face him. I wouldn't face him. Not yet, anyway. I got dressed as covertly as possible, did a half-assed braid in my wet hair, and headed to the café with my mini laptop and e-reader.

While sipping my coffee and nibbling on a sesame bagel with cream cheese, I glanced around the crowded coffee shop in wonder. So this was what other people did at eight thirty on a Sunday morning while Nicholas and I were unconscious in bed. Forcing thoughts of Nicholas out of my head, at least for the time being, I clasped my hands together, intertwined my fingers, and stretched my arms out in front of me. I was ready to dig deep into my edits.

In the original version, my protagonist Laurel became so fed up with her boyfriend Henry for never putting her needs ahead of those of his dysfunctional family that she cheated on him in a moment of weakness and bad judgment. In the new draft, I nixed the cheating in favor of her blogging about her frustrations— resulting in a flood of bad advice from her followers she ends up taking out of desperation. Although misguided, none of Laurel's actions would be considered by readers to be unforgiveable or fatal to her happily ever after with Henry. At least I hoped not. This version was also much funnier.

When my phone pinged the receipt of a text message about forty minutes into my writing session, I knew it was Nicholas. Ignoring the increase of my heart rate, I leisurely reached into my bag and read the message.

"Where are you?"

I quickly wrote back, "I'm writing," and tossed the phone back in my purse.

Before my fingers had time to make contact with my keyboard, he responded, and I retrieved the phone from my bag once again.

"So early? I'm impressed."

"The early bird gets the worm." I rolled my eyes and made a mental note never to use the phrase in my writing. It was so cliché. I placed the phone on my table in front of me and stared at it while awaiting another text. When about a minute passed with nothing, I closed my eyes and took a deep inhale determined to focus on the book. I would deal with Nicholas later.

Ping.

Or I would deal with him now. I read the text.

"I'm sorry about last night, Kimmie."

I let out a long deep breath. The apology was welcome, but it didn't change the reality. I could escalate the drama by saying "I'm sorry" didn't fly, but what good would it do? We couldn't jump in a time machine and redo the night, complete with a shot of espresso after dinner or Red Bull and vodka instead of wine. Besides, reaming the guy out for falling asleep was over the top. Nicholas was too tired to have sex last night. Big whoop. He was an ambitious guy trying to get ahead in his career. Exhaustion came with the territory. Last night was not our one and only opportunity to sleep together. It was one night. I knew this to be true, but the ache in my gut suggested it was so much more than a one-off.

Not knowing what else to say, I responded: "It's okay." When in doubt, take the passive-aggressive route.

I could almost hear the scratch of a broken record when I read his next message. "I'll make it up to you. I promise."

My mind went to the final season of *Sex and the City* when Aleksandr Petrovsky insisted he would make more time for Carrie Bradshaw "as soon as..." Was Nicholas my Aleksandr Petrovsky? I thought he was my Mr. Big.

Practicing Jonathan's twenty-second rule to avoid saying something I would regret, I asked the woman next to me to watch my computer while I went to the bathroom. When I returned to my seat, I wrote back: "I know. No worries. I'll be home later."

"K. I might head to the office for a bit."

Mumbling, "What else is new?" to myself, I buried my phone at the bottom of my bag and vowed not to look at it for the rest of the morning.

Needing a break from my edits, I read a few chapters of the latest novel in my review queue. I was pleasantly surprised by how much I was enjoying Olivia Geffen's new release, mostly since I was underwhelmed with the *New York Times* bestseller's previous book, but also a tiny bit because Ginny Webber said there wasn't a market for *A Blogger's Life*, and I feared it would bias me against one of her clients. After I made a decent dent in my reading, I reviewed the slew of submissions flooding my inbox in response to my advertisement for an associate reviewer. In only a few days, I received almost fifty applications. The majority of them were not of *Pastel Is the New Black* caliber, and many more were well written but lacked the *je ne sais quoi*. I chuckled to myself. *Je ne sais quoi?* I sounded like Hannah Marshak.

One submission stood out tall from the others—Pia Chin. Her review of *What a Fool Believes* sparkled. Not only was it grammatically correct, it was thorough and witty. She even included her casting for the main and supporting characters. I notified her by email that she made the short list and asked when she would be available for a video chat or phone call.

Pleased with my level of productivity despite my emotional turmoil over Nicholas, I checked my Facebook account to find a message from Hannah herself. Maybe her ears were burning.

I hear congratulations are in order for your little book. I knew Felicia loved me, but even I didn't realize the extent of my influence. We should celebrate. Cocktails and snacks at HanGawi. Wednesday night, 7:30. (I'm on a vegan cleanse.)

Bisous Bisous.
Hannah

PS: I'm finalizing the schedule for my blog tour. What day did you plan to post on Pastel Is the New Black? *I'd prefer a Monday to take advantage of #MondayBlogs or Friday for #Fridayreads on Twitter.*

A pang of guilt washed over me as I realized my intention to thank Hannah for the introduction to Felicia had yet to come to fruition. After so many years of discomfort at her hands in junior high and high school, being indebted to Hannah seemed as unlikely as me being the tallest girl in a room full of grown-ups. If someone had told me back in high school that Hannah would willingly and voluntarily pave the way toward me securing a literary agent in a decade's time, I'd have dismissed it with a hearty laugh and possibly a punch in the nose, but here we were. I couldn't decline the invitation. (Although in typical Hannah fashion, she didn't even ask if I was available so much as assume it as a given.) Being Hannah's plus-one for an evening left me unsettled, but it was not negotiable. I owed her. Before I could change my mind, I wrote back and told her I would meet her.

Chapter 25

Rob lowered the contract onto his desk and fixed his gaze upon me. "It looks pretty standard."

My heart slowed down marginally. I was afraid Rob would spot a deal-breaker in the contract that would force me to open up negotiations with Felicia. What if asking for modifications to the agreement resulted in Felicia reneging her offer?

"There is one thing I'm not sure you noticed," Rob pointed out.

I leaned forward in my chair. "What is it?" Please don't be a deal-breaker. Please don't be a deal-breaker.

Rob gave me a soft smile. "Don't panic. It's nothing unreasonable. She included a clause reserving the right to terminate the agreement if the rewrites aren't up to snuff. Sorry if I sound cynical, but it's not a done deal yet."

I let out a sigh. "I'm well aware. I sent the revised draft to her this morning and have been glued to my email waiting with bated breath ever since." As heat warmed my neck, I backpedaled. "In between diligently handling my work assignments, naturally."

Rob rolled his eyes. "Naturally."

Ignoring his sarcasm, I asked, "So should I sign it?"

"I don't see why not." He picked up the agreement, and I watched his eyes scroll the length of the document. "It covers all the bases: you're giving her agency exclusive rights to seek a publisher and a buyer of film rights..." His eyes met mine again. "I assume the squad will be invited to the Oscars when the movie is nominated for an Academy Award?"

"Maybe not the *entire* squad," I said, smirking.

Rob smiled knowingly and began reading again. "She gets

fifteen percent of the profits. The term is twelve months after which both sides can terminate with thirty days' notice. Blah blah blah." He handed the contract to me across his desk. "Like I said: standard. I would recommend signing it unless you're having doubts about this agent and want to keep querying. What did Nicholas say?"

"I didn't show it to him. He offered, but he's been so busy lately, and I didn't want to waste what precious time we had together discussing legal stuff."

Rob narrowed his eyes. "But it's perfectly acceptable to take time out of your eight-hour workday to pester *me* about it?"

I dropped my chin toward the ground. "I'm sorry, Rob. Rest assured, your work is getting done. And besides, you're a far more experienced attorney than Nicholas."

"Flattery will get you everywhere."

I smiled. Rob loved compliments on his legal prowess.

"Except when you rub my more advanced age in my face."

Cringing, I said, "You know that's not what I meant. I'm so grateful for your guidance, but when it comes time to review the publishing contract, I promise to go to Nicholas. Okay?" Hopefully, I would be over the events of the past weekend, and Nicholas and I would be in a better place by the time that happened. If it ever happened. Four days after the fact, and I still hadn't confronted him. How do you say, "I'm hurt you fell asleep in the middle of sexy time" without sounding like a silly, needy girlfriend? And, really, what could he say in response that he hadn't already told me? "I'm so sorry, Kimmie. Work is crazy. I promise to make it up to you." So instead of calling him out, I was going through the motions of being his happy-go-lucky girlfriend even though I felt like a volcano about to erupt.

Bringing me back to the present, Rob said, "And this is the agent you want?"

"Definitely." Not only did Felicia love *A Blogger's Life*, she wanted to invest in my writing career moving forward. And her great editorial contacts would hopefully help her sell it to a great publishing house. Once I stopped being a gushing fangirl, we established a smooth author/agent rapport. She was "the one." Getting to this point made all of the rejections, even Ginny Webber's, worth it.

"Just sign it, Long. And then revise the bills I left on your chair. If nothing else, it will be a welcome distraction from worrying about whether Felicia approved of your rewrites."

I stood up. "You got it, Boss Man. Thank you again."

For the entirety of the afternoon, I was a model secretary. After I finished inputting the changes into Rob's bills, I entered his time for the month and opened up billing numbers for all of his new clients. Then I went online and bought him a World's Best Boss trophy. Shopping for yourself might not fall under the "model secretary behavior" umbrella, but shopping for your boss certainly would. I only broke concentration from my tasks when my phone rang. It was Bridget.

"What's up, chica?"

As I refreshed my Gmail account for the hundredth time that day, torn between anticipating and dreading the arrival of Felicia's email, I said, "Same ole. What's going on?"

"Log onto your website."

As instructed, I went to my favorites and instinctively clicked on *Pastel Is the New Black*.

Reading my mind, Bridget said, "Not *Pastel Is the New Black*. Kimberlylong.com."

"Oh." I bopped up and down in my office chair like a hyperactive toddler while entering the login and password she gave me, keen to witness Bridget's magic at last. She had insisted on creating a dummy author website for me, refusing any predesign guidance, but promising to accept and act upon my feedback after the fact—even if it meant redoing the entire project. She wouldn't even hint at her ideas.

As my computer screen refreshed, I squeezed my eyes shut, wary of what awaited me on the other side of my closed eyelids. I peeked at the monitor with one eye open, taking in as much as I could with only half of my vision. As my jaw dropped in wonder, my other eye flew open. "The color, Bridget. It's...It's..."

"Electric blue," Bridget interrupted. In a soft voice, she asked, "Do you like it?"

I had been tempted to ask Bridget to design my author site to match *Pastel Is the New Black*. She had masterfully designed the blog site to suit my vision to a T. The pastel swirl background was pretty enough to eat, yet not so busy as to cause headaches from staring at it too long. (I would know, since that's exactly what I had done when it first went live almost three years earlier.) Although I kept my fear to myself, I doubted whether another website she built for me could be anything more than second best. Despite my concern, I was determined to create a separate writer identity, so I told her to take the author website in a different direction.

Encouraging a response, Bridget said, "If you hate it, I'll change it."

"Don't you dare." Lowering my voice, I said, "It's perfect."

"Are you sure? Because I won't be insulted if you don't like it."

"I don't *like* it, Bridge. I love it." I didn't think it was possible to be as enchanted by another website with the same fervor as *Pastel Is the New Black*, but like parents could cherish their first-born child with everything they had and somehow possess equal love for their second, third, fourth (and so on) offspring, my heart had expanded to fall eyebrows over toenails for Kimberlylong.com. Bridget had used the perfect shade of blue for the background—neither too pale nor too bright, yet undeniably feminine. And the minuscule flecks of glittery silver served to create a mood that was romantic without being mushy—just like my novels. Make that *novel*, at least for the time being. In case she missed it the first time, I repeated, "I love it."

"Hooray!"

I grinned. "You know me so well."

"I told you so," Bridget said matter-of-factly.

"And you didn't have to tell me twice. I gave you free rein without any argument. Remember?"

"True. Although you did threaten to chop off my hair in my sleep if you hated it and I refused to make it right."

I giggled. "Guilty as charged. But only because I had the utmost faith in you. I love your hair too much to bet against it."

"Shall we celebrate tonight?"

I gulped. "I wish I could, but I can't."

"Big plans?"

I tugged on a piece of my hair and twirled it around my fingers. "Not really. Dinner with Nicholas." I lifted my chin skyward, silently asking God to forgive me for lying to my best friend. Since I considered my evening out with Hannah nothing more than an obligatory get-together, I saw no reason to ignite a flame by telling Bridget the truth at this point. She'd be upset and undoubtedly dwell on how evil Hannah was in high school. Between waiting for Felicia's feedback and my absentee boyfriend, I had enough stress already. But I would fess up after the fact, and we would share some laughs over Hannah's famous one-liners.

"Are things better with you guys?" she asked hopefully.

I had told Bridget about the unfortunate climax of my celebration with Nicholas. Although anticlimactic was a more accurate description. "Things are as good as they can be for a couple who barely sees each other. When we first started dating, I was in awe of Nicholas's drive, but it's gone from wild ambition to all-consuming, and I don't know where I fit in anymore." I choked down the urge to sob.

"You should talk to him, Kim. He probably has no idea you're this bothered."

I sighed. "I've tried. He always promises to make it up to me as soon as things calm down."

"Better to be busy at work than getting busy with another chick, right?"

"I suppose so. Unless 'Work' is the first name of his hot, nubile new colleague." With an exaggerated laugh, I said, "Wouldn't that be a riot?"

Bridget chuckled. "Not likely. Nicholas is not the cheating

type. And what parents would name their child 'Work,' anyway?"

"If Jason Lee can name his kid Pilot Inspektor, anything is possible."

"Ha ha. Use the opportunity to confide in him tonight. And have fun."

"Thank you." I swallowed hard, nearly certain my guilty conscience over lying to Bridget would make enjoying myself a challenge—even more arduous than a night out with Hannah would be on its own.

"Maybe slip an energy booster into Nicholas's drink so he doesn't doze off on you."

"Great idea." And maybe I'd try it if I were really having dinner with Nicholas.

Since I wasn't meeting Hannah until seven thirty, I slipped into a vacant lawyer's office at the end of the workday and invited Pia Chin, my top pick for the associate reviewer gig, to a video chat so I could gauge our compatibility. Her passion for chick lit and decent writing skills were evident from the sample reviews she supplied, but I needed to confirm she wasn't a lunatic. Since conducting psychological testing required professionals, I settled for relying on my instincts and scheduled a chat.

The moment her face popped up on the screen, she flashed me a smile and bowed her head. "I'm so honored to meet the famous Kim Long: Blogger Extraordinaire."

Waving her off with a laugh, I said, "Eh, I'm not extraordinary."

"Oh, but you are. And I'm not sucking up. I wanna be you when I grow up." Her porcelain-like cheeks turned crimson, and her brown eyes opened wide. "Not that you're old."

I chuckled again. "No offense taken. And I'm twenty-nine, which makes me on the cusp of ancient. How old are you?" I pegged her for under twenty-five.

"Twenty-three. I'm studying for my MFA at U of M, but I

swear I have enough time to contribute to *Pastel Is the New Black* if you'll have me. My thesis is on the development of literature with the advent of the internet and social media. I can chalk up the time spent to research."

She spoke really quickly, jumbling her words together and dropping off the letter "t" as if afraid she'd be interrupted before completing her sentence.

"You have the cutest accent," I said.

Pia whipped her head back. "Michiganders don't have accents. Now, New Yorkers...you guys have accents."

"Meshuganah? Wha?" She spoke so fast and slurred her words together, I had no idea what she said.

Slowing her voice down, Pia said, "Michiganders. People from Michigan. Also known as Michiganians."

"Oh." Pia was an itty-bitty thing, even compared to me—another itty-bitty thing, but where I was thin yet curvy, she was waif-like. Her long stick-straight hair was black with random strands of orange, and her bangs fell in a clean line directly above her sparse brows and almond-shaped brown eyes. Between her flawless complexion, tiny stature, and her adorable accent, she gave off an almost doll-like appearance, and it was impossible not to like her. "I'll have you." This time, it was me who blushed. "On *Pastel Is the New Black*, I mean. For a trial run. How about I assign you three books, and we'll see how it goes?"

"Awesome." Pia raised her hand in a fist pump. "I can't wait to see what books you assign me." Shaking her head, she said, "I keep hearing about Hannah Marshak's upcoming novel, *Tearing at the Seams*. I'm not sure what all the hype is about. I thought the first one was overrated, to be honest."

My lips curled into an instant grin. "I love you. You're hired." I glanced at my watch. "Speaking of Hannah, I'm meeting her for dinner later and should get going."

Pia's mouth opened, and her face turned pink again. "Oh, shit. I didn't realize you two were friends. Please don't hold my lack of enthusiasm for her writing against me."

I gave her a closed-mouth smile. "Trust me, that won't be a problem."

After a quick summary of the novels I'd be sending her, we agreed on deadlines and concluded our chat just as a reminder popped up on my screen that my dinner with Hannah was in thirty minutes. As I touched up my makeup and switched out my flats for four-inch platform shoes—to minimize the significant height differential between five-foot-seven Hannah and me—I tried not to think about the oddity of voluntarily meeting Queen Bee Mean Girl Hannah Marshak for a one-on-one girls' night out. I shuddered at what my fifteen-year-old self (or even my twenty-eight-year-old self) would have to say about that.

Chapter 26

As it happened, I could have left my high heeled shoes at home, since patrons of HanGawi were required to leave their footwear with the hostess before being escorted to the dining area. Rather than sit in chairs, diners kneeled at the table, and the room was filled with natural artifacts intended to bring harmony to the body and mind. Hannah's essence was far from Zen-like, and I would never have guessed she'd be into this scene. Not for the first time over the course of a year, the girl surprised me.

Hannah raised her mojito to her mouth and then pulled it back at the last second. "We should toast your success, no?"

Apparently, her cleanse did not include abstaining from alcohol. I raised my own mojito in the air. "I'm afraid to jinx myself. Felicia hasn't approved my rewrites yet." I cursed my alcohol-induced loose lips. I'd always made it a point to keep my insecurities out of Hannah's earshot lest she use them against me, yet here I was—a willing accomplice to her stomping on my ego. She might not be my enemy anymore, but it was still a stretch to call her a friend, and I wouldn't underestimate her ability or desire to cut me down.

"It's no biggie. I had to make edits to *Cut on the Bias* after she offered me representation too." Hannah took a delicate sip of her drink and flipped her hair across her shoulder. "Of course, mine weren't *rewrites*, per se. Felicia adored my book at first sight. But I knew it could still be better, and so she agreed to give me time to make adjustments. So...it's not exactly the same thing, but still, I wouldn't fret."

I nodded at Hannah, suppressing a giggle. God forbid she admitted to being anything less than perfect.

"Anyhoo," she continued, "I'm happy for you." Raising her glass again, she said, "To little Kim Long."

We clinked glasses as I beamed at the new-and-improved Hannah in surprise. Her personality tweak wasn't exactly lobotomy material, but she was a far cry from the girl who publicly ridiculed my stick-straight hair as unwashed and greasy and then showed up the next day bragging about the new hair-straightening iron her folks bought her in Italy. "Thank you."

Hannah put down her glass and looked at me with an earnest expression. "Although I should be annoyed you're copying me, I'm not. It's okay." She smiled and gave a faint shake of her head. "Who would have thought we'd both be authors of chick lit? Crazy, right?"

And she's back. "It's a bizarre coincidence, yes. But I didn't copy you, Hannah."

She lightly tapped her hand over mine. "It's totally fine. Even though you never let on in high school—with that cool act you and Bridget had going on—I always knew you secretly looked up to me."

Stupefied, I blinked at her, saying nothing as a blast of red heat blanketed my face. I had two choices.

I could deny her bogus accusation that I was a copycat, and laugh in her face in response to her claim I secretly admired her. As if. While Hannah was busy terrorizing preteens in middle school, I was already writing books, and I had numerous unfinished manuscripts on the top shelf of my closet to prove it. I could also remind her of the day she *coincidentally* showed up at Starbucks months after our high school reunion wearing the shoes I had worn that night—the shoes she had complimented. Who was copying who?

Or I could let her believe her own bullshit, thank her for referring me to Felicia, and politely change the subject.

My decision made, I gave her a warm smile. "I really appreciate you hooking me up with Felicia. Do you know what you're going to order?"

Even though I'd only "looked up to her" in a literal sense, Hannah was partially responsible for pushing me outside of my comfort zone whether I liked it or not. And besides, if I told her I'd actually been writing since junior high, I'd also be admitting I was too cowardly to do anything about it for over a decade. The truth was, I'd become somewhat accustomed to Hannah's need to feel superior, and it no longer bothered me. Much. Nevertheless, my previous conclusion about the positive changes to her personality might have been premature.

Twenty minutes, one mojito each, and a shared platter of assorted gluten-free appetizers later, conversation had blessedly moved on to less tumultuous topics, like shopping. We even shared our favorite sites for buying discount designer clothes online. I was impressed Hannah actually admitted to searching out deals and would have guessed she paid full price on principle.

Leaning slightly across the table, her eyes darted the length of my body. "Great dress. You do have style, Kim."

"Thanks." I gazed down at my outfit—a black, white, and blue swirl-print chemise above-the-knee dress with three-quarter sleeves.

"Do you need to shop in little-people stores?"

As my head jerked back, I repeated, "Little-people stores?"

"Not dwarfs or anything. Just specialized stores for..." She cleared her throat. "Height-deprived people."

I pursed my lips. Never once when we had discussed our favorite stores mere minutes earlier had I mentioned shopping at "Little People 'R Us." How silly of me to forget Hannah's tendency to deliver left-handed compliments. Though I regrettably lacked the ability to censor her, I could at least control how I reacted to her jabs and focus on her positive attributes, however few of them there were.

Letting the insult roll off my back, I said, "I shop in the petite section in regular stores. Although my tailor could probably subsist on my clothes alone," I confessed with a chuckle.

Hannah nodded. "I get it. Almost every clothing item I buy

needs to be taken in because I have such a small waist." She shrugged as if being slim was her cross to bear.

Wishing I had recorded this conversation to enjoy later, I excused myself to the bathroom, giggling silently all the way. Hannah was always good for a laugh, even if she didn't know it.

After relieving my bladder and running a brush through my hair, I exited the restroom ready to conclude the evening. Even though there was no evidence to suggest Hannah was bent on destroying my writing career—quite the contrary actually—she was still the same ole Hannah in so many ways. Too much "Hannah time," chock full of insults disguised as compliments, was a recipe for a wicked tension headache, and I already felt the stirrings of one in my temples. Yes, small doses of Hannah was the way to go.

As I approached our table, I heard a very familiar voice call out my name.

Shit.

Chapter 27

I turned around very slowly to face Bridget, who was grinning broadly at me. "I can't believe you're here."

You and me both. After a subtle glance over my shoulder, I faced her with a timid smile, wondering how I was going to get out of this. "Hi."

Following my line of vision, Bridget looked past me. "Is Nicholas here? Jonathan's at our table in the back. We should sit together." Studying my face with concern, she said, "Unless you're having your heart-to-heart now."

I shifted my feet. "Um..." It was moment-of-truth time. Did I lie to Bridget and hope to God she and Jonathan were sitting far enough away from my table and the exit to allow me to escape the venue without her ever knowing I was there with Hannah? Or did I fess up and face the consequences? As I debated my choices for what felt like a dog year, Bridget's eyes widened before me, and I didn't need twenty questions to decipher the reason.

"I should have known." Hannah stood before us, her slender hands on her hips as she looked from me to Bridget and then back at me.

"You were gone so long, for a split second I thought you walked out on me." She laughed. "But c'mon. Why would you do that? Then I worried you were puking or something. You probably have the alcohol tolerance of a child." She laughed again. "I should have known Bridget would turn up. Some things never change."

As I tried feverishly to make eye contact with Bridget, and she worked tirelessly to avoid making eye contact with me, neither of us responded to Hannah.

Darting her eyes back and forth between us, Hannah frowned. "Did I say something wrong?"

"I, um…" I was so busted, and the words escaped me.

Hannah sighed impatiently. "While you two pals do whatever it is pals like you do, I'm going to the ladies' room." She sashayed her skinny hips (and tiny waist) in the direction I had come, and I was left alone with Bridget in silence.

Bridget gawked at me.

I blurted out, "This isn't what it looks like."

Her brows furrowed. "Seriously? So you're not really out with Hannah after telling me…correction, *lying* to me about having dinner with Nicholas?"

I bit my lip. "I only lied to you because I knew you'd be pissed. I was planning on telling you later."

Bridget's face turned the color of her hair. "Damn straight, I'm pissed. You don't lie to your best friend. Ever. Unless Hannah is your BFF now," she said, mumbling the last part.

"C'mon, Bridget. She wanted to take me out to celebrate Felicia signing me. I owe her."

"You owe her?"

"If it wasn't for Hannah, Felicia would never have even read *A Blogger's Life*."

She snorted. "I'd say it's a fair exchange for all of her shenanigans in high school."

"Yes, Bridget. In *high school*. As in ten years ago. Maybe it's time we cut the girl some slack."

"Never in a million years would I think you'd sell out and kiss Hannah's ass because she's a published author."

My heart racing, I raised my voice. "I'm not kissing anyone's ass, Bridget. But I'm not stuck in the past like you."

Bridget dropped her chin. "Remember when we fantasized about all of her hair falling out in the shower after watching *The Craft*?"

I smiled. "Of course I remember."

Her somber eyes met mine again. "And now you're hanging with her all shoeless and fancy-free."

"She's not that bad. Although she's not that go—"

"And lying to me about it."

"I only lied because I knew you'd react like this," I said between my teeth.

"Like what?"

"Like a child. You give Hannah way too much power. Get over it already." I whipped my head around, afraid we were causing a commotion in the restaurant.

"You're such a hypocrite."

I placed my hands on my hips. "What are you talking about?"

"I give Hannah way too much power. When Nicholas said the same thing to you about Daneen, you didn't take it too well as I recall," Bridget said, cocking an eyebrow.

"It's different," I said, biting my lip. "Hannah is in our past, and Daneen is in my present."

Motioning over her shoulder toward the ladies' room, Bridget said, "It seems Hannah is in your present too." She shrugged. "I should get back to Jonathan."

"Afraid if you leave him alone, he'll meet someone else he actually wants to marry?" I pressed my hand against my mouth the minute the words came out. "I'm sorry. I didn't mean—"

With a shake of her head, Bridget said, "It's really sad how small your world is—how you can't possibly comprehend someone not wanting the same things as you. Jonathan might not want to marry me, but at least he wants to spend time with me. Too bad I can't say the same about Nicholas."

I muttered "Cheap shot" under my breath.

"When I said you had nothing to worry about with Nicholas, I was being nice." As Hannah rejoined us, Bridget looked at us both and said, "You girls have fun now," before walking away.

"Did I miss something? What's got your slightly taller Siamese twin's curls in tangles?" Hannah asked.

I shrugged and trailed her back to our table, striving to find the humor in the evening's irony. No matter how many times Hannah had endeavored to drive a wedge between Bridget and me during our secondary education years—with baseless rumors of one's betrayal and deceit upon the other—our alliance had held strong. Our bond was unbreakable, our trust nonvulnerable to outside interference. Now, when Hannah no longer cared if we took our friendship to the grave or even came out as lesbian lovers, we were fighting over her.

What little patience I had stored away for Hannah before I went to the bathroom was gone by the time we returned to our table, along with my appetite, and we parted ways less than fifteen minutes later. Hannah said she would try to put in a good word with Felicia to accept my rewrites, and I pretended to believe Hannah's influence over Felicia had that far a reach. As I made my way outside, I tried to catch Bridget's eye, but both she and Jonathan had their backs to me. She was no doubt telling him what a horrible friend I was. I hoped Jonathan would stick up for me, but considering it was Bridget who stroked his sausage and not me, my expectations in that regard were managed. Hopefully Nicholas would side with Team Kim, but I didn't have high hopes of him being around to hear my version of the facts.

What if Bridget was right about my future with Nicholas? She knew I was uneasy about our relationship at the present time, but whether or not her primary intent was to hit me where it hurt didn't mean there wasn't truth to it. Things with Nicholas were not ideal. Maybe I was losing both of them.

The lights were off in my apartment, and it was quiet except for the barking German Shepard/Siberian Husky mix in the neighboring apartment and the squealing of brakes on the street below. After turning on the television, I went to the kitchen for a glass of water. On the refrigerator was a note from Nicholas: *I got out of work early tonight, but since you weren't home, I called George. Sorry I missed you!*

My stomach sank. I yearned to crawl onto Nicholas's lap and cry about my fight with Bridget while he stroked my hair and wiped away my tears. He'd gently coax me to make the first move and call her. It was me who lied, after all. And even though her jab about Nicholas was below the belt, I was the one who made the first nasty comment about Jonathan. Bridget and I had argued before, but this was the first time we'd fought, and I was scared. I needed my boyfriend to assure me it would all be okay, but I couldn't wait for him to come home and hold my hand while I called. I had to put on my big-girl panties and do it without his support.

She didn't answer her phone—probably screening my call. I left a message for her to call me so we could talk. Then I glanced around my empty living room, indubitably aware of how lonely I was. Much more so than I ever was when I lived alone. Only one thing could save the night—a message from Felicia saying she loved my rewrites. It had been hours since I checked my email. At least my disastrous night out with Hannah and resulting argument with Bridget served to distract me from constantly refreshing my account. It wasn't much of a consolation, but I was desperate for a silver lining.

My hopes soared when I saw the new email from Felicia. As my heart thumped against my chest, I raised my head skyward, closed my eyes, and repeated, "Please, please, please." Then I exhaled deeply before clicking on the email.

Dear Kim,

Great headway on the rewrites. I was hoping for a bit more conflict though. We want the readers to earn the happy ending, so throw a couple more stumbling blocks in Laurel's way. You know when you're in the ocean and crushed by wave after wave, unable to get your bearings? It should feel like that.

I know you can do it! Call me if you need to brainstorm.

F

Fight with Bridget—check, absentee boyfriend—check, dissatisfied agent—check. I was zero for three. Desirous to put the day behind me, I got in bed and was on my stomach, my head buried in the fluffy pillow, when Nicholas got home and joined me.

"You up, Kimmie?" he whispered.

Without lifting my head, I said, "Yes," but the sound was muffled by the pillow.

Nicholas laughed. "I think that was a yes."

I flipped over onto my back. "Hi."

On his side facing me, he said, "Hi, stranger," and softly swiped a finger across my cheek.

"Have fun tonight?"

"Yeah. We hung out at Sarah's friend's bar."

Sarah was George's girlfriend. Her friend Tim from culinary school was a bartender at an uptown Italian restaurant. "Free drinks?"

"But of course." He smiled. "How was your night?"

"Epic."

Nicholas raised an eyebrow. "You seem rather gloomy for someone who had an epic night."

"Epically bad. I got in a fight with Bridget, and Felicia said my rewrites weren't good enough."

"I'm sorry. Let's discuss this more tomorrow. I'm ready to drop, but I'm sure you'll make up with Bridget. You guys are solid as a rock." His lips turning up, he added, "Did you know that song only made it to number twelve on the U.S. Billboard Hot 100?"

My body tensed and through gritted teeth, I said, "So on the one night you don't work late in God only knows how long, you have enough energy to go drinking with George, but you'll talk to me 'tomorrow'? Thanks, Nicholas. Thanks for nothing." I turned on my side so he was facing my back.

Nicholas exhaled. "Of course I have time for you, Kim. Tell me what happened."

I flipped over on my other side. "Hannah asked me out to dinner, and I didn't want to tell Bridget—"

Nicholas yawned. "Excuse me," he said, covering his mouth with his hand. "You had dinner with Hannah?"

A painful lump in my throat, I conceded defeat. "Get some sleep, Nicholas. I'll tell you tomorrow."

"You sure?"

I longed to ask if he still loved me, but too afraid to risk another disappointment, I said, "I'm sure."

Nicholas removed his pillow from the sham and tossed it on the floor before slipping under the covers. Kissing me on the shoulder, he said, "Tomorrow will be a better day" and closed his eyes.

I nodded. I began to say, "From your lips to..." but Nicholas was already asleep before I could even complete the sentence.

Chapter 28

The next morning, I woke to the sound of Nicholas's footsteps throughout the apartment. I stretched lazily for a moment until the events of the night before came rushing back, and I sat up in a panic remembering my duel with Bridget. Last night was the first time we'd ever gone to bed angry with each other, and we'd both said terrible things. I shouldn't have lied to Bridget, but she shouldn't have taken it so badly. She had no reason to be so jealous and insecure. It wasn't as if Hannah could ever replace Bridget. Bridget was the wind beneath my wings. My comment about Jonathan was royally mean, but she packed a punch with her jab about Nicholas too. As far as I was concerned, we'd both screwed up, but it was no reason to throw away more than a decade of friendship. Hopefully Bridget came to the same conclusion after sleeping on it, and we could put the awful night behind us and lock it away somewhere never to be revisited again. I'd call her again later and make the (second) first move.

Nicholas was sitting at the table tapping at his phone when I joined him in the kitchen. "Morning," I said with a touch of apprehension. I ached to confide in him but worried he'd be in a hurry to get to work. Or worse, not remember our conversation from the night before at all.

"Feeling better today?"

I released a breath of relief. He did remember. "Not really," I said, sitting down next to him.

Glancing at his watch, Nicholas said, "I have a few minutes before I need to leave. What happened?"

"I had a nasty fight with Bridget last night." The hollowness in my chest deepened as I said it out loud.

Nicholas cocked his head to the side. "About?"

"Hannah Marshak."

Nicholas gave me a slow smile. "Well, I'm certain a dispute concerning Hannah won't mark the end of your friendship with Bridget."

I bit my lips. "The thing is...we fought about other things too."

"What other things?"

Jonathan. You. Us. My stomach twitched as I searched for the right words to tell him how I'd been feeling lately—how much I missed him and how afraid I was that by giving his all to work, he was not reserving enough energy to nurture us. If I told him, maybe he'd take me in his arms and vow to find a way to make time for the two of us without threatening his position at work. But what if he didn't?

"Kim?" Nicholas glanced at his watch again.

"Do you have to get to work?"

"Kind of, yeah." He stood up and pushed his chair toward the table. Kissing the top of my head, he said, "Call Bridget. You'll feel better."

I gulped. "Okay."

I arrived at work determined to right all of my wrongs before they suffocated me. First, I would call Bridget again and put an end to our squabble. Then, I would attack my work in progress by adding more choppy waters to my heroine's journey and, by doing so, keep my readers guessing and on high alert until the very last page. Finally, I would muster the confidence to instigate a heart-to-heart with Nicholas. My insecurity paralyzed me in the kitchen earlier, but I couldn't fret silently for much longer.

The goal was to accomplish all of this by the stroke of midnight.

Unfortunately, Rob had me running around like a last-minute

shopper on Christmas Eve—dashing back and forth between my desk to print out documents, the copy room to make enough sets to supply a baseball team, and the conference room to sort and collate—and by the time I picked up the phone to call Bridget, it was nearly two o'clock. Before I had the chance to complete the call, Rob was upon me once again, this time with Daneen at his side. I slipped my phone back into my desk drawer and looked at them expectantly. "Busy day, eh?"

"Trial preparation usually is," Rob said with a shake of his head.

I offered a half-assed frown. It was hard to take pity on Rob knowing he secretly lived for the frantic pace and the high stakes that came with big cases, but it was part of what made Rob Rob. I glanced from him to Daneen. "What can I do to help?"

Rob handed me a piece of paper with his mostly illegible-to-the-untrained-eye handwriting. "Hotel and flight reservations. Book us anywhere with a four- or five-star rating within a fifteen-minute cab ride from the Dade County Courthouse. I wrote down all of the dates and addresses you should need. Please take care of the two of us." He angled his head toward Daneen. "And David."

By far, my favorite work-related task was choosing where Rob stayed while away on business. I loved to research different hotels for their business amenities, gym facilities, and on-location restaurants. I also enjoyed the challenge of booking flights with the least layovers and the most points. Ready to work, I sat up straighter and circled my shoulders back. "On it."

"Thanks, Long," Rob said before walking back to his office.

Following him and with barely a glance in my direction, Daneen mumbled, "Yeah, thanks."

Perhaps I would "accidentally" book Daneen at a Best Western.

I reached my arms over my head for a moment before reading Rob's note. I read it once and then again, squinting my eyes the second time to better make out the dates Rob had indicated they would be heading to Florida. It had to be a mistake. With the note in my hand, I walked to Rob's office and stood at the entrance. "Um, Rob?"

He looked over Daneen's head toward me. "Yes?"

"This says you're leaving the day after tomorrow."

Daneen whipped her head around to face me. "What of it?"

Ignoring her, I twirled a strand of hair around my finger. "Um, this is the Orange Essence case, right?"

Rob nodded. "Correct."

"I wasn't aware the trial was coming up so soon. Is, um, is Nicholas going?" I carefully breathed in and out and then repeated the motion. Surely if Nicholas was joining them in Miami, he would have told me by now. In and out.

"Yes. He's going. Why?"

One side of Daneen's mouth quirked into a smile. "Yeah. Why, Kim?"

"No reason." But the steam coming out of my ears defied the words leaving my mouth.

As soon as I got back to my desk, I called Bridget. Despite our current circumstances, Bridget was my best friend, and I needed her. Voicemail. "Bridget. It's me. I know you're mad and I'm sorry, but I really need you. Please call me back."

The afternoon crept by without a return call from Bridget. It took me over an hour to book flights for Rob, Daneen, and David, and to reserve three rooms at the Mandarin Oriental. I finally took a lunch break at three thirty, during which I drafted a broad outline of possible roadblocks to throw in Laurel's way. I also finished *From Tuscany With Love*, the latest book in my review queue. But I'd probably need to leaf through the last chapter again before writing my review because the entire time I was reading about the main character's travels in Italy, my mind was on Nicholas's impending trip to Miami. Why hadn't he told me he was going away on a business trip—in two days? It wasn't as if he didn't have ample opportunity, like this morning. Nicholas often claimed he didn't want to bore me with "work talk," but failing to provide the details on discovery and evidence was one thing; omitting the news he would be leaving the state for several days was another. If there was a reasonable explanation, I couldn't find it. The answer was with Nicholas, and as I walked the steps to our apartment later to confront him, my heart was jumping in my chest. I had sent him a text asking what time he'd be home, and even though he said he'd leave work at a "reasonable" hour, I was surprised to see him sitting at our breakfast nook when I walked in the door.

He glanced up at me from the book he was reading and smiled. "How was your day?"

I threw my keys on the counter and shrugged out of my coat. "It was fine," I said, not meeting his eyes.

"Want me to make—"

"I lied. My day wasn't fine."

A frown creased Nicholas's forehead as he closed his book. "What happened?"

"Were you planning on waiting until the plane took off to tell me you were going to Florida?"

Nicholas let out an audible breath. "I didn't tell you about my trip?"

I shook my head. "No."

He ran a hand through his hair. "I totally thought I mentioned it to you. The trial should only be a few days, but I might meet up with some folks from company headquarters while I'm out there."

My eyes bugged out at his nonchalance. "Do you have any idea how embarrassing it is to hear these things from Daneen instead of my own boyfriend?"

Nicholas rolled his eyes. "Are we still on that? Daneen is not a threat to you."

"Tell that to Daneen. You tell her everything else about me."

Nicholas jerked his head back. "What do you mean?"

"I don't appreciate you divulging all of the details about my book stuff to her—like getting rejected by Ginny Webber. It's none of her business."

Rubbing his temple, Nicholas said, "I know. I'm sorry. But what does it matter now? You've got Felicia."

I grabbed a fistful of my hair and pulled. "Do you also confide in Daneen about your daddy issues?"

Raising his palms, Nicholas asked, "What daddy issues?"

Pacing the kitchen, I said, "With your unsupportive parents, you guys have so much in common besides the law."

"Not everyone is blessed with a perfect family like you," Nicholas muttered.

"My family is not perfect."

Nicholas let out a loud sigh. "This is silly. Why are we fighting about this? I'm sorry I said anything to Daneen. But, seriously, stop giving her so much power."

"I don't give her..." I pressed my lips shut as my mind flashed back to using the same words on Bridget about Hannah. It wasn't exactly the same thing, but close enough. Maybe I was a hypocrite, but it didn't make me any less upset with Nicholas. "Why is it so difficult for you to keep me apprised of what's going on with you? I want to be your partner—not just your slam piece."

Nicholas stood up and walked toward me. "You're not just my..." His face contorted in laughter. "Slam piece?" He chuckled. "That's a new one."

"It's not funny, Nicholas." I turned away to wipe a tear from my cheek.

"I'm sorry, Kim." His hands massaged my shoulders from behind. "What can I do to make it up to you?"

"You can't fix everything with sex," I whispered. Especially when you can't stay awake long enough to close the deal.

"It's a start though, right? A woman's got needs." He pinched my sides.

I released myself from his embrace and faced him. "I'm being serious. We're so disconnected lately. Even when you're with me, you don't seem present because you're so focused on work."

This time it was Nicholas who turned his back on me. "There's a lot riding on this trial. That's all."

I grabbed him by the elbows and guided him until he was facing me again. "You can talk to me about it, you know. Maybe I can help. Rob always says I'm his right arm." I grinned. "Actually, he says I'm his right stump."

Nicholas laughed halfheartedly. "I appreciate it, Kimmie, but I've got it covered."

"Are you sure?"

"Positive. But thanks."

I swallowed back my disappointment that he was shutting me out of his work again. "I sure hope you win the damn thing."

"Me too. And I'm sorry I didn't mention the trip to you earlier. It was an oversight. But on a bright note, the flight will give me time to start reading your book."

My lips curled up slightly. "Really?" I had printed out the revised version just in case.

Nicholas nodded. "Really. We good now?"

Nodding, I said, "Uh huh." This was a lie, but the part of Nicholas I always counted on to sniff out my needs when I couldn't or was afraid to express them was lost, at least temporarily, to the big bad trial. Hopefully, he would return from the Sunshine State with his more sensitive and intuitive side in tow. And with any luck, he'd revert to the typical overworked attorney I fell in love with and leave the workaholic I barely recognized back in Florida with the palm trees and retired senior citizens.

I couldn't wait as long to make things right with Bridget. Since she'd made it clear she wasn't going to answer the phone when I called or return my numerous messages, I proceeded to Plan B and called Jonathan the following day. Unlike his stubborn girlfriend, he picked up on the first ring. "Hey, Kim." The resigned tone of his voice suggested my call was not much of a surprise.

"Put her on."

After a brief pause during which I clearly heard Bridget say, "Tell her I'm not here," Jonathan said, "She's...she's not home."

"Either you're lying to me, or you're cheating on Bridget with another girl who just said 'Tell her I'm not home.'"

Jonathan groaned. "She doesn't want to talk to you. I told her she was being silly, but she won't listen."

"Please tell her Nicholas is going to Florida tomorrow for a trial and didn't see the point in telling me. I had to hear it from Rob and Daneen." I was totally playing the pity card—hoping Bridget would set aside our fight over Hannah to comfort me in my moment of need.

I listened to Jonathan repeat what I said to Bridget. Then I heard Bridget say, "Give me the phone." I smiled. Friendship was thicker than water.

As soon as I heard her breathe into the phone, I said, "Thank God. I'm so sorry—"

Cutting me off before I could complete my apology, Bridget said, "Wow, Kim. I was only half-serious when I said you were losing Nicholas, but it doesn't look good for you. At all. Sorry."

Except she didn't sound sorry. She sounded smug. I opened my mouth to say something, but no words came out.

"It's a good thing you have Hannah."

As all of the blood in my body seemed to converge in my face, I balled my free hand in a fist, as angry as I'd ever been with Bridget in almost two decades of friendship. "Why are you being such a bitch? Are you that jealous of Hannah?"

Bridget snorted. "As if."

"You know what, Bridget? I'm sorry I lied, but considering how you're acting, maybe it's good I did. At least now I know what you're capable of."

"Whatever—"

"And maybe I am in danger of losing Nicholas, but you're not fooling me at all. Your love nest with Jonathan is all blissful and cozy right now, but eventually, his aversion to marriage and kids will sink in, and you guys will implode too. Don't come to me when that happens. I'll be with Hannah." As I pressed "end" on the call with force, I wished it was a rotary phone I could slam for effect.

Chapter 29

With the entire squad in Florida, most of my work-related responsibilities the following week were limited to covering the phones, and so I spent much of the daytime hours working on my edits. Since there was no one waiting for me at home, and I wasn't on speaking terms with my best friend, most of my nighttime hours were also spent finalizing my revisions, either at my kitchen table or the coffee shop. After reading the final draft out loud in my living room in a dramatic monologue and giving myself a standing ovation when I finished, I knew I'd nailed it. Now that I'd reached the "after" phase of the process, I was actually happy Felicia had rebuffed the original version because I knew the novel was better for it—something I was too blinded by fear of failure to appreciate in the "before" stage. Even if she volleyed it back to me for more changes, I would get it right eventually—no matter how many rounds it took. Knowing I was capable of giving my all to something when it really mattered was electrifying, and even the muddled conditions of my personal life couldn't take that victory away from me. Nicholas would be so proud, if only he were paying attention. For now, I would have to be proud for the both of us.

With the updated version of *A Blogger's Life* fired off to Felicia, I had time to prepare for the approaching dinner with Caroline. I had been so consumed with my own drama that I didn't have the chance to obsess over her secret. She'd promised it wasn't bad, but "bad" was a relative term. For instance, she might think moving her permanent residence to the Galapagos Islands was the best news ever, but I'd be crushed. But at least I knew she wasn't suffering from a terminal illness because that would be tragic no matter the perspective. Hopefully, she'd be so animated in delivering her news she'd fail to notice the tension between Bridget and me. Although she'd have to be blind, deaf, and seriously clueless to miss it. I had no plans to cause a scene, but I also did not intend to offer Bridget a white flag. When I flashed back to the icy tone of her voice when she predicted the end of my relationship with Nicholas, I was struck with an urge to pull out every strand of hair from her head by the roots. I still regretted my impulsive decision to keep my dinner with Hannah from her, but my sole motivation was to protect Bridget from unnecessary distress, and I had apologized—more than once. Her initial reaction made perfect sense, as catching me "in the act" with Hannah after being told I was having dinner with Nicholas must have hurt, but how many times could I say "I'm sorry"? And how many times should a girl need to apologize before her friend—her best friend—forgave her? Once the shock wore off, Bridget should have accepted my apology, offered her own regret for the nasty words she uttered, and called it a day, but instead she turned a minor tiff into an all-out war.

I hoped Parlor Steak House, where Caroline had made a seven o'clock reservation, wouldn't have a strict policy about not seating diners until the entire party had arrived, as I purposely showed up ten minutes late. If the odds were in my favor, rather than withstand several minutes of awkward conversation standing at the bar avoiding eye contact with Bridget, I would be led directly to our table where I could distract myself with the menu during any lulls in the conversation. If luck was not on my side, I would be the rude member of our group who showed up tardy, resulting in everyone else standing elbow to elbow listening to their stomachs growling.

I didn't see any familiar faces at the crowded bar to the right of the restaurant's entrance, and so I approached the hostess, who informed me my party was seated mere moments earlier. I followed her to the back of the restaurant where I caught sight of Caroline's face at a circular table. She talked animatedly as three other heads bobbed up and down in response to whatever she was saying. I increased my pace, excited to see her after so many months, and then abruptly stopped short as the other faces came into view—Bridget, Jonathan, and...who was the brown-eyed guy with shaggy dark hair and full eyebrows? Whoever he was, he was adorable, despite the overuse of hair gel. Could he be the big surprise? I was so accustomed to Caroline's independent spirit—albeit not necessarily by choice—it never dawned on me her secret might involve a guy.

The four of them stopped talking as the hostess pulled out a chair for me and placed another menu on the table. I remained standing, uncomfortably aware of all eyes on me, as I thanked her. After she walked away, I beamed at Caroline. "Hi."

Caroline stood up and embraced me fiercely, shaking me from side to side. When she pulled away, she smiled. "I'm so glad you made it. We only sat down a couple of minutes ago."

I shrugged out of my coat and sat down at the empty seat between Caroline and Jonathan. "I'm so sorry I'm late." Glancing at the others at the table, I said, "Hi, everyone."

To my left, Jonathan nodded. "Long." Then he turned to Bridget nervously.

Her eyes flicked to mine briefly before she looked away, but the second of contact was enough for me to sense her discomfort rivaled mine.

My stomach hardened as I wondered if Caroline and her "friend" noticed the tension. Clearing my throat, I jutted my chin in the direction of Caroline's "surprise" and smiled. "Hi. I'm Kim." I sized him up, guessing from his attire—a slim-fit denim short-sleeved shirt and red jeans—that he was European. He confirmed this when he greeting me with, "All right?" in a British accent.

Caroline placed her hand over his. "This is Felix. He's the reason I invited you all out for dinner tonight," she said, glancing around the table. Focusing on me, she said, "I'm sorry Nicholas couldn't be here. Bridget mentioned he was in Florida for a trial."

I timidly looked in Bridget's direction, but she had her head down. I swallowed hard. "Yeah. I'm on my own tonight. But no worries. Tonight's not about me. It's about you."

Caroline grinned. "Thank you. You've probably already guessed my news involves Felix here." She paused as we all nodded. "I don't know quite how to say this, so I'll just blurt it out. Felix is my..." She bit her lip. "Felix is my husband."

I burst out laughing. "No way." I waited for the others to chime in, but Bridget and Jonathan were silent as they gawked at Caroline and Felix, and Caroline and Felix grinned so wide, I could see their wisdom teeth. While the waiter poured prosecco in each of our glasses, I stopped laughing. "Wait. You're serious?"

Caroline and Felix exchanged a private smile while he slipped a diamond ring on her finger right before our eyes.

Felix winked at me. "Quite serious."

Caroline extended her hand toward Bridget, who peered at the ring with wide eyes. "Wow."

Jonathan regained his bearings first. "I'll take the liberty to congratulate you while Bridget and Kim pick their jaws off the floor." He raised his glass in the air. "Congratulations."

Caroline chuckled. "I know it's shocking news. When I left, I was as single as a nun and not only did I meet someone, but I married him. It's the craziest thing I've ever done, but I couldn't be more ecstatic." She kissed Felix on the cheek, running her fingers along his skin.

I had a barrage of questions requiring answers, the first one being, "Are you out of your freaking mind?" But for now, there was only one thing to say, so after taking a gulp of prosecco, I planted on a smile. "Congratulations. I'm so happy for you guys." And I would be—as soon as I was certain Felix wasn't a serial killer or using Caroline for a green card.

"Me too. Congrats, guys," Bridget said, with what I knew from experience to be forced enthusiasm. Our eyes locked, and I saw my own shock mirrored in her expression. Our differences were temporarily forgotten as she widened her eyes at me as if to say, "Holy crap."

Jonathan said, "Since the resident lawyer is not in attendance, I have to ask. Is this marriage legal?"

Her brows squished together, Caroline asked, "Why wouldn't it be?"

My own half-assed legal mind waking up, I chimed in. "Yeah. Aren't there immigration laws in play? Will Felix need to apply for a Green Card to live here?" I certainly hoped Carolyn planned to stay in the country once their world tour came to an end.

"I have dual citizenship," Felix said with an easy grin.

Caroline nodded. "He's been living here for ten years now but was visiting family while traveling for work. We sat next to each other on my flight to London, hit it off, and after spending a few days with his folks, he met up with me, and we've been together ever since. We flew directly to Vegas and have been married two days now."

Okay, so the green card issue was off the table, but there was still a possibility he was a serial killer on the America's Most Wanted list. "What was the hurry? Didn't you want to get married in front of friends and family?" They hadn't even known each other an entire season. At this stage, Caroline wouldn't know if Felix had seasonal affective disorder unless he volunteered the information. And he might not be aware of how bitchy Caroline got when Aunt Flo was in town.

Caroline smiled with her eyes as Felix squeezed her hand. "Neither of us cared about a big ceremony, but we'll probably have a party when we come home for good. For now, we'll treat the rest of my trip as our extended honeymoon."

I wondered how Felix managed to get so much time off from work. "What do you do for a living, Felix?" Noting how parental and potentially stuck-up the question sounded, I winced inwardly.

But Caroline's grin didn't falter. "You'll love this, Kim. Felix is a writer like you."

"I write for a travel magazine, actually. After I met Caroline, I pitched a new feature. I'm writing a travel blog about discovering the world with my new bride. I'll report on the grub in China, the posh hotels in Hong Kong, and the rugby in Australia and New Zealand." He flashed his pearly whites in unabashed delight. "All while getting off with Caroline. Brill, right?"

I only understood about half of what he said, but his spirit was contagious. "Totally."

Caroline's whirlwind romance with Felix read like a Harlequin novel, but I worried marrying a virtual stranger wasn't the most infallible way to ensure a happily ever after. Still, as conversation halted while the waiter took our dinner orders, I observed Caroline and Felix and couldn't deny the color in their cheeks and the width of their grins. Even if their relationship lasted the length of a novella rather than an epic novel, nothing could take this moment away from them.

While Bridget was busy telling the waitress she wanted the tuna nicoise medium, I stole a glance in her direction. She delivered her order, all the while holding Jonathan's hand. When he gave it a squeeze, she looked up at him in surprise and beamed as he bent down to kiss her nose. Despite her own long-term boyfriend's disinterest in ever making their relationship legal, Bridget didn't appear to be envious that mere moments earlier, her close friend announced her spontaneous marriage to a guy she practically just met. Perhaps her claim of not caring about getting married wasn't a lie or self-delusion after all. I observed them affectionately with a smile playing on my lips until her eyes met mine, and her head jerked back in surprise. Embarrassed to have forgotten we were in a fight, I quickly shifted my chair closer to Caroline to better examine her solitaire-shaped diamond ring.

"It's so sparkly," I said.

"Thank you."

"What did your parents say?" Bridget asked.

Caroline smirked. "My dad has no business saying anything considering he's married to a woman my age. My mother wasn't pleased." She dropped her gaze and fiddled with a roll.

Felix placed his arm around her and drew her close. "She thinks we're both barmy, but I'll win her over. You'll see."

Laughing, Jonathan said, "You sure don't sound like you've lived here for ten years." I was glad he said it and not me.

"If I have anything to do with it, he'll never lose his accent. I love all of the British slang. It's so sexy," Caroline said, her cheeks flushed.

Once again, I was glad she said it and not me. Felix was my close friend's boyfriend—correction, *husband*—but I could certainly appreciate his appeal from a no-touching distance. Bridget and I would have so much fun dishing about his adorable accent, chiseled jaw, and ease with which he sported colored jeans later—if only we were speaking.

For the remainder of the meal, I made it a point to focus the conversation on Caroline and Felix—details about their wedding, observations from their travels, et cetera. Bridget did the same. Even while in a feud, it was as if we made a silent agreement to work together for a common goal—not to let our contention get in the way of Caroline's big night. Under normal circumstances, Caroline would have seen through it, but she was so preoccupied with Felix and under their love spell, she didn't seem to notice Bridget and I never spoke to each other directly.

At the end of the night, we huddled outside the entrance to say our goodbyes. "Take lots of pictures of the pyramids," I demanded, after giving Caroline a tight hug. They were jetting to Egypt the following day.

"I promise to post on Facebook and Instagram," Caroline said.

"Perfect." I gave her a thumbs-up. "So nice to meet you, Felix, and congratulations. Take care of our girl or I'll hunt you down and—"

"What? Punch him in the knees?" Jonathan interrupted, laughing.

Playfully shoving him in retribution, I said, "I own a stepladder, and I know how to use it."

Felix crossed his heart. "On my John Thomas, I promise to treat her like a princess." He leaned down and kissed me on the cheek. "You're a brilliant friend."

As I stepped aside to give Bridget room to bid her farewell, Jonathan edged closer to me.

I gave him a halfhearted shrug.

He tilted his head to the side. "What are you going to do about your little situation?" he asked, gesticulating between Bridget and me.

Crossing my arms over my chest, I said, "*I* don't plan to do anything about it." With a darting gaze toward Bridget, who was still saying her goodbyes, I whispered through my teeth, "I tried to make peace, and she got nasty with me. I'm done." My brain ordered me to stand strong even as my heart ached for my best friend.

Jonathan's lips pressed together in a slight grimace. "She'd never admit to it, but she misses you like crazy. She keeps trying to make me act more like you. I love the girl, but I'm not watching real housewives of anywhere, and I don't care about her damn period."

I chuckled despite myself, even as my chin trembled dangerously. I gave him a quick kiss on the cheek and a fleeting smile. "I need to get out of here." Raising my voice to get Caroline and Felix's attention once more, I said, "Safe travels, guys. Congrats again," all the while avoiding eye contact with Bridget.

"Cheerio," said Felix as the two of them waved goodbye. Before the onset of tears could give me away, I turned on my heel and flagged down an oncoming taxi.

Chapter 30

"Thank you! You won't regret this!"

As Pia's screeching voice attacked my eardrums, I winced and put the phone on speaker. One would think she was nominated for a Golden Globe award as opposed to being made a permanent reviewer on *Pastel Is the New Black*, but my lips turned up at how charged she was. I had planned to wait at least a month before making a decision, but after reading Pia's first two probationary reviews, I was convinced she was the closest I was going to get to cloning myself. "You're very welcome. I'm so grateful for the help."

"So many books, so little time, right?" she said.

"Exactly." With a dishrag in hand, I did a sweep of my living room to see what else could use a good dusting. I was attempting to keep myself busy to avoid obsessing over Bridget, Nicholas, or my revised manuscript sitting in Felicia's inbox.

"I was shocked by your latest blog post. I had no idea."

I had published a post making my writing aspirations public for the first time ever. I assured my readers I would not be abandoning my role as a book reviewer/blogger, but would be doing double duty as a blogger and an aspiring novelist. I also told them my author website would be launched in the upcoming future. It remained to be seen whether it would be the stunning website of Bridget's creation or if I would be forced to find a new web designer. I refused to acknowledge my desire for the former since I was on a mission not to obsess over Bridget. "I haven't wanted to talk about the writing gig so early in its gestation," I confessed.

"Well, I can't wait to review your book. I'm sure I'll give it five pink champagne flutes."

"Ha. It might be a bit of a conflict of interest for you to review it on *Pastel Is the New Black*. But feel free to do so on Amazon, Goodreads, and Barnes and Noble. If I ever get to that point."

"For sure. So exciting. Do you have an agent? Do you want to publish traditionally or self-publish? The book is chick lit, right?"

I swallowed hard, debating how much to share with her. Even though I was bursting to announce I had already signed with Harrison & Gold, I kept my blog post very vague, wanting to discuss it with Felicia first. What if she preferred I keep the title a secret until the book was sold? What if she insisted I change the title before the novel went on submission? What if she lost patience with my multiple rounds of rewrites and dumped me as her client?

"The book is chick lit," I said, hoping she'd be satisfied with the answer to just one of her many questions, or at least take the hint I didn't want to answer the others.

"I'll take your vagueness as a sign you don't want to talk about this," Pia said with a chuckle.

I let out a huge breath of relief. "Thanks." Hoping to keep the conversation going, albeit in a different direction, I said, "So, what are all the cool graduate students at University of Michigan doing tonight?"

I felt a wave of sadness as I realized how desperate I was for a friend—someone to talk to. My circle of close friends had always been limited—a logical result of having such a long-standing relationship with Bridget. From the age of thirteen, we had relied almost entirely on each other for female companionship. As I stood between the walls of my 700-square-foot apartment, desperate to keep Pia—someone I would likely never meet face to face—from ending our call, I wondered if it was karma's way of kicking my butt for engaging in such an exclusionary clique of two.

"Going to the Jolly Pumpkin. A bit more upscale than some of the college bars."

I removed my phone from the coffee table and headed to the

bedroom. Stripping the bed without another set of sheets on deck meant I'd be forced to do laundry later, but it needed to be done. "Sounds fun. Tell me about it."

As Pia rambled off a description of the Jolly Pumpkin—it was a bar and brewery combined into one—I continued cleaning my bedroom. I removed various items of Nicholas's clothing from the floor and straightened the pile of *Mad Magazines* on the top of his dresser.

"Maybe I'll meet a mature twenty-five-year-old man instead of the usual frat boy who considers chugging beer after beer followed by sloppy drunk sex an ideal Saturday night," Pia continued.

Laughing quietly, I said, "You might want to aim for older than twenty-five if you're seeking maturity." I bent down in front of Nicholas's dresser to return some of his items to their rightful place.

"Maybe twenty-eight. Thirty is way too old."

Remembering when I too thought thirty was over the hill, I rolled my eyes in amusement as I opened Nicholas's top drawer. Expecting to see folded pairs of boxer shorts and undershirts, my stomach clenched at the sight of the revised copy I had given Nicholas of *A Blogger's Life* and I gasped out loud.

"What's wrong?" Pia asked, a catch in her voice.

The messed-up part was it wouldn't have upset me to see the book sitting untouched in his dresser if Nicholas hadn't mentioned his intention to read it on the plane. But knowing he cast it aside in favor of, what, another pair of shoes, prickled my skin.

"Kim? You there?"

"Sorry. I'm still here." My breath caught in my throat, and I longed to confide in someone. I needed someone to assure me it was okay to want more from Nicholas than he was currently giving me, to remind me of how supportive I'd always been of his career and understanding of his late hours, and to confirm I wasn't imagining Nicholas's distance over the last few months. I wished more than anything that someone was Bridget, but Pia would have to do since she was currently my only source of female comradery, or at least the most convenient seeing as we were already on the phone. I gave her the short version of the facts, concluding with finding the manuscript in his dresser after he'd told me he planned to take it to Florida.

"I'm sorry, Kim. You should talk to him."

"Bridget said the same thing."

"Who's Bridget?"

"My best friend." My stomach dropped. I couldn't bring myself to clarify the statement with the word ex before best friend. "I've tried, but he's either been too focused on work to give me his full attention, or I lose my nerve. And he's in Miami at a trial anyway."

"Maybe simply talking isn't the answer. Why not go big?"

"Like a grand gesture?" I recalled Caroline's words from the year before: pretend you're a heroine in a chick lit novel, and write your own happy ending.

"Yeah. Something dramatic to get his attention."

I sighed. "I did that already." But even as I pouted over the injustice of once again being responsible for turning our relationship around, an idea was brewing. My eyes spotted the framed photograph on the wall of me, Erin, and my parents. It was taken when my folks first moved to Florida, and it was the only time my sister and I visited them together. "I suppose flying to Miami would be too dramatic, right?" I snorted.

Pia clapped. "Genius. Genius," she repeated, sounding like the curator at the museum in Paris when Aleksandr Petrovsky revealed his light installation in *Sex and the City*. "You must do it."

I laughed. "I wasn't serious."

"Why not?"

I opened my mouth to provide a credible reason and snapped it shut. Why not, indeed? It wouldn't be the first time I impulsively flew to Florida. I had done it the year before after finally acknowledging my dream to be a writer and escaping to my parents' house and the warmth of Boca Raton to complete the paranormal young adult novel I had started in high school.

"I'll do it," I said, logging onto Expedia to hunt down flights.

The last time I took a day off was when Ginny Webber rejected my query, and Rob always preferred when my absentee days from work coincided with the days he wasn't in the office anyway. He wouldn't mind. I hoped Nicholas would appreciate I was digging into my barely there savings to rescue our floundering relationship. I wouldn't expect him to reimburse me or buy me jewelry, but some groveling and assurances to never take me for granted again would be appreciated.

"Yay," Pia said, clapping again. "You need a plan."

I frowned. "What sort of plan?"

"Do you know where he's staying? Are you going to tell him you're coming or surprise him?"

She had more questions than I had answers for, and I rubbed my queasy belly. "He left me his hotel information, so that won't be a problem, but I hadn't thought about whether to tell him I was coming." Considering it had been less than five minutes since I made the decision to meet up with him, I hadn't thought about much. Thinking out loud, I said, "If I told him I was flying there without an explanation, he'd discourage me. He's busy with the trial and meetings with the company bigwigs and such. I think simply showing up is the way to go."

"That's sexier anyway. Maybe you can knock on his hotel room door wearing a trench coat and nothing else. What better way to corral his undivided attention?"

I grinned. Seducing Nicholas in Florida might present the perfect opening for an honest-to-goodness rap session about the state of our coupledom. I'd wait until he was at his most vulnerable—after we had gone several rounds and he was completed sated. This could work. Then again, the last time I tried to sex things up with Nicholas, he conked out before we even got naked. But what were the chances of a thirty-one-year-old healthy straight man falling asleep during his girlfriend's seduction twice in the same month? I swallowed hard and then quickly shook off the possibility. This time would be different.

"You're ingenious," I said as I visualized how things would go down when I got there. The trench coat idea was hot, but I had to devise something scorching. "Thank you so much, Pia. I should start packing." A carry-on would be sufficient since I didn't plan on wearing much clothing while I was there, but I had a lot to do before I went to sleep if I was going to catch an early plane the next day. First things first: book my flight. Then I would leave a voicemail for Rob. I'd thank him profusely for his understanding and insist he not tell Nicholas. Or Daneen. That bitch would love nothing more than to watch me and Nicholas implode.

"Keep me posted," Pia squealed, her enthusiasm booming through the phone.

High from our girly scheming session, I laughed with her. "You got it."

Chapter 31

Arriving at the Fontainebleau Miami Beach, I paid my cab driver, trying not to worry about the increasing balance I was putting on my credit card, and dragged my pink La Vida vintage carry-on tote behind me into the lobby. Practicing fiscal responsibility, I wisely bypassed the swanky shops and walked directly to the set of elevators that would take me to Nicholas's room in the Chateau Tower of the hotel. Maintaining a calm and confident gait, with a small smile playing on my lips as if I belonged there, I purposely avoided contact with the porters. Sneaking into one's boyfriend's hotel room was a private, covert operation. The last thing I needed was a bellhop offering assistance. Actually, the last thing I needed was to run into a member of the squad, but since I was the one who booked all of their rooms—in a different hotel—it was unlikely they would be here. Rob had told me they won the trial, and in response to subtle prodding on my part via text, Nicholas had informed me his plan for the day involved a jog up Collins Avenue to burn off last night's victory dinner at Joe's Stone Crab, followed by a meeting with some executives from his company for most of the afternoon. Rob and crew did not qualify as executives or even employees of his company. By my calculations, Nicholas would be with his colleagues for at least the next hour or two, leaving me time to sneak into his room and set the mood.

The lobby had the energy of a Vegas casino, complete with loud music and long lines to check in and out, and it was quite easy to blend into the crowd and into the elevator. My confidence soared until I couldn't get the elevator to move no matter how many times I pressed the button for Nicholas's floor.

With three unsuccessful attempts at getting beyond the lobby under my belt, I offered a pursed-lip smile to a fifty-something-year-old man who stepped into the elevator wearing Bermuda shorts and a bright yellow t-shirt. He acknowledged me with a nod of his head before slipping his room key into the slot and pressing the button for his floor, which was, regrettably, different than Nicholas's. The door closed.

I gave the man a pleading look. "Um, I hate to ask, but would you mind pressing the tenth floor for me? My boyfriend arrived yesterday and has both of our keys. I caught an earlier flight than planned and wanted to surprise him, but I didn't realize I needed my room key." I shifted my feet. "We're in a long-distance relationship and haven't seen each other in weeks. I'm sorry to ask. I swear I'm not trying to break in to someone else's room." Aside from Nicholas's.

The man gave me a onceover. "You don't strike me as the criminal type. Not that unlawful people don't come in small packages sometimes." He smiled. "But...what the hell." He slid his key in again and pressed the button for the tenth floor.

"Thank you." If only the tenth floor were my final destination. I still needed to get into Nicholas's room. Without a key. One step at a time.

Before exiting on the seventh floor, my new friend smiled. "Enjoy your trip."

"Thanks. You too. And thanks again for your help." As I watched his back disappear behind the closing door, and the elevator continued its ascent to the tenth floor, I felt my heart in my chest. Writing one's own happy ending was idealistic in theory and exhausting in practice.

When the doors opened, I stepped into the hallway and headed right toward Nicholas's room. My calming breaths battled my rapidly beating heart with each room I passed until I arrived at 1027. I turned the knob as if anticipating a miracle, but of course, it was locked. I leaned my carry-on against the door and peeked down the hallway, spotting a housekeeping cart a few rooms down.

I slowly walked in the direction of the cart, mentally rehearsing my speech. If I was lucky, the housekeeper would take my claim to have misplaced my room key at face value and let me in with her master key. But what if she lumped me in with some of the ritzy entitled guests who probably turned down their cosmetically modified noses at her? Or what if the room she was currently cleaning was left in shambles—clogged toilet, semen-stained sheets, broken glass, et cetera—leaving her in a lousy mood? She'd be well within her rights to send me on my way with a self-satisfied smirk, or worse, sic hotel management on my ass. I knew Nicholas wouldn't let them arrest me for attempted trespassing, but it really wasn't the ideal scenario.

And then I saw it—a square of yellow on top of a pile of white terrycloth towels. If it was what I thought it was, it would be a serendipitous moment. I took longer strides until I was close enough to the cart to confirm the yellow I saw was, in fact, Sophie Kinsella's newest novel. A smile spread across my face as I felt for my own copy on the bottom of my purse.

I stuck my head in the entrance of the room and knocked lightly. A woman with blond hair held back in a loose ponytail wearing a pale-blue housekeeper's uniform stepped out of the bathroom. "Yes, miss?"

She looked young enough to be my peer, and we had at least one thing in common. Perhaps the stars would align. "Is that your book in the cart?"

Her eyebrows furrowed. "Yes. It's mine. I brought it from home. Is something wrong?"

From her defensive tone, I worried I had sounded accusatory and shook my head vigorously. "No, I was coming down here to ask for assistance, and I couldn't help but notice we're reading the same book." I removed my copy from my bag and waved it at her.

I followed her into the hallway where she glanced at the contents in the cart. I watched her eyes light up when she saw her book was still there. "Do you like it?" she asked.

"Sophie is my favorite author."

"Mine too. I read on all of my breaks." She looked down the hallway in both directions and whispered, "I love chick lit, but some of the other staff members tease me."

I nodded empathetically. I had my share of experience with genre snobs. "I love it too. I have an entire blog dedicated to it."

The woman peered at me. Then she did a double take. "*Pastel Is the New Black*? Are you Kim?"

My eyes bugged out. "Yes, I am."

She put her hand to her heart. "I love your blog."

Trying not to choke up, I said, "Thank you so much. This is wild. No one's ever recognized me before."

The woman blushed. "I really love chick lit."

I nodded. "You and me both."

"Did you say you needed my assistance?"

Having momentarily forgotten my true mission, I blinked. "Oh, yes. I'm trying to get in room 1027. I've misplaced my room key, and my boyfriend is at a business meeting. Can you help me?" I hoped she would take my fidgeting to mean I needed to go to the bathroom and not that I possessed a guilty conscience for asking her to be my accomplice to breaking and entering. Although it had been several hours since I last peed.

"Is your boyfriend the dark-haired man with the kind brown eyes and the scruffy jaw?"

Dreamy-eyed, I said, "And a smile bright enough to light up a pitch-black sky?"

She nodded.

"Then the answer is yes. I'm actually surprising him." I crossed my fingers behind my back, praying she'd appreciate my honesty and help out her favorite blogger.

"Lucky lady." Shutting the door of the opened guest room behind her, she headed in the direction of Nicholas's room. "Follow me."

I practically skipped to the door.

She unlocked the room and motioned for me to come inside. "Please don't tell."

I crossed my heart and zipped my finger across my lips. "And hope to die." I reached into my purse and slipped her a twenty-dollar bill. "Thank you again."

Smiling brightly, she said, "Enjoy."

"That's the plan."

After letting the door close behind me, I leaned against it and took a long-overdue deep breath. Once I confirmed I was in the correct room, I stripped off my clothes and jumped in the shower. I wanted to wash off the grime from the flight, but I kept my head covered with a shower cap, afraid I wouldn't have time to properly restyle my hair from scratch.

Freshly clean from my shower and cozy in the hotel robe, I removed the red interoffice envelope I had borrowed from work from the bottom of my carry-on and spilled the contents on the bed. Inspired by my teenage years of creating friendship boards with Bridget, I had rummaged through a collection of old magazines the night before and cut out words corresponding to a favorite Beatles' song, "Strawberry Fields Forever." I removed the robe and placed the words strategically over my private parts. Even though no one would describe the area as a "strawberry field"—the color was off, and a strip was more accurate than a field—I knew Nicholas would appreciate the symmetry. I lay down carefully on the bed, my hands stretched out in front of me so I could read Sophie's new book while I waited.

Once everything was in place, the inevitable occurred—I had to use the bathroom. In all likelihood, I didn't physically need to pee, but once my mind believed I did, my bladder was certain to follow. I groaned. Tossing the cutouts to the side, I vaulted off the bed and ran to the bathroom. After completing my mission, I ran back to the bed and lay still. C'mon, Nicholas. Hurry up before I have to pee again.

I read a few pages with half-assed concentration, looking up from the book each time I heard a sound coming from the hallway, but the walls were pretty thick, and I couldn't hear much of anything. This was good news for people walking by after

Nicholas's arrival—for obvious reasons—but not very helpful now, when any advance notice would be to my advantage.

After about eighteen minutes—a short enough period of time to avoid another urge to urinate, but a long enough interval to place my sanity in jeopardy—I heard a click in the door. I quickly glanced down at my body and made last-second adjustments to the placement of the cutouts. Then I raised myself slightly forward so I could witness Nicholas's expression when he saw me. As discontent as I had been over the last few months, when I tried to pose lasciviously, my cheeks insisted on smiling goofily instead in anticipation of seeing him.

I fully planned to wait for him to notice me, but the moment I saw his form walk through the door, I blurted out, "Surprise!"

Nicholas whipped around toward the sound of my voice at the exact same moment I noticed the two men in suits behind him. He yelped, "Kim!" as I shouted, "Oh my God," and in what felt like an out-of-body experience, I clumsily pulled the comforter over my naked body.

I locked panicked eyes with Nicholas—who was rendered catatonic and gaping at me. Through my peripheral vision, I saw the two men raise their hands to their mouths in a mixture of amusement and embarrassment and hightail it out the door.

Finding his voice, Nicholas said, "Kim...I...Shit. I'll be right back." He ran into the hallway, leaving me alone in my own state of catatonia.

Chapter 32

What the hell just happened?

Shaking off my stupor, I was certain of one thing: I was a complete and utter failure at seduction, and now I might have cost Nicholas the respect of his colleagues. I jumped out of bed and dressed as hurriedly as I could. After scrawling, "I'm sorry" on the hotel-provided notepad, I threw my purse over my shoulder and pulled my carry-on bag behind me out of the room, down the hallway, into the elevator, and to the lobby as fast as I could. Thankfully, a room key was only required to go up.

While I imagined Nicholas making excuses for his girlfriend and pleading for his job, I gave the cab driver the address of my parents' house in Boca Raton an hour and a half away. The fare was more than I could afford, but my dad would pay for it in a heartbeat as soon as he saw my face. As the yellow cab pulled out of the hotel onto Collins Avenue, the humidity caught up with me, and I pulled my hair into a bun on the top of my head. Then I called my mom.

She answered on one ring. "Hi, sweetie."

"Are you home?"

"Yes. Why?"

"Stay put, okay? I'm on my way."

"What? What time does your flight get in? Your dad and I will pick you up. Is Nicholas with you?"

I winced at his name and choked back the tears. "I'm in a cab."

"A cab?"

I clarified. "From Miami." I slipped out of my sweater, under which I wore a more weather-appropriate tank top, and fanned myself.

"You've lost me."

"I'll explain when I get there."

"Okay."

"And Mom? Can you spot me fifty bucks for the fare?" The driver locked eyes with me through the rearview mirror and raised his eyebrows. "Er, make it a hundred?"

"Of course. Are you all right?"

I blew a stream of air out of my mouth. "It depends on your definition of 'all right.' See you soon."

I ended the call as the phone rang again. It was Nicholas. Lost for what to say and not keen to have the conversation in front of the cab driver, I dismissed the call. I leaned my bare back against the seat, thankful the air conditioning was on to cool off the black leather, and closed my eyes. I wished for sleep to wipe away the image of myself sprawled across the bed with the phrase "Strawberry Fields" adorning my nipples.

"Miss."

My body shuddered as an agitated man's voice woke me from my sleep. I forgot where I was until I realized the voice was coming from the cab driver. His body was still facing forward, but he had turned his head toward the backseat. Pointing out the window where palm trees decorated a sunny suburban street with matching white ranch-style houses, he said, "You're here."

I wished I could muster more enthusiasm for this impromptu visit to my folks' lovely over-fifty development, but whereas sleep allowed me to forget the circumstances under which I was there, it was only a temporary fix, and I was awake now. "How much do I owe you?" I placed my wallet on my lap.

"One hundred and fifty-four dollars plus tip."

I sighed. As I removed my phone from my bag to call my mom to bring cash (or a credit card not close to being maxed out), I noticed the three missed calls and four texts. I flipped through them. All from Nicholas.

"Where are you?"

"Are you okay?"

"I'm worried. Please call me back!"

"Kimmie. Call me. Now."

"Miss?"

I turned away from the phone and toward the cab driver. "Yes?"

"One hundred and fifty-four dollars."

I swung my head back. "Huh? Oh, Right."

While my mom settled with the cab driver, I went into the house, plopped myself on the bed in the guest room, and sent Nicholas a text. I assured him I was fine and with my parents and told him I hoped things were okay on the work front. I yearned to go back to the ignorant and blissful sleep state I had abandoned in the cab, but I knew my parents were worried sick and waiting for details. Well, my mom wanted details—I was surprised she hadn't pounced on me already. Once my dad was assured I wasn't assaulted or beaten and my problems were romance related, he would go back to reading his novel and leave the details to my mother. I reluctantly joined them at the table by the pool. A bottle of something—most definitely alcoholic—was chilling.

While my dad stood up to give me a hug, my mom pulled out the bottle from the bucket and poured me a glass of white wine.

I separated from my dad and sat down. "Thanks," I said, taking a sip of wine. "Thanks for covering the cab. I'm sorry it was so expensive."

"As long as you're safe," my dad said.

"As you can see, I'm in one piece," I said, glancing down at my body.

"He means both physically and emotionally," my mom said with probing eyes. "Don't you, Peter?"

My dad gave me a pursed-lip smile and nodded. "Of course."

I chuckled. "I'm fine. I just had an unfortunate mishap with Nicholas in Miami and thought it was better if I came here."

"What sort of mishap?" my dad asked.

I imagined my dad's response to hearing I taped cutouts from a magazine on my breasts and genital area. He might faint. Then I visualized his response to hearing I accidentally exposed myself in this condition to two male strangers. He might have a heart attack. "The kind of mishap one does not tell her father."

He cocked his head.

"Trust me. You don't want to know."

His face turning red, my dad stood up and tucked his book under his arm. "You don't need to beat me with a stick." Taking his glass of wine with him, he said, "I'll be inside."

My mom looked at me with amusement. "This should be good."

"I'm not entirely comfortable sharing it with you either, Mom."

"Now I really need to know."

I closed my eyes, but in the darkness of my mind, I could still see Nicholas's shocked expression at realizing his colleagues had a clear view of his girlfriend in the buff. If Lucy attempted a sexy surprise on Desi in a twenty-first-century adaption of *I Love Lucy*, it would probably go down exactly like this.

"As long as it doesn't involve hamsters, I can handle it," my mom continued.

I opened my eyes. "Gross, Mom."

"I read *Fifty Shades of Grey*. Apparently, anything goes," my mom said, a twinkle in her eyes.

I laughed despite myself. "I think Nicholas and I are having some problems." I grimaced. It was the first time I had voiced my concern so definitively.

"Sexual problems?" my mom asked.

"No." Cringing at the memory of the day's happenings, I said, "This afternoon notwithstanding, I don't think sex is the issue." The events of the last twenty-four hours took their toll on me, and my shoulders slumped. "I really don't want to talk about it right now, Mom, I'm sorry." I stood up. "I'm tired. You mind if I take a nap?"

My mother frowned at me, her forehead creased with concern. "Sure, baby. Get some rest. I'm here if you need me."

I forced a smile. "I always need you, but I'm beat from the flight and..." My head spun as I mentally ran through the additional causes of my fatigue. My life had been on overdrive for the past few months—between Felicia's offer of representation and my corresponding rewriting efforts, my fight with Bridget, my failed attempts to maintain my boyfriend's attention, and keeping up with my day job and *Pastel Is the New Black*—it was no wonder I was burned out. "I'm just pooped," I said, keeping it simple. I leaned down and kissed her on the cheek before trudging inside.

Chapter 33

The creak of the door opening woke me. My mom popped her head in the room. "Kim," she whispered. "You have a guest."

My eyelids still heavy from my nap, I raised my arms over my head and yawned. "Who is it?"

Nicholas walked in and closed the door behind him. "Just me." He had changed out of his suit into black shorts and a Steely Dan t-shirt.

"Hi," I said, burying my head in the pillow.

Nicholas sat next to me on the bed with his feet dangling off the side. Patting my legs under the covers, he said, "Hey, Kimmie. Or should I say Strawberry?" He opened his hand and dropped the cutouts on the bed.

Squeezing the pillow tighter over my head, I said, "Ugh. I'm mortified. And so sorry."

"It's true, when I envisioned you meeting my colleagues, I pictured something else entirely," he said while rubbing my back. "But at least the important bits were covered, and if anything, they think I have the sexiest girlfriend ever. I tend to agree with them."

I threw the pillow off my head and stared up at him. "I didn't get you in trouble, did I?"

Despite the flirtatious words a moment ago, his expression was all business. "No, but I had some awkward explaining to do. Why didn't you tell me you were coming?"

"I wanted to surprise you." I threw my hands up in the air. "Surprise!"

Nicholas gave me a halfhearted smile. "Under normal circumstances, I'd be thrilled to discover you naked in my hotel bed, but..."

"But your colleagues were with you. I know. It never occurred to me you'd bring them back to your hotel room." I grimaced at the memory.

Nicholas ran a hand through his hair. "Your near peep show was one thing, but the fact you're here in the first place is what I'm confused about. What's going on?"

"I missed you, Nicholas."

Raising an eyebrow, Nicholas said, "You flew all the way here to tell me you missed me? Not exactly stellar timing."

Clenching my jaw, I said, "When is the timing ever good? When you're in a hurry to get to work and obsessively glancing at your watch? Or how about during the rare occasions we share a meal together, and you're compulsively checking your email? Or after a fourteen-hour day of work when you fall asleep the moment your head hits the pillow? Would the timing have been better then? I'm sorry my timing is less than impeccable, but we're in trouble, Nicholas, and I thought if I surprised you here, we could reignite our flame."

Nicholas's eyes opened wide. "Reignite our flame?" His lips quivered, and his face turned pink. "Sounds like a page from one of your books." Abandoning his attempt to keep it together, he cracked up.

As I watched him laugh, a lump formed in my belly, and I swallowed hard, trying to identify my feelings. I didn't share Nicholas's amusement. Was I sad? Angry? "I'm glad one of us is entertained." I raised my voice above his laughter. Yeah, I was pissed. "I came here to show you what you've been missing, and you don't act like you miss it at all. Or me."

Nicholas opened his mouth to speak, but I raised my hand in protest. "I know you're busy at work, but you were a busy lawyer when we started dating, and we were good." I closed my eyes. "So good." I opened my eyes.

Nicholas wasn't laughing anymore. "I know things have been crazy, and I'm sorry."

"Long hours I can handle, but this? Even when you're with me, you're not fully there. You've shut me out of your work stuff and don't bother to even fake interest in my writing."

"Of course I care about your writing—"

I dropped my gaze downward. "I found my book in your dresser. So much for reading it on the plane."

"Kim, I—"

I waved him off. "It's fine. The book is the least of it." Staring at the wall, I said, "I don't want to guilt you into reading my novel or even spending time with me, and let's face it, you're only here because I embarrassed myself in front of your work buddies and you feel bad. Or maybe it's so you could yell at me about my poor timing. You stood up my sister and brother-in-law for dinner because you 'lost track of time,' with a promise to make it up to me with a trip to Boston you've never mentioned again. You only took me out to celebrate getting an agent because you forgot to tell me you were going to the Patent Prom. And then you fell asleep before we could do it."

Nicholas nodded. "Yes, I did. It made me question my own manhood." He closed the distance between us and brought his lips to mine. He whispered, "You sexy thing" against my mouth.

My breathing quickened as I responded to his kisses. He tasted so good. I pushed him away. "I can't go on like this, Nicholas."

He drew back. "What?"

"I love you, but I need more than good sex."

"Good?" He put a hand to his heart. "I'm offended."

I rolled my eyes. "I'm serious, Nicholas. The relationship we're in is a crumb of what it used to be. If I'm asking too much, so be it. I kept hoping it was temporary, but there's always another justification—this project at work is insane, the trial is killing me, bear with me, I'll make it up to you. Blah blah blah. By the time you get around to 'making it up to me,' we'll be eligible for residence in a retirement community."

Nicholas lowered his head but looked up at me. "Jeez, Kim, I had no idea you felt so neglected."

"I've been so upset and afraid. Ask Bridget. We're still in a fight, by the way—Bridget and me."

Nicholas's mouth dropped open.

"Yeah, but how would you know that? And how's this for shocking news—Caroline is married."

This time, his eyes bugged out as his mouth formed an "O."

"And it's not only you who hasn't a clue what's going on in *my* life. I only know how your trial is going because Rob told me. And I wouldn't have known about the spa gift certificate we bought for your mother's birthday if she hadn't addressed her thank-you card to both of us. I know she's your mom and not mine, but it's just another example of how we might be living together, but we're not living *together*. Pia suggested I do something dramatic to try to fix things between us." I noted the lack of recognition on his face at Pia's name. He didn't know about her either. "Pia's my new assistant at *Pastel Is the New Black*, and I confided in her since Bridget's not speaking to me, Caroline's on the other side of the world, and Erin's...Erin."

Nicholas's lips curled up slightly.

"Anyway, my karaoke performance last year did wonders, and an undercover operation to break into your hotel room is equally dramatic. But last year, I was in the wrong and needed to show you in big block letters how sorry I was so you'd know I was serious." I paused. "It's different now. Whether I sing to you in a bar full of people or strip down to my skivvies in front of your coworkers, only you can decide if our life together is worth making some adjustments to your schedule, and I don't think you're willing to do that."

Frowning, Nicholas asked, "What are you saying, Kim?"

What was I saying? I rubbed my eyes and studied Nicholas's gorgeous but currently very sad face. I loved him so much. "I don't know. I think I need some time to figure out what I want."

"Time?"

I nodded. "Yes, I need time away from you. To think."

"Kimmie. I love you. Please let me prove it to you." He held my gaze with a pleading expression on his face.

My hopes soared. Perhaps he was willing. "If you mean it, my flight back isn't for a couple of days. Maybe you can start now. Rob said the trial is over. We can frolic in the pool, get a couple's massage. Or order room service from one of the hotel rest…" I noted the crease in Nicholas's forehead and stopped talking.

"I'm sorry, Kim, but even though the trial is over, I still have work obligations. I'll be tied up in meetings almost constantly for the next two days."

"You can't skip any of them?"

Shaking his head, Nicholas said, "It's not a good idea. I already blew off a meeting to come here, and I need to put in my time if I want the General Counsel gig."

Confused, I cocked my head to the side. "Is the General Counsel leaving? Retiring or something?"

"Not that I know of, but—"

"This is about your dad, isn't it?"

Vigorously shaking his head, Nicholas said, "Of course not. If it were up to my dad, I'd quit the law and go to medical school. This is about me wanting to reach my potential." He rubbed his finger against his uncharacteristically freshly shaven chin and grinned. "Being made General Counsel would be for me what getting a publishing deal is for you. You know?"

He looked so hopeful, smiling at me while his face seemed to shine, and my heart broke. It broke for the little boy inside of Nicholas who craved his father's approval. And it broke for me as I realized I was fighting a battle I'd already lost. I slid out of the covers and sat next to him on the bed with my feet dangling. I looked at him thoughtfully.

"You know, what drew me to you initially was your sex appeal."

Nicholas ran his fingers slowly along his jawline and smiled at me wickedly. "I know."

I playfully swatted his side with my elbow. "I still think you're the most delectable specimen in the land."

"Second to you, of course."

I blushed despite myself. "But it quickly became so much more. You saw beyond my boobs and truly cared about me. Because of you and your relentless and sometimes annoying encouragement of my writing, I grew as a person." I glanced down at my feet, which barely reached the ground. "Figuratively speaking, of course."

Nicholas chuckled, but his eyes were sorrowful.

"You pushed me to take life by the steering wheel and drive, and now I have two completed manuscripts under my belt and an agent. Without you, my writing dreams would still be packed away on a shelf in my closet along with countless unfinished books. You were good for me. Everyone saw it. Even before I did. And I was good for you too. I made you laugh even when lawyer stuff weighed on your mind. And I restored your faith in women."

A piece of hair had escaped my ponytail during my nap, and Nicholas twirled it around his finger. "Then why are you doing this, Kimmie?"

I took a deep breath to compose myself. "Because we're not the same couple anymore. It's like you led me to my dream, and now that it's within my grasp, you've lost interest. But I still need you."

"I'm still here," he argued.

I shook my head. "You're not though. Or maybe you are, but it's different. I can't talk to you the way I used to. I hold back sharing things with you because I don't want to bother you or add to your stress. And you keep me and work completely separate as well, which would be fine if your job wasn't so all-consuming. You reveal more to your dad than you do to me." I almost said "and Daneen too" but stopped myself. "If we can't talk about our passions—aside from the one we share for each other's naked bodies—what else is there?" I shrugged. "I'm probably not making any sense."

Nicholas let his head fall back and blew out a stream of air. "You're making sense, but..."

"But what?" I whispered.

He shook his head timidly. "I wish you wouldn't make me choose between my career and you."

An ache rippled through my tummy. "I'm doing nothing of the sort, Nicholas."

"It sure feels that way," he said flatly.

Raising my voice, I said, "I've always encouraged your career and even the long hours it often comes with, but not this. What you're essentially telling me is you're willing to sacrifice the quality of our relationship until you get promoted—something not likely to happen for years. And if you're doing it to impress your dad, decades. Or until you get your medical degree." I sucked in my breath, knowing I'd hit Nicholas where it hurt and regretting it immediately. In a softer voice, I said, "I'm not the one pitting me against your career, Nicholas. You are."

Nicholas stared straight ahead. "I don't know what to say."

I knew what I wanted him to say—that he was sorry and would find a way to make us better. My lips trembled as the ramifications of this heart-to-heart set in. "Me neither."

"You just need time though, right?" Nicholas asked hopefully.

I blinked back tears. Even though the very thought of a permanent split from Nicholas made my chest constrict as if my heart were being stepped on by someone wearing four-inch stilettos, no amount of thinking would convince me to accept the status quo. I deserved better than a relationship in which the finest moments were already behind us.

Taking my silence as a "yes," Nicholas buried his head in his hands and mumbled, "Logistically speaking, how are we going to do this? I mean, we live together."

I hadn't thought of that. We spent so little time together, I had practically forgotten we shared a living space. "I'll move out."

"Where will you go? You're fighting with Bridget, and Caroline is out of the country. And married." He widened his eyes. "I can't believe Caroline got married. Who's the groom?"

"A British guy she met on a plane. Crazy, right?"

"Crazy." He exhaled. "You stay put. I'll move out."

"Absolutely not. This is my doing. And besides, it was your apartment first."

"I need to know where you're going before I agree to this. I'm still your boyfriend, and I'm not letting you sleep on the street."

I smiled faintly. "I won't sleep on the street." I placed a hand on his bare knee before quickly drawing it back. "I promise to keep you apprised of my living arrangements. Okay?"

He nodded. "Okay. But let it be known I'm vehemently opposed to this plan and will do everything I can to change your mind. I love you, Kim." He looked firmly into my eyes.

Considering he had put work ahead of our relationship once again mere minutes ago, I doubted he would do anything to change my mind. Just the same, I met his gaze. "I love you too, Nicholas."

We stared into each other's eyes for a moment in silence before Nicholas broke away and stood up. Sticking his hands in the pockets of his shorts, he said, "I guess I should get back to Miami."

"I'll call you a taxi," I said, standing up too.

While we waited for the cab, we sat side by side on my parents' porch swing. The sun had set, and I gazed at the stars. It was hard to believe Boca Raton shared the same sky as New York City, where stars weren't visible to the naked eye.

"When do you head back to New York?" Nicholas asked.

"Day after tomorrow." I didn't know where I'd go, but I had two days to figure it out.

Nicholas nodded. "Me too." Then he lifted his chin toward the street. "Cab's here," he said, standing up.

I glanced toward the street where the yellow car was waiting at the edge of the driveway. There were tears in Nicholas's eyes, but I felt mostly numb. I wondered how long it would last. Probably about as long as it took Nicholas to get in the cab and drive away. I stood up with him and swallowed hard, trying to think of something to say. What did one say in these circumstances? I ran through my virtual list of chick lit novels for inspiration and came up empty. "Be safe."

Nicholas whispered, "You too, Kimmie."

I leaned my head against his chest and shook it against his t-shirt. My tears would not wait until he was gone. I felt him kiss the top of my head and pull away from me, but I kept my head down and my eyes closed. When I opened them next, he was gone. I stared down the quiet, empty road and wiped my damp cheek. I headed to the guest room and put on my bathing suit. A swim would do me good. If nothing else, a wet face would help me to hide my tears.

Later, after a classic Florida dinner of blue crab and rock shrimp, followed by key lime pie, all courtesy of my dad's surprise trip to the grocery store while I was with Nicholas, I relaxed in the reclining chair watching a movie on Netflix with my folks. Wondering why Nicholas hadn't returned to the house with me, my parents had asked where he went. I calmly explained I had broken up with him and then promptly burst into tears, hence the reason my mom agreed to watch *Love Actually* for the fifth time and my dad consented to watch it at all.

I hadn't checked my email since before I'd checked (broke) into the Fontainebleau, so after the movie, I grabbed my charging phone from the dresser in the guest room, and returned to my comfy chair in the living room. I scrolled through the messages—most were review requests. The trip had set me back a few days in my review schedule. I knew it would, but assumed it would be worth it. Silly me. Letting my head fall backward, I looked at the ceiling and rolled my eyes. I skipped over a note from Pia with the subject line: *How did it go??* Rob always said bad news couldn't wait, but I think even he'd make an exception in this scenario. Only paying half attention, my eyes glazed over an email from Felicia and quickly went back. Bad news from her couldn't wait.

Only it wasn't bad news this time, and as I skimmed the message, I sat up straight in the chair.

Kim,
You added conflict like a rock star. I knew you could do it!

We're good to go. I'm going to submit to Three Monkeys first because I think they're a great fit, but if they don't bite, I'm attending the Los Angeles Times Festival of Books and will pitch there.

I'll keep you posted, of course. In the meantime, keep plugging away at your second book. And work on your author platform.

Cheers,
Felicia

I jumped out of my chair. "Oh my God. Felicia is submitting my book to publishing houses. It's really happening."

My mom launched off the couch and grabbed me into a hug. "I'm so happy for you," she said, squeezing me tight.

My dad approached me with a broad grin. "That's my girl."

While hugging my father, I thought of something, and I pulled away with a frown.

My mom noticed it immediately. "What's wrong?"

I sat back down on the reclining chair with my butt on the edge of the seat and ran my palm along my ponytail. "She's submitting to Hannah's publisher first. What if they reject me?"

Nonplussed, my dad said, "I'm not exactly a publishing savant, but even I know there's more than one publisher. If Hannah's publisher doesn't want it, another one will." He paused. "Who's Hannah?"

My mom looked at my dad incredulously and swatted his arm. "Seriously, Peter? How many times must we go over this? Hannah went to high school with Kim and tried to make our little girl miserable—Kim and Bridget both."

My stomach dropped at the mention of Bridget. Hannah might have attempted to make us miserable in high school, but she inadvertently came between us last week.

Nodding, my dad said, "Ah. It's all coming back to me now. Your sister likes her though, right?"

"Erin's got a girl crush on her," my mom and I said at the same time before giggling.

"But she's also the one who referred me to Felicia. She's not all bad," I conceded in a soft voice. Even so, a rejection from Hannah's publisher would sting like a jellyfish, especially if she found out. She must never find out. As I shook myself out of my daydream of assumed failure, with a reminder there was a possibility Three Monkeys would want to acquire *A Blogger's Life* and would offer me a five-figure advance, I reached out for the phone my mom was handing me. "Who is this?" I mouthed.

"Your sister," my mom whispered. "We have to share the good news. Put it on speaker."

Blood rushed to my face as I took hold of the phone and placed it on the coffee table in front of me. I would have preferred to wait until I was offered a deal before telling Erin. "Hey, Erin."

"Hey, sis. What's with having a family reunion without me?"

I knew she wasn't really wounded by the tone of her voice. "I surprised the folks."

"A habit of yours lately," Erin said, laughing.

"Ha ha. Yeah, I was in Miami with Nicholas and figured I would take the opportunity to see the parental figures." Not wanting to discuss Nicholas, I cleared my throat and quickly changed the subject. "Mom wanted me to call and share some good news."

"Do tell."

"I have an agent who's going to be submitting my book to publishers."

"Hannah's agent," my dad piped in.

I glared at my dad for providing this unnecessary bit of information.

Feigning ignorance, he said, "I wanted to see how Erin would react to hearing Hannah's name."

As if on cue, Erin said, "No way. You and Hannah share the same agent? That's beyond cool."

My dad smiled and whispered, "I told you so."

I shook my head at him while my mother chuckled into her hand. "Yeah. I took your advice and asked Hannah for help, and she referred me to her agent, who loved the book."

"See? You should listen to your little sister more often."

I rolled my eyes. "Yes, sometimes you are worth something."

"Hardy har har. So, what happens now?"

"Felicia, the agent, pitches the book to a bunch of publishing houses, and hopefully one will want it." More to myself, I added, "It would be super cool if it went to auction, but I won't be greedy." If more than one house wanted a book, it would go to the highest bidder.

Erin squealed. "Maybe it will be published by the same company as *Cut on the Bias* and *Tearing at the Seams*."

My mom began saying "Hannah's publisher is the agent's first choi—" before cutting herself off and glancing at me apologetically.

"I'm so coming to your book launch," Erin said.

I beamed in response to my sister's confidence in me.

"I assume Hannah will be there, right?"

As my dad laughed from his seat on the couch, I walked over to him and kicked his foot.

"I suppose." At the rate I was going, Hannah might be my only friend, but I didn't want to think about celebrating the release of my debut novel without Nicholas or Bridget by my side. "But let's not get ahead of ourselves."

"Congrats, Kim. What?"

"What what?"

"Huh? Oh, I was talking to Gerry. My husband's having a breakdown because some character got eaten on *The Walking Dead*. I need to comfort him. But keep me posted, okay?"

"I promise."

As I lay in bed later, I clasped my phone, fighting the urge to call Nicholas and tell him I was another step closer to being a published author. Nicholas was generally a happy person, but he reserved his biggest smiles for me—when I walked into a room, when I said something funny, when I delivered good news. I knew this latest disclosure would make him grin so wide, and my cheeks hurt vicariously just thinking about it. But I was remembering the old Nicholas. The new Nicholas wouldn't have time to be happy for me until the conclusion of his business meeting, until the jury reached a decision, until the judge issued a sentence. I released the phone with my hand and curled into the fetal position, my heart equal parts bitter and sad. And I missed Bridget so much, my heart throbbed. If a dream came true and you had no one to share it with, was it really a dream come true?

Chapter 34

I second-guessed my decision as soon as I stood outside her apartment and the cab drove away, leaving me on the curb with my pink carry-on luggage next to me. It wasn't so much a choice to go straight to Bridget's apartment from the airport as a reflex I couldn't control. I swallowed hard and rolled my bag into the lobby. "Hey, Joe," I said to Bridget's doorman as I approached the elevator. Since I was a regular fixture at Bridget's apartment, the doormen never bothered to call up first. Only a few years older than us, Joe was my favorite, although before I moved downtown, we went to the same gym, and I sometimes did a double take when I saw him in workout clothes, his sweaty brown hair matted against his head. It was a far cry from his black doorman's uniform.

"Kim. It's been a few weeks. How've you been?" Joe called out from behind the front desk.

"Never better," I said cheerfully, trying to disguise the tremor in my voice even though I was positive Joe wouldn't pick up on my anxiety. Why would he? Bridget and I never fought. Until now.

"Good to hear," he said as a pizza delivery guy walked into the building. I heard him say, "Delivery" into the intercom as the elevator door opened before me, and I stepped inside. I held the door for the pizza guy and acknowledged him with a smile before staring straight ahead, my feet tapping against the ground until we reached Bridget's floor.

Before I could chicken out, I knocked three times and held my breath as I heard Jonathan say, "Coming."

"Kim," Jonathan said, his mouth falling open. "What are you doing here?"

"I need to see her." I peered inside, a waterfall of tears threatening to drop at any second.

Jonathan scratched his shaved head with one hand and pulled up his black sweatpants with the other. "Are you sure you're not twins?"

I gently shoved him out of the way and walked inside the apartment. I felt Bridget's absence instantly.

Jonathan shook his head in amusement. "She's not here."

"No duh. Where is she?"

"It's a funny thing…" Jonathan said, an odd smile plastered on his face.

I placed my hands on my hips and waited for him to continue. "Well?"

"She went to find you. We were watching *Hot Tub Time Machine*, chomping on microwave popcorn, and out of nowhere, she jumped off the couch, grabbed her purse, and headed for the door. I asked where she was going and she said, 'Kim. I need Kim.' Before I had a chance to respond, she threw her jacket over her arm and slammed the door behind her."

"She went to find me," I repeated and looked down at my shaking hands. "I gotta go." I ran out the door. As an afterthought, I called out, "Thanks," hoping Jonathan had heard me.

Unlike Greenwich Village where I lived with Nicholas, cabs were plentiful on the Upper East Side where Bridget resided with Jonathan, and I hailed one the moment I stepped out of their lobby and onto the sidewalk. I gave the driver my address and sat upright watching the neighborhoods change from midtown, to Gramercy, to Union Square, and beyond out the window. Halfway there, I second-guessed my hasty decision to head downtown. What if Bridget had been to my place, found it empty, and was now on her way back uptown? I debated telling the taxi driver to turn around, but my thoughts on the matter were so scattered that before I knew it, the cab was parked in front of my brownstone, where a girl with long, rusty-red hair was sitting on the stoop with her head bent down between her legs.

I paid the driver and climbed out of the cab, calling out, "Bridget," before I could stop myself.

Bridget's head popped up, and she scrambled to her feet.

I ran toward her, my arms outstretched until she was directly in front of me. As she stood immobile, I stopped short. What if it wasn't a desire to reconcile that prompted Bridget to race out of her apartment to meet me, but an urgent need to attack my friendship skills in person?

As we faced each other, less than ten inches between us, visions from a friendship past flashed before my eyes: The day we became friends, after I caught her peering over my shoulder in seventh-grade science as I read *The Power of Three*, the book based on the *Charmed* television series; the nights we spent in each other's childhood bedrooms (mine pink and hers multicolored, of course) high on Fruitopia as we pored over the latest *Delia's* catalog and took countless relationship quizzes in *YM* magazine despite having zero experience with boys; the times we stood up strong against the big bad Hannah when she pulled every trick out of her hat to exploit our vulnerabilities, including my (lack of) height and Bridget's (lack of) money; the night at the end of my sixteenth year when I called her only minutes before and then an hour after I lost my virginity to Jonathan with a mixture of excitement and horror over "going all the way." Her friendship was my most significant relationship to date, including Nicholas, and I wasn't ready to pull the final curtain. But what if Bridget was?

As if reading my mind, she threw herself forward and engulfed me in an embrace. The smell of apricot from her hair tickled my nose, and I heard a muffled, "I'm so sorry, Kim. Please forgive me."

"I'm sorry too," I mumbled into her shoulder before I lost control of the tears I was holding back. We held each other tight, both of us sobbing as we rocked from side to side.

Bridget let go first, but a moment later, she pulled me toward her again and squeezed me hard. "Thank God." When we separated the second time, I noticed she was shaking. "I'm freezing," she said, her teeth chattering.

I grabbed her chilled hand and led her to the entrance of my brownstone. "How long have you been waiting?" It was unseasonably chilly for late spring and way too cold to be outside for an extended period of time.

Crossing her arms across her chest while I fumbled in my purse for my keys, she said, "Jonathan called and told me you were on your way. I didn't want to miss you."

I opened the door, and we hugged again at the foot of the stairs, garnering chuckles from the young couple whose path we blocked. "They probably think we're lovers," Bridget said with a laugh.

"You could do worse," I said as we trudged up the stairs, me falling behind Bridget due to my luggage.

Twenty minutes later, Bridget was cozy on my pink "lady couch" with an afghan over her legs and a cup of tea while I packed a bag to bring back to her place.

"I can't believe you broke up with Nicholas, Kim. The things I said about you guys..." She frowned. "I didn't mean them. I was being a bitch."

"Yeah, you were," I agreed. When Bridget's lips trembled, I sat on the couch next to her. "I forgive you."

She slid closer to me and put an arm around my back. "I sunk beyond low, Kim. Besides being jealous, I was seriously angry at you." She blew on her tea and took a timid sip.

"With good reason. My comment about Jonathan was way out of line. Watching you guys at dinner with Caroline and Felix, it's clear you're happy the way things are, and I'm happy for you. Your dreams are no less valid than mine even if they're different. I'm sorry for being so shortsighted. I promise not to bug you about it anymore."

Bridget swiped her brow. "Thank God. I know the concern

came from a good place, but I hated having to justify my decisions to you."

I swallowed hard. "And I shouldn't have lied to you about Hannah. It's how we got into this mess in the first place."

Bridget let out a sigh. "I'm not excusing it, but I understand why you felt the need."

"She asked if I shopped in little-people stores," I said, staring straight ahead at the queen-sized bed I shared with Nicholas. I wondered if we'd ever sleep there together again. I couldn't remember if we'd even cuddled the last time we lay there together, much less had sex.

"What the hell does that even mean?"

I turned to face her. "It means she will never ever replace you. Not even close."

"I believe you."

I stared at her intently. "Do you really though?"

Bridget dropped her gaze downward and nodded before taking another sip of tea.

I tapped her on the shoulder. "Because, Bridget, you have to know something."

Bridget cocked her head to the side. "What is it?" she asked, her green eyes opened wide in uncertainty.

I inhaled deeply and let out a breath before speaking. "Hannah was horrible in high school, but she's not so bad anymore. Yes, she's the president of her own fan club, except for Erin, maybe..." I paused, and we laughed together. "For sure, she still has this way of making compliments sound like insults and insults sound like flattery. And I have no desire to spend more than twenty minutes in her company at a time, but she's done some really nice things for me."

Bridget nodded. "All true."

"Do you think you can let go of the past, then?" I pleaded with my eyes. "If not for you, then for me?"

Bridget nodded and, her voice shaking, said, "Recent behavior notwithstanding, I'd do anything for you, K."

I smiled softly. "I don't doubt it." I stood up and walked over to the bed where my suitcase was half-filled with enough clothes to last a week. I blinked back tears.

Rising from the couch, Bridget said, "Damn Nicholas. I'm so pissed at him."

"I have my best friend back. I have an agent. Why isn't that enough?" I gulped.

"Because it's not." Wrapping her arms around my neck, she whispered, "Stupid boys."

Relaxing into her hug, I wiped my eyes and repeated, "Stupid boys."

"As long as we're speaking of boys, can we talk about Felix now? Is it acceptable to refer to someone's husband as a 'boy'?"

I zipped my suitcase and faced Bridget with my hands on my hips. "I suppose 'man' is more appropriate."

She clucked her tongue. "Hot man?"

I smiled. "Very hot man. Our Caroline did a fine job."

"A *fine* job, indeed," Bridget said, and we laughed together, a sound I had missed with fervor.

I was a long way off from convincing myself having my best friend back and an agent was good enough, but as Bridget and I dragged my luggage down the stairs and into yet another cab, I conceded it was a decent start.

We sat in silence in the taxi, lost in our thoughts, but every so often, Bridget would squeeze my hand as if reminding me she was still there. I returned a text from Nicholas, whose flight home from Florida had just landed, asking about my whereabouts, and told him I had resolved my issues with Bridget and would be staying with her and Jonathan temporarily. Then I checked my Gmail account. When I saw the unopened email from Hannah, I sucked in my breath, troubled by the timing. I glanced at Bridget, who was busy texting someone—probably Jonathan—and opened it.

Bonjour Kim,
I trust you're past whatever caused that scene with

Whatshername—Strawberry Shortcake—at HanGawi by now. It was super awkward for me, but I forgive you.

As you know, the release of Tearing at the Seams *is August 11th. In case Candace hasn't reached out to you yet, I've attached an advanced copy review in MOBI format. I can arrange a paperback like last time if you prefer—in exchange for a five-pink-champagne-flutes review, of course. Jk.*

Enjoy!
Cocktails soon?
Hannah

I snorted and quickly covered my mouth with my hand, but it was too late.

"What?" Bridget asked, turning away from the window.

I hesitated, but now was as good a time as any to see if Bridget meant what she said about moving on. "Hannah sent me a copy of *Tearing at the Seams* for review. She didn't ask me to review it as much as assume it as a given. So very Hannah of her." I failed to mention Hannah's reference to Bridget, not by her name, but by "Whatshername Strawberry Shortcake." Mostly because I didn't want to give Bridget a reason to renege on her promise, but also because "Strawberry Shortcake" reminded me of "Strawberry Fields Forever," and I was trying to keep my mind off of Nicholas.

Bridget pursed her lips and shrugged. "Surprise surprise. But at least this time around, you're okay with liking the book."

"Hannah's a lot of things and, for better or worse, being a good writer is one of them." I gave her a wry grin. "I still hope it doesn't make my top-ten list."

"Maybe I'll read it too," Bridget said, her voice steady.

My mouth dropped open.

Breaking into a huge smile, Bridget said, "Gotcha."

I placed my hand over my heart. "You scared me."

Bridget chuckled. "I said I'd cut the chick some slack, but a girl's got to have limits."

Chapter 35

Later on, I sat in the middle of Bridget's purple couch, with Bridget on one side and Jonathan on the other. Jonathan had picked up Italian food from Uva for dinner, and Bridget had cracked open a bottle of pinot noir. They were both being extra nice to me. I expected it from Bridget—she was still making up for her past behavior, even though I told her it was forgotten—but when Jonathan agreed to watch back-to-back episodes of *The Real Housewives of Orange County* with us, I asked Bridget to check his temperature.

"I'm not sick. I'm just glad you guys made up. And I'm sorry about..." He walked over to the windowsill with a cigarette before completing his sentence.

Twisting my head so I could still see him from my comfy spot on the couch, I said, "What are you sorry about?"

Jonathan took a deep drag of his cigarette and then flicked it in the tray. "You and Nicholas." His face turned red.

Despite a newfound familiarity with the heaviness I felt in my chest whenever his name was mentioned, I was lost for a response and tempted to apologize to Jonathan for putting him in the awkward position of wanting to comfort me. I wondered if it would be the same way at work the next day. Had Nicholas told them what happened? If so, I knew Rob would tread carefully and not mention anything unless I did first. Although well-intentioned, I feared David and Lucy would be in such a rush to share their regrets they would unknowingly move in like vultures. And Daneen. Well, Daneen would be like Nurse Ratched on steroids ready to pounce.

Her elation at this new gossip likely had her so riled up, she'd have to take a Valium to fall asleep tonight. I was only mildly consoled in the knowledge that whether or not I was in the picture, Daneen would never take my place in Nicholas's heart or bed. As my tummy dropped, I visualized Daneen and Nicholas huddled together over a bottle of wine, comparing notes on whose parent was less praiseful of their respective career achievements.

I jolted at the sound of the buzzer ringing and Bridget's doorman calling, "Delivery." Since Jonathan had picked up our food, the three of us glanced at each other with confused expressions until Bridget said, "Send him up."

"I wonder who it is," Bridget said.

I looked up from my e-reader. "You'll find out soon enough." I was reading *Tearing at the Seams* during commercials and brought my eyes back to where I had left off on the assumption whatever was being delivered wasn't for me. It was probably some home-office gadget one of them had purchased online and forgotten about.

Hannah had provided just enough backstory in *Tearing at the Seams* to avoid confusing people who hadn't read *Cut on the Bias* in a while or were reading the sequel as a standalone, but not too much history to feel repetitive. I was impressed—with both the book and my ability to compliment Hannah without wanting to throw up in my mouth. How far I'd come.

When the commercials ended, I placed my e-reader on my lap to return my focus to *RHOC*, and I didn't look up when the doorbell rang. Although I faintly heard Bridget thank the guy and close the door, I paid no attention until she stood before me, blocking my view of the television set. "What's up?"

Holding a vase of assorted pink flowers, she gave me a closed-mouth smile. "These are for you."

My eyes opened wide, and I repeated, "For me?" My brain directed me to stand up, but my butt remained glued to the couch.

Standing up from next to me on the couch, Jonathan raised an eyebrow. "One guess who these might be from."

Bridget walked toward the kitchen island and gestured for me to join her. "Open the card. I'll cut the stems and put the flowers in water."

My body cooperating at last, I lifted myself to a standing position and followed Bridget into the kitchen, the soles of the rainbow-colored fuzzy slippers I had borrowed from her scratching against the wood floor with each step. Grasping the small white envelope, which contained the card, I leaned my head into the combination of roses, hydrangeas, dahlias, and ranunculuses, all in various shades of pink, and inhaled deeply through my nose. It smelled like the Botanical Gardens after a rainy day.

"They're gorg," Bridget said, nudging Jonathan.

He jerked away from her. "What?"

"You don't bring me flowers...anymore," Bridget sang, sounding nothing like Barbra Streisand.

"Break up with me, and maybe I will," Jonathan threatened.

"Not gonna happen," she said, throwing herself into his arms.

Wishing they would take the PDA into the bedroom, I ripped open the envelope and read the card, my heart beating in rapid succession.

Dear Kimmie,
I love you more than you love pink.
Please come home.

Love,
Nicholas

I swallowed back a tear. I loved pink a lot.

"What did he say?" Bridget asked. "Unless it's pornographic, and in that case, what did he say?"

"Nicholas is too classy to ask a florist or a One Eight Hundred Flowers customer-service rep to write a pornographic note," Jonathan said. Then he grinned sheepishly as a film of pink blanketed his face.

I beamed at Jonathan. "That's so nice of you to say." I had no idea he thought so highly of Nicholas.

Jonathan shrugged. "Read the damn note, Long."

"You don't have to be embarrassed over your bro crush on Nicholas," Bridget teased.

Quite enjoying the opportunity to mock Jonathan, I smirked at him. And then I remembered a bromance between Nicholas and Jonathan wasn't so cute now that we wouldn't be double-dating and did as he asked—I read the note out loud.

"Short, sweet, and to the point," Jonathan said, nodding knowingly. "Classy."

Bridget put a hand to her heart. "He loves you, Kimmie. Are you going to make up with him now?"

After placing the envelope on the counter, I walked back to the living room and reassumed my position on the couch. "We're not in a fight. We don't need to 'make up.'" I turned the television back on.

Bridget sat down next to me, removed the remote from my lap, and muted the TV. She didn't say anything, but she didn't need to. We had perfected our nonverbal mode of communication years ago.

"The point isn't whether he loves me or not, Bridget. The issue is since we've been living together, he's put work ahead of us—way ahead of us—and he's too blinded by his daddy issues to see what's happening. And then he shrugs off all of my attempts to take an interest in what he's clearly so passionate about." More passionate than he is about me. "He claims he doesn't want to bore me."

"It's pretty boring," Bridget said, tapping her feet on the floor.

"But I'm making an effort, Bridge. If Nicholas is going to be so wrapped up in his work, he should let me decide if it's too boring. I know he loves me, but he's so obsessed with not letting his father down that letting me down is a lesser evil." Motioning toward the kitchen where the bouquet was displayed prominently on the island, I said, "The flowers are beautiful, and I appreciate the gesture. I really do. But his note said nothing about working on us. Neither have any of his texts or voicemail messages. Nicholas just wants to kiss and make up and return to normal. Well, I hate our new normal and want a revised one. I don't think Nicholas can give it to me." I cocked my head toward her. "You know?"

Bridget nodded. "I hear you, K. It sucks more than sixteen-year-old Hannah at a high-school party."

Too depressed to agree with or dispute Bridget's statement, I stood up and removed my phone from the coffee table.

"Where are you going?" Bridget asked.

"I should thank him for the flowers. You mind if I use your bedroom?" I glanced at Bridget and then at Jonathan. They lived in a one-bedroom apartment, and I would be sleeping on the very couch we were sprawled out on. I was grateful to be taken in by my best friends, regardless of the conditions, but I needed a private space to talk to Nicholas.

"Of course not," Jonathan said, frowning. "Sorry, Long."

I shrugged and then headed toward the bedroom.

I knew thanking Nicholas was the right thing to do, but I didn't know what to say to him. I couldn't say what he wanted to hear—that I was coming home—even though I really wanted to. I could jump in a cab and be in his arms in twenty minutes, and I'd be lying if I said I wasn't tempted. Nicholas would undoubtedly give me his undivided attention for the night. He might even turn off his phone, but he'd probably have to put in more face time at work for the next week to make up for all the texts and emails he ignored. The flowers were a temporary bandage for our relationship, but underneath the gauze was a deep wound.

Chapter 36

As it turned out, if I had hurried downtown upon receipt of the flowers—pent-up passion waiting to explode in response to Nicholas's "grand gesture"—I would have rushed into an empty apartment, since when I called Nicholas to thank him, it came up in our brief conversation that he was still at the office. He claimed being in the apartment was too painful without me there. I believed him, but I also had no doubt the main reason he was working late was because he almost always worked late. Anyway, I told him as gently as possible the flowers were lovely, as was the sentiment, but I needed time to mull things over.

I almost pined for my earlier relationships—when it was easy to walk away when the going got tough or when asking for space was a deliberate ploy to get some power back. But my relationship with Nicholas had reached a level never attained in the past—one I hoped would lead to marriage. Acknowledging the reality Nicholas might not be "The One" hurt with a ferocity I had never experienced before, and I couldn't fathom the possibility of falling harder for any other man walking this earth. The part of me that feared what I had with Nicholas was probably as good as it was going to get implored me to pack my bags and go back to him before he stopped asking. But the memory of how well we had managed to meld our busy schedules for the first several months we dated made it impossible for me to accept as permanent the sour direction he had allowed our relationship to take.

"Kim!"

My body twitched in response to the boom of Daneen's voice. I looked up from my computer, where I had been entering Rob's time while simultaneously mooning over why I finally met the man of my dreams only for him to go and ruin it, and met her annoyed gaze. "I didn't hear you. I'm sorry." This was my least favorite phrase when it came to communicating with Daneen, but pondering why God hated me was not part of my job description, and she was within her rights to raise her voice in response to being ignored. But if she so much as mentioned Nicholas as it related to the two of us as a couple, I would pluck every perfectly groomed hair from her eyebrows with my bare fingers. Since she was close to a foot taller than me, I'd have to stand on my tippy toes and maybe even jump to reach, but I'd make it happen.

Daneen dropped a pile of assorted butterfly-clipped documents on my desk. "We need these scanned to the W drive. Open a new folder under Dalton Exhibits, and file them there. Return the originals to me when you're done." Without so much as a "thank you," she walked away, but I would prefer a lack of gratitude over a dig aimed at my doomed love affair with Nicholas ten times out of ten.

After scanning the documents, I returned to my desk to save the attachments to the W drive as I was told. I had gotten as far as creating the Dalton Exhibits folder when my cell phone rang, and Felicia Harrison appeared on the display. My hands shook as I removed the phone from my desk and swiped my index finger across the screen to accept the call. This was the first I'd heard from Felicia since she informed me she'd be pitching *A Blogger's Life* to publishers, starting with Three Monkeys Press. I'd been tempted to follow up several times, and in fact, had two unsent emails in my drafts folder gently asking her for a progress report, but I didn't send them due to fear of coming across as a stalking client. If Felicia had something to tell me, she would have reached out, and if she had nothing to say, sending her periodic reminders wouldn't change things. My life was chock full of other "distractions" at the moment to keep me from obsessing too much, but the day had arrived: Felicia was on the other end of the phone line, potentially ready to deliver life-changing news.

Breathing heavily, I answered the phone. "Hi, Felicia." My heart went *thump thump thump*.

"Hi Kim," she said, her voice quavering.

My stomach dropped, as I couldn't imagine the words "We got an offer" would follow such a taut greeting.

"I have some news."

I swallowed hard, bracing myself. "Yeah?"

"Three Monkeys passed on *A Blogger's Life*."

My stomach sank. "Did they say why?" I asked the question before contemplating whether I wanted to hear the answer.

"The editors thought the characters were credible, the plot good, and the pacing well-executed. This is good news, Kim."

"But they passed." I might not (ever) be a published author, but I was sufficiently versed in the English language to understand that "passed on" when uttered in the current context was the equivalent of a rejection. "How can a rejection be good news?"

Felicia sighed. "They don't want to acquire more romantic comedy right now because they're overloaded in the genre. But they liked the book. It's merely a matter of timing."

With one sentence, she had crushed my dream. There was nothing "merely" about it, but I swallowed back my tears. There was no crying in publishing—at least not while I was on the phone with my agent pretending to be a confident author worthy of her representation. All bets were off after we hung up. Trying to sound chipper, I said, "Well, that's something. What happens now?" Please don't fire me. Please don't fire me.

"I have several other worthy houses in mind. Bigger ones than Three Monkeys. Don't fret, Kim. We'll find a home for *A Blogger's Life*."

I dabbed my eyes with a tissue. "Thanks for not giving up on me," I said, my voice wobbly. Pursuing my writing dream coupled with falling in love had turned me into such a crybaby. I momentarily longed for the days when I convinced myself being a secretary/part-time blogger and calling my ex-boyfriend for whom I had no feelings for a booty call made me happy. Dream-chasing Kim was killing me.

"Kim. If I dropped every author whose book I wasn't able to sell to the first house I approached, I'd have a very small client list and a lot less money in the bank."

"I think I love you," I said, meaning it.

Felicia laughed. "If you love me now, you'll want to marry me when I'm done with *A Blogger's Life*. Now keep writing your next book, and leave the rest to me."

I chuckled. "You got it." I hung up the phone with a smile. Today would not be the day I updated my Facebook status to announce my book had been sold to a publisher, but Felicia seemed confident that day would come. I wasn't thrilled to be rebuffed by the publisher who housed Hannah's books, but sharing an agent and a publisher with Hannah Marshak was a closer relationship than I (or Bridget, I suspected) could handle, anyway.

After I attached all of the exhibits to the Dalton file I created, I reluctantly went to return the original documents to Daneen. When I passed Nicholas's old office, I was hit with a wave of homesickness. For an instant pick-me-up, I flipped my shoe to catch a glimpse of its red sole. I rarely wore my Christian Louboutins, but they were an instant mood elevator for when my life was falling to pieces. Between missing Nicholas like mad and the news of Three Monkeys' rejection, it seemed I chose the perfect day to match my favorite shoes with a stylish fitted black zip-front long-sleeved dress. My high-fashion exterior was a perfect disguise for my inner disarray.

When I reached Daneen's office, I knocked gently on the open door until she looked up from her computer. "Yes?"

I approached her desk and handed over the documents. "Here you go. Scanned copies are on the W drive."

"Thanks, Kim." Daneen's lips curled up, resulting in an expression with which I was not familiar, at least when directed at me.

The facial tic combined with her declaration of thanks rendered me temporarily speechless, but after a brief hesitation, I croaked out, "No problem" and turned around for a quick escape. Before I made it out the door, I heard her say, "Oh, Kim?" to my back.

I should have known it wouldn't be so easy, and my shoulders sank. I closed my eyes for half a second before doing a one-eighty and facing her once again. "Yeah?"

She handed me another document. "Can you please scan this to Nicholas?" She paused for a beat. "I would ask you to deliver it in person, but I heard you moved out of his place." She shook her head sympathetically, but her eyes shone with glee.

With supersonic speed, I leapt onto her desk and yanked a fistful of her hair while simultaneously kicking her pointy chin with the heel of my shoe.

Daneen stared at me in horror, her hand clutching her chin while blood seeped onto her winter-white cashmere sweater.

Okay, so maybe resorting to physical violence was too much even for Daneen. But in an alternate universe, it would be fun.

With the self-restraint of someone three times my size, I removed the papers from her hand and smiled. "No problem, Daneen."

I was choking back tears by the time I reached my cubicle. The girl was high-school Hannah on crack, and she manipulated me into a false sense of security before pouncing. I was especially impressed with her subtle reference to "his" apartment. I could have imposed a gag order on her with the simple yet honest statement that it was my idea to move out of *our* apartment, but it wasn't worth it. Sure, it would feel good to put Daneen in her place, but at the end of the workday, I would still go home to Bridget and Jonathan instead of Nicholas. On the bright side, my scanning the documents to Nicholas was preferable to Daneen handing them to him in person over drinks and deep conversation.

I dropped my head onto the rough exterior of my desk, wishing I had a fluffy pillow.

"Kim?"

I muttered, "Mmph."

"I don't speak that language," Rob said.

I lifted my head. "Sorry. Do you need something?" I hoped he wouldn't respond with a smart-alecky comment like, "Yes, I need you to do your job." But I couldn't blame him if he did.

Rob furrowed his thick dark eyebrows. "I was going to ask you to make me a lunch reservation for tomorrow, but it can wait." He pointed toward his office. "Let's talk." When he turned his back on me and walked away, I assumed he wanted me to follow him, and I begrudgingly complied.

I sat on one of his visitor chairs and sighed.

Sitting in his chair across the desk from me, Rob crossed his arms behind his head. "What's bothering you?"

"Let me count the ways," I said emotionlessly.

"Start at number one."

I gave him a rundown of my "break" with Nicholas. "And Daneen threw it in my face. I can't believe Nicholas told her. What are they, BFFAEUDDUP?"

Rob regarded me in confusion before shaking his head. "It didn't happen that way. If anything, it was my fault. Since you were so elusive in your voicemail, I asked Nicholas where you ran off to. When he said you were in Florida, I asked if you wanted to join us for dinner. And when Nicholas said you were with your parents in Boca Raton, I dropped the subject." He gave me a wry smile. "Not that I have no interest in your whereabouts, but it didn't seem important at the time."

I pressed my lips together. "Gotcha."

"Anyway, Nicholas was uncharacteristically detached at our post-trial meeting. He's typically very hands-on, but he deferred all of the decision making to us. I normally prefer when clients take a backseat and let me do my job, but it was so unusual for Nicholas that I was compelled to confront him. He told me you had asked for a temporary split and he was distracted. If Daneen overheard, it was my fault, not his."

I shrugged. "The end result is the same. Daneen used it against me. Surprise, surprise."

"Nicholas didn't, um, cheat on you, did he?" Rob cleared his throat. "I don't mean to be nosy."

"It's fine," I said, offering a small smile. "No, he didn't cheat. Unless work can be considered 'the other woman.' If so, he's perfected infidelity to a science." I averted eye contact. In Rob's world, prioritizing career ahead of loved ones was probably a no-brainer.

"Have you told him how you feel?"

I pressed my fingers to my temples. "Repeatedly. He keeps telling me he loves me, but I think he loves his job more. He certainly spends more time with it."

"Lawyers tend to work long hours, Kim. Something you of all people are acutely aware of."

"Which is why I waited until I was twenty-eight to date one. I should have waited forever." Heat crept up my neck. "No offense."

Rob smiled. "None taken."

"When we first started dating, Nicholas was swamped, but then you hired Daneen, and it freed up some of his time. He was thrilled to get out of the office at a decent hour a few times a week so he could have dinner with me. He was devoted to his job, but he wanted a life outside of the office, and he genuinely enjoyed his time off. Sure, he worked less set hours than, say, a bank teller, but I was cool with that. I have a life too, you know? And we kept up with each other by text. Our text messages were so playful and..." I coughed. I was going off on a tangent. Rob didn't need to know about our sexting. "The point is, I never doubted for a second that no matter how committed Nicholas was to his job, he preferred his time with me." Tears blurred my vision, and I struggled to catch my breath. "He'll never admit it, but I don't think he feels that way anymore. I'm afraid he'd rather be at work than with me."

A moment of awkward silence ensued, and I instantly regretted confiding in Rob. How could I possibly expect him to understand, much less take my side? I lifted myself to a standing position and wiped my eyes. "Any preferences for lunch tomorrow?"

Seemingly unfazed by the rapid change of subject, Rob said, "Not really. Somewhere in the area. Table for two. One o'clock."

"You got it."

"Thanks, Kim."

I waved him away. "Just doing my job."

After reserving a table for Rob's lunch meeting the next day, I found myself paralyzed to release the email I had prepared to Nicholas attaching Daneen's document. I was torn between including a personal greeting and defaulting to the all-business "Please see the attached." My usual closing, "Love, Kimmie" was not an option. Although my love for him wasn't in question, it seemed inappropriate under the circumstances. Yet resorting to formal communication was too cold and suggested we weren't even on speaking terms. I was fairly certain the attachment was meaningless and merely a prop Daneen had used to remind me of my current living situation—as if anything short of early-onset Alzheimer's disease would allow me to forget—but I wasn't going to take the risk. Knowing the firm would not pay me overtime for staying late to debate such an esoteric matter, I settled on:

Dear Nicholas,
Daneen asked me to send this to you.

Talk to you soon,
Kim

I clicked send and took the much needed breath I had been holding. Nicholas responded before I even had a chance to exhale.

Thanks, Kimmie.
I love you.
See album: Some Girls, *track 1.*

Naturally, my first course of action was to search "Album Some Girls" on the internet. I learned that *Some Girls* was a Rolling Stones album and, according to Wikipedia, the first track was "Miss You." *I miss you too, Nicholas.* Narrowly escaping following my heart's desire (along with that of my lower extremities) before my brain was fully onboard, I logged off, said goodbye to Rob for the day, and headed to my temporary home.

Chapter 37

"Yes, married life is amazing," Caroline said, her cheery face supporting her claim.

It was our first video chat with Caroline since her visit to New York City. I still hadn't quite wrapped my head around her spontaneous marriage. I feared her whirlwind nuptials would result in an annulment or divorce before they reached their first anniversary, but I kept my cynical outlook to myself. I didn't want to be the shark in her calm waters. I also wondered if I was projecting my floundering love life on her.

Bridget, who was sitting next to me on the couch, didn't share my filter. "Aren't you a little afraid you're living *The Bachelor* experience? It's all champagne and hot tubs now, but what happens when you return to real life?" she asked unapologetically.

I was afraid Caroline wouldn't respond well to such unsolicited pessimism. As much as we adored Caroline, our comfort level with her did not reach Kim/Bridget levels. I swiped Bridget's leg with my foot as a silent warning.

Bridget flinched. "I'm sorry. I didn't mean to compare you guys to *The Bachelor*. Although Felix can hold his own with any of the guys on that show." Her face turned red. "Not that I'm attracted to your husband." She stuck her fist in her mouth. "I'll just shut up."

"Good idea," I muttered before chuckling.

"It's all right, girls," Caroline said, her smile unwavering. "I'm used to the doubts by now. My mom made sure to tell me she's still friendly with her old divorce lawyer. Of course, she tossed it out in the conversation randomly as if I wouldn't know she was suggesting I'd need one." She rolled her eyes. "There are no guarantees in life or love, but my money is on us."

Knowing how much money Caroline made, I hoped she wasn't being literal.

"My sister's support came as the biggest surprise. I'm hoping she'll encourage my mother to be more accepting of the situation." She shrugged. "But enough about me. What's going on with you guys?" She glanced from Bridget to me.

"Your life is more exciting than ours," I said.

Bridget turned to me with a quizzical expression on her face. "Not entirely true."

I was unsure what she was alluding to with that statement. We had agreed to skip over our temporary feud—there was no reason to relight a fire that had been extinguished and forgotten—but I didn't know if Bridget was referring to my split with Nicholas or something else. I returned her questioning look and silently penetrated her brain space. I had my answer in no time. "I moved out of Nicholas's apartment."

First, Caroline's mouth opened, and then her brows furrowed. "Why?"

Trying to be as succinct as possible, I explained what had happened, taking care to express how lonely coupledom had been for me over the last several months so she would understand why I felt inclined to take such drastic measures and why it wasn't simply a matter of Nicholas asking for forgiveness and me accepting his apology.

"Nicholas hasn't hung up his boots yet though." Urging me on, Bridget said, "Tell her, Kim." She beamed at me.

If I didn't know better, I'd think she was enjoying this a little too much, although if I was being honest, I was beginning to enjoy myself too. I told Caroline about the flowers and the texts and was about to share the latest when Bridget interrupted. "Tell her about the comment on your blog."

Caroline's eyes opened wide. "What comment on your blog?

Wait. Which post? I'll open a new window and read it on my other monitor."

"Please tell me you didn't delete it," Bridget said.

"No way." My eyes filled with tears as I recalled the comment Nicholas had left earlier in the afternoon on my latest book review. "It's the book review for the new Betsy Harbick novel, *Driving With Old Boyfriends*." I wiped my eyes.

"Okay. Give me a sec to find it," Caroline said.

While we waited, I scooped a handful of M&Ms from Bridget's candy bowl, putting the green ones to the side. Urban legend or not, I was horny enough without help.

"Here we go." Caroline read, "'Serena Dawson gave up on love after her college sweetheart, Michael, disappeared after graduation without so much as a Dear John note. But when the unexpected death of a fellow classmate requires her to take a cross-country—'"

"Can we please skip the review and go directly to the comments?" Bridget rolled her eyes.

Caroline shrugged. "Sorry. I was thinking of downloading it and wanted to know what Kim thought."

Always pleased to hear when someone relied on my book recommendations, I belted out an enthusiastic "Thank you."

Waving her arms animatedly, Bridget said, "Five pink champagne flutes. Okay? Now get on with it." With a guilty look, she added, "Please."

"Fine," Caroline said. "There are fourteen comments. Which one is from Nicholas?"

"Eleven," Bridget and I said at the same time. Even though I had read it a dozen times, my heart raced in anticipation, and I took a deep breath to calm my nerves.

Caroline laughed. "This had better be good. You're certainly hyping it up enough."

"It's good," Bridget promised.

"Found it. Here goes: 'Your review was great, Kimmie. Here's mine: I thought the couple had amazing chemistry and enjoyed the slow burn—the witty banter and flirtation that eventually led to a night (and morning) of mind-blowing sex, despite a misunderstanding involving a rather bitchy girl from high school. I thought I had it figured out until they fought—totally his fault. I nearly pissed my pants when she sang to him and was blown away that she chose Crystal Gayle. Most chicks would choose someone obvious like Taylor Swift or Whitney Houston (R.I.P.), but not my girl...I mean, the heroine. Anyway, I'm reserving my review for when Part II comes out. It's fairly predictable though: the hero's totally gonna win her over. She can't resist his scruff. I have it on good authority it has grown in quite nicely just for her. Other parts are being groomed for her pleasure.'"

Caroline looked up, an amused expression on her face. "He's a pisser."

"I know," I said, blushing and barely suppressing a smile.

"You're totally caving," Bridget said knowingly.

I pursed my lips. "I totally am. Damn." My walls were crumbling like a cookie, and I hated myself for it, because Nicholas still hadn't said a thing about making more time for me. Would giving in now be equivalent to accepting the status quo of our relationship?

By the time I went to bed, Bridget's charcoal chunky wool blanket curled snugly around me like a second skin, I'd made up my mind to move back in with Nicholas. Even though he hadn't directly promised to readjust his priorities, his endeavors over the past week convinced me his workaholic tendencies had nothing to do with his affection for me as I'd feared. Nevertheless, a relationship needed to be nurtured by both parties in order to survive, and I would reunite with Nicholas only on the condition he make a conscious effort to do his part. For the first time in weeks, I fell asleep eager to wake up the next morning knowing I would be next to Nicholas in the bed we shared—although underneath or on top of him would work fine too—in twenty-four hours' time.

Chapter 38

"Okay, let's talk."

I had drafted and redrafted my text to Nicholas, debating how specific it should be, and finally settled on "Okay, let's talk" because it suggested I was open to discussion, but it wasn't a done deal. Holding my breath, I brought my finger to the phone, but quickly drew it back as I heard muffled voices approaching from around the corner. I recognized Rob's authoritative tone and Daneen's grating one and then a deep, soft, and sexy-as-hell voice that could only belong to...Nicholas? As my pulse raced, I quickly smoothed out my hair, wishing Rob had warned me Nicholas would be coming into the office. The voices and the clanking of Daneen's high-heeled shoes increased in volume, and I deleted my text and sat up straighter in my chair.

The three of them walked by my cubicle on their way to Rob's office, and Nicholas acknowledged me with a nod and a sad smile. I responded with a lame wave, since the timing for a personal discussion was way off. As I drank him in, from his beautiful head to his perfect feet, I wondered if the matching black and white gingham shirts we were wearing were a sign everything would work out. Before I could contemplate further, Rob said, "Hold my calls" and beckoned the others to follow him inside. Daneen honored me with a self-satisfied smirk before closing the door behind them.

Clearly, I wasn't going to get any work done with Nicholas less than thirty feet away from me. With every second and then minute that passed, I sat in my uncomfortable swirly chair willing myself not to call Rob and demand he cease bogarting my boyfriend. At last, the door opened, and Daneen walked out. I waited for Nicholas to follow, but Daneen closed the door again, leaving Nicholas alone with Rob. Not wanting to invite conversation with her, I pretended to be busy typing a document, but either seeing through my façade or not caring if she interrupted my concentration, Daneen stopped at my desk and hovered.

I removed my fingers from the keyboard and looked up at her. "Can I help you?"

She shook her head at me in undisguised mock sympathy. "Poor Kimmie. Must be difficult seeing Nicholas, considering..."

I clenched my jaw in response to hearing Nicholas's nickname for me from Daneen's thin lips. It wasn't the first time and wouldn't be the last, but it never ceased to rankle me. I raised an eyebrow. "Considering...?"

"Breakups are never easy," she said, before walking away with a swagger.

My first instinct was to race after Daneen and tackle her to the ground, but Daneen's livelihood practically subsisted on these jabs poorly disguised as kindness, and I didn't want to feed her diet. And besides, I was not in the midst of a breakup. On the contrary, as soon as Nicholas left Rob's office and I got him alone, we would kiss and make up. And later, he would help me move my stuff out of Bridget and Jonathan's apartment. Granted, my "stuff" was the equivalent of a suitcase and a wilting bouquet of pink flowers, but once I told Nicholas I was ready to move home, I knew he'd want to keep me close.

It was approaching one o'clock, and on any other day, I would head down to the cafeteria for my lunch break, but I didn't want to risk not being there when Nicholas finally came out. To most people, the firm's lunchroom was merely a convenient place to grab soup, salad, a sandwich, or even a decent warm meal at a reasonable price without ever leaving the building, but it held a sentimental significance for me too. On more than one occasion before we were dating, Nicholas would spot me at a table reading on my e-reader or writing a blog and would ask if he could join me.

Even though I relied on my lunch breaks to stick to my self-imposed strict blogging schedule, my crush on Nicholas from afar was epic, and I happily fell behind on my reviews for an opportunity to get to know him better. Nicholas typically worked through lunch, but I later learned he'd been keen on me from a distance too and welcomed the chance to talk one on one. I hoped yearning for those early days, when Nicholas considered time with me as valuable as his billable hours, wasn't a fool's dream.

My stomach was rumbling from hunger, and if Rob didn't release Nicholas soon, I might need to pee in a bucket. Needing a mindless distraction, I flipped through the pages of a magazine left in Rob's mailbox even though I had zero interest in anything written in the International Trademark Association's biweekly bulletin unless one of the firm's attorneys or Nicholas got a mention.

Finally, I heard the squeak of a door opening, and my body warmed in anticipation. I assumed Nicholas would come by to offer another tempting reason why I should come home and was eager to see his eyes light up when I said yes. I was already smiling when he walked out and certain he'd know what I was thinking without my needing to say a word.

But Nicholas didn't even see my face. From the moment he stepped out of Rob's office, he kept his head down and walked swiftly past me without so much as a wave. Risking whiplash, I turned around and watched him disappear into the hallway. Thinking maybe he had to use the bathroom too, I waited for him to come back until I heard the ping of the elevator and then silence. It wasn't like Nicholas to ignore me. Worried something ominous happened during his meeting with Rob, I sent him a text asking if he was all right before approaching Rob's door with shaky legs and knocking gently.

Rob swung around in his chair. "Shouldn't you be at lunch?"

Tapping my foot against the carpet, I said, "I'm taking a late lunch today. Is...uh...is Nicholas coming back?"

Rob shook his head. "Not unless he left something behind."

It was on the tip of my tongue to declare Nicholas had, indeed, left something behind—me. "Is everything okay?"

"Yeah. Why?" Rob asked. His blank expression worsened my fear that Nicholas shunning me likely had less to do with the status of his company's trademark portfolio and everything to do with the status of us.

"Nothing." I headed back to my desk without another word.

Needing some air, I spent my lunch hour sitting on a bench in Madison Square Park, a public park located a few blocks from my office. My meal consisted of a bottle of water as the smell of burgers wafting through the air from the neighboring Shake Shack was not enough to pique my appetite for anything more than answers to why Nicholas had walked right by me without saying anything. Rob appeared unfettered by whatever was on Nicholas's mind when he left his office, which suggested it was not work related. But even if he was distracted by work, he would have at least acknowledged me, especially considering the state of our relationship. Not responding to my text because of his job was not the key to getting me back. Instead, it was a reminder of exactly why I moved out in the first place. Maybe my decision to move back in with him was premature. More disturbing was the possibility Nicholas no longer cared. What if the comment on my blog was his last attempt at wooing me, and when I didn't respond, he cut his losses and moved on?

I relayed the details to Bridget over the phone later. "And that's the story." For the fiftieth time in as many minutes, I checked my phone, but so far, Nicholas hadn't returned my text.

"I'm baffled," Bridget said.

"Maybe I should have given in sooner."

Raising her voice, Bridget said, "No way. Don't make this your fault. You're stronger than that."

Up until then, I agreed with Bridget, but I wasn't so sure anymore. "Even you tried to persuade me to forgive him after he sent the flowers."

"I changed my mind once you explained things so clearly. You weren't ready to give in before. If Nicholas loves you, he'll do whatever it takes to prove his devotion to you and won't give up so easily."

"Maybe that's the problem," I said dully.

"What is?"

Placing my palm over my forehead and leaning over my desk, I whispered, "Maybe he doesn't love me."

"Of course he does."

"Then how do you explain his behavior earlier today and his continued silence all afternoon?"

"He's busy at work?"

I sat up. "So busy at work, he has no clue the wreck he's made me? It's like he's the defense attorney and the star witness for the prosecution all at once."

Bridget snorted. "Spare me the legal mumbo jumbo, please. Creative types like me don't follow that jargon."

I sighed.

"Let's do something fun tonight. Cocktails?"

"Maybe," I said as I maximized the screen for my Gmail. There was an email from Hannah. As I clicked on the message, I seriously hoped she wasn't nudging me for an expedited review of *Tearing at the Seams*. I had already pushed the book to the top of my TBR out of a sense of obligation, but if I had known accepting her proposition for an in with Felicia came with the unspoken cost of forever being her beck and call girl, I might have declined the offer. Or not. But I didn't like the idea of Hannah taking advantage of the situation, even though it didn't surprise me.

"A new gastropub opened up on the corner of 84th and Third," Bridget was saying.

"One second, Bridget. I have to read something."

"Okay, K."

Kim,

A little birdie told me Felicia is submitting your book to Three Monkeys. My fingers are crossed for you. You couldn't ask for a better home, as they are the premier press for romantic comedy and light women's fiction.

Bonne Chance,
Hannah

P.S. The not-so-little birdie was your sister, Erin.

I couldn't tell if Hannah's use of "not-so-little" was a dig at Erin—whose frame was, admittedly, not so little—or at me since unlike me, my sister surpassed sixty inches and then some. Regardless, she had insulted either me or my sister, but I was too concerned with the implications of the email to feel the sting: Hannah knew Felicia had submitted *A Blogger's Life* to Three Monkeys Press, which meant sooner or later she would find out they rejected it and, by extension, me.

To Bridget, I said, "This day couldn't get any worse. Do you think any of Jonathan's pot-dealing friends can get a hold of an IV so I can mainline alcohol? I don't have the patience to drink it the old-fashioned way."

Chapter 39

Two nights later, I still hadn't heard a peep from Nicholas. In typical heartbroken fashion, I was curled on the corner of Bridget and Jonathan's couch with a pint of Ben & Jerry's Spectacular Speculoos. "I suppose I'll need to find a new apartment now." Too bad I hadn't insisted on keeping my studio in order to maintain my independence like Carrie Bradshaw. Then again, even though Nicholas made a good living, it didn't compare to the likes of Big or Petrovsky. Who was I kidding? My life would never resemble an episode of *Sex and the City*. Except the really sad episodes, like when Big told Carrie he was marrying Natasha or when Berger broke up with Carrie on a Post-it note. And, unlike Carrie, I wasn't a published author. I shoved another spoonful of ice cream into my mouth and shivered as a cold rush blasted through my head. "Ouch." A little ice cream still in my mouth, I mumbled, "Brain freeze" in response to Bridget's questioning gaze.

"Oh." She giggled.

"Not funny." I pouted.

"I'm sorry, K." She frowned. "I wish I knew what to say."

Bridget and Jonathan had been wonderful the last couple of days. They doted on me from the moment I walked in the door after work until we all retired for the night—making me dinner, giving me power over the remote control, plying me with cookies. I was almost afraid they would suggest I cuddle with them before bed, but more afraid I would take them up on their offer.

Even when I first expressed my need for time away from Nicholas—back in Florida—my heart ached at the thought of a permanent break, but I was prepared to go through with it if I didn't see things getting better. But even then, I never imagined Nicholas would shut me out so harshly. No word from him for two days—not even a quick text in response to mine—shattered me to my core.

At the sound of my phone ringing, I practically flew off the couch to grab it from the coffee table. It had to be Nicholas. Although, unless he had a compelling reason for going AWOL on me, it might be too little too late.

Only it wasn't Nicholas. It was Pia. "Hi," I answered unenthusiastically as I settled my frame back into the indention it had left on the couch.

"Have you seen it?" she squealed.

I wiggled a finger in my ear. Not wanting Pia's screaming to wreak permanent damage on my hearing abilities, I put more distance between the phone and my ear. "Seen what?" I wasn't in the mood for Pia's exuberance.

"Oh my God. You haven't, have you?"

I sighed. "What are you talking about?"

Bridget muted the television, and she and Jonathan regarded me with curiosity. I shrugged and mouthed, "Pia."

"Go on YouTube right now," Pia demanded.

"I'm not online." Sitting up, I said to Jonathan, "Can I borrow your computer for a second? Pia's insisting I go on YouTube."

Jonathan nodded and walked his laptop over to me.

"Okay. I'm on YouTube. What exactly am I looking for? Is it a book trailer or something?" I sometimes attached fan-created book trailers to my reviews.

Pia chuckled. "Not exactly. I can't believe you haven't seen it. It's on its way to going viral."

I put my phone on speaker. "What's it called?"

"Just search, 'guy asks his girlfriend for a second chance.'"

My fingers reacted to her words before my brain could catch up, and it wasn't until I was staring at a screenshot of Nicholas hovered over his piano that my mouth dropped open. The video already had more than 100,000 views since it was posted earlier in the day. "Oh my God!" I called out, prompting Bridget and Jonathan to race to my side. "Nicholas made a YouTube video," I said, in a semi state of shock.

"I know. Play it!" Pia screeched, and I could visualize her dancing around her dorm room in excitement, her nonexistent hips shaking from side to side.

I exhaled a nervous laugh. "Okay. Okay." I glanced at Bridget and Jonathan hesitantly, and they nodded their encouragement. I clicked "play" and held my breath.

Chapter 40

Nicholas gazed earnestly into the camera. "It's been brought to my attention that, through no fault but my own, my girlfriend is under the misconception I enjoy my time at work more than my time with her."

I pressed pause on the video. "Rob." When Nicholas and Rob were behind closed doors, they must have been talking about me.

"Why are you stopping it?" Bridget yelled before practically throwing herself on my lap to gain access to the keyboard.

As instructed, I resumed the video. I wondered who was filming him. Or was it a selfie?

"Kim." He paused. "There is nothing further from the truth." He held up his hand. "If you're watching, I know you're thinking actions speaker louder than words."

I glanced at Bridget and Jonathan and shrugged. It was precisely what I was thinking.

Nicholas continued, "I'm so sorry you thought for one minute there was anything in this world I would rather do than you." He smiled. "Now you're thinking it's not all about sex."

I rolled my eyes but let a small smile escape.

"I apologized for making you feel neglected without ever acknowledging that you were neglected." He shook his head. "So much time I could have, no, *should* have, spent being accepted unconditionally by you was wasted seeking the elusive approval of someone whose opinion, quite honestly, doesn't mean nearly as much to me. Yes, I love this person. But I don't want to date this person. And when this person rides me hard, it doesn't feel nearly as good as when you do." He cracked up.

I clamped my hand to my mouth as my face warmed in embarrassment.

His expression serious again, Nicholas said, "My work is important to me and has been since well before you first walked into my law firm. You, with your smoking-hot pencil skirts and button-down tops I mentally unbuttoned each time we shared the same air space. You, whose eyes danced whenever the word 'book' was spoken within a mile radius. My ambition is not what changed. You did not change. We are not what changed. I alone am responsible for the near destruction of our relationship, and Rob made me understand what I risked losing if I didn't get my priorities in order. I'm embarrassed I needed to be told, but I'm glad Rob pointed it out to me."

Rob was so unresponsive when I confided in him, but he was secretly super concerned. What a faker. Oh, how I adored him. Bridget handed me a tissue, and I mouthed, "Thank you" before dabbing my eyes.

"There is not another person in this world I'd rather spend my time with than you, Kimmie Long, and it pains me to have you doubt my love for you for even a second. My negligence in letting it go on this long is something I'll have to live with, but I hope I can make you forget—a little bit each day—if you'll let me. The thing is, Kimmie, we're both quite capable of achieving success in our professional endeavors without losing what makes us so damn great together, and I'm determined to prove it to you beginning now. My first order of business..." He grinned, his eyes shining with light. "...is to sing you a little ditty."

I giggled. For Bridget and Jonathan's benefit, I muttered, "Private joke." On our first date, Nicholas demonstrated his immaturity by confusing my use of the term "ditty" to describe a short song with the slang term "diddies," which means "breasts."

Nicholas lowered his gaze toward the piano and started playing. Within the first few chords, I recognized the song: Player's

"Baby Come Back." His song choice was as corny as mine the year before, but I choked up anyway as he sang, "I was wrong, and I just can't live without you" in near-perfect pitch.

Nicholas didn't play the song like a professional pianist—his rhythm was a bit choppy, and he missed a few notes—but in my eyes, he was a rock star. By the time he sang the last words and played the final notes, I was halfway to the West Village— metaphorically speaking, since I was being held hostage on the couch by Bridget, who had grabbed hold of my hand halfway through the song.

Jonathan broke the silence. "I'm so screwed." He walked to the window, a cigarette already dangling from the side of his mouth. "Nicholas has set the bar quite high for a grand gesture. No apology I ever offer will compare."

"Just don't do anything which would require a grand gesture, and you'll be fine," Bridget said. "And besides, Nicholas was just living up to the standard Kim set last year when she sang to him. Remember?"

"Performing karaoke to a controlled audience does not compare to making a YouTube video accessible to an infinite number of views," Jonathan said, taking a long drag of his cigarette before blowing out the smoke in a slow exhale.

"Nicholas can take down the video any time he wants," Bridget argued.

I was contemplating the swiftest path to Nicholas's arms and was only half-listening to their debate. I was considering the advantages and disadvantages of taking the subway, car, or an Uber when Bridget's intercom rang.

"Hey, Joseph," Bridget said into the speaker.

"You have a Nicholas in the lobby. Can I send him up?"

"Yes," I volunteered, vaulting off the couch. "I'll call you later, Pia. Thanks," I said before hanging up the phone. My short legs reached the front door in record time, and while I waited for Nicholas, I wiped a smudge of ice cream off my chin. After a few minutes, I was certain he must have gotten stuck in the elevator.

Impatient, I swung the door open with force, coming face to face with a startled Nicholas.

At the sight of him, I sucked in my breath. "Hi," I said, sounding more like a shy tween meeting the lead singer of a boy band than an almost-thirty-year-old woman.

Nicholas ran his tongue along his lower lip. "Hi yourself."

I tore my eyes from his mouth and, noticing his attire, broke into a huge smile. "Nice shirt."

He glanced down at his very snug-fitting pink t-shirt with the words "Strawberry Fields Forever" written in green atop a red strawberry design. "This old thing? Lucky for me Amazon has two-hour delivery."

I raised an eyebrow. "You do realize it's a girl's shirt, right?"

His cheeks turning red, he said, "I bought it for you?"

"It will look nice next to my Penny Lane shirt," I said, referring to the shirt I had worn when I sang "Don't It Make My Brown Eyes Blue" to him at karaoke in front of all of our colleagues. All self-control lost, I launched myself into his arms. "I missed you so much," I whispered.

Squeezing me tightly, Nicholas said, "I take it you saw the video?"

I pulled away. "Did you mean what you said?"

"Every word."

I planted a soft kiss on his lips before nibbling on his neck. I breathed in his scent with every peck.

"Will you please come home now?"

"Yes." I lightly tugged on his earlobe with my teeth. "I just need to pack my stuff." I replaced my teeth with my tongue and sucked gently.

I heard a thumping sound from behind me and broke away from Nicholas to find Bridget standing beside my bag. "I packed your suitcase. Here's your hat. What's your hurry?" Then she closed the door behind her.

I looked at Nicholas and shrugged. "I guess my visitor's pass has expired."

From the other side of the wall, Bridget shouted, "Call me tomorrow."

Grabbing my bag with one hand, Nicholas placed his other hand on the small of my back and led me toward the elevator. "Let's get you home where you belong."

Chapter 41

We froze as one, spent from vigorous makeup sex. Our heavy breathing was the only evidence of life until I released a sob.

Nicholas untangled his legs from mine and pushed himself up on his elbows. Peering at me with concern, he asked, "What's wrong, Kimmie? Did I hurt you?"

Surprised by my own reaction, I shook my head. "Not at all." I wiped the wetness from my eyes. "I'm just emotional, I guess."

"Things are going to get better from here on out. I promise," he said.

"I thought you gave up on me."

"Never," Nicholas said, shaking his head.

"You didn't return my text." I sat up against the headboard. "The other day. You ran out of Rob's office without a word to me, and when I texted to see if you were all right, you ignored me. I was going to tell you I wanted to come home, and I...I thought you changed your mind." I reached over to the nightstand for a tissue.

Nicholas sighed. "I couldn't face you. After what Rob told me—that you thought I would rather be at work than with you—I was so ashamed. I knew I had to fix it. So I went home and played the piano until I got it right." He gave me a sheepish grin. "It took me a while to find the perfect song. And then learning to play it on the piano wasn't easy either."

Smoothing out a hair on his head that was sticking straight up, I said, "The effort did not go unnoticed, but a simple sincere apology and promise to try harder would have been enough. You didn't have to go all grand gesture on me." I kissed his cheek. "But I'm glad you did."

"We're even now. Between 'Don't It Make My Brown Eyes Blue' and 'Baby Come Back,' I'd say we're a shoo-in if there's ever a contest for the couple with the oddest taste in music to serenade your lover." He chuckled.

I raised an eyebrow. "Not to mention outdated. We should be closer to fifty than thirty based on our song choices."

"Nothing wrong with that. The Beatles would have been over fifty by now. I prefer the term 'classic' to "outdated.'"

"Fair enough," I said.

"Kimmie?"

"Nicholas?"

He flashed me a sexy grin and inched even closer to me on the bed. "Can we do it again now?"

Shaking my head in amusement, I said, "I'd love to. But..." I paused. I didn't want to harp on an issue he'd promised to resolve, but I wasn't sure it would be as easy as Nicholas seemed to think.

"What's wrong?" Nicholas asked with concern.

I bit my lip. "I'm so happy you've acknowledged what's been happening between us and I love that you've sworn things will be different from here on out, but how do you plan to accomplish that? How can you be sure we won't revert to old habits and find ourselves in the same place two months from now?"

Nicholas nodded. "It won't always be easy, Kimmie. I do have a demanding job. But like you reminded me in Florida, I was a busy attorney when we first started dating and I managed to make time for you. I worked late some nights so I could be with you on others. I delegated assignments where possible. I don't have a Daneen anymore, but there are junior people at my company I can rely on more than I have lately."

I tried not to grimace at the mention of Daneen.

Nicholas pursed his lips. "I know I can make it work. Especially because now I've experienced what it's like to lose you and I can't bear it happening again. If we have plans, unless my job is truly at stake or someone's life is on the line, I'll be there." He grinned. "And unlike my dad's job, the likelihood of someone's life being at stake and me being the one to save it is pretty small."

"Speaking of your dad..." I raised an eyebrow. I didn't think additional clarification was necessary.

"I'll take care of my father. Trust me on that. He has to be proud of me for who I am now, not who he wants me to be. If he's not capable, I'll learn to live with it." His lips curled up. "I'm pretty sure my mom loves me best at least. Don't tell my siblings."

"You have my word," I said with a chuckle as I ran my thumb and index finger across my lips. I was glad Nicholas was going to stop trying so hard to earn Dr. Strong's approval both for the sake of our relationship and because a parent's approval shouldn't take so much work, but I also knew joking was Nicholas's way of coping. It made me sad.

"I can't promise to have a nine to five existence five days a week nor can I guarantee a work event will never get in the way ever again, but you have my sincere vow to make it the exception and not the norm. I also promise to share my schedule with you so there will be less surprises. And I will confide more about the work gig and take more active interest in your publishing journey than I've been doing lately. Can you live with that?" He looked at me hopefully.

I pressed my lips against his and whispered, "I can."

Waking up early the next morning, I reached for my phone on the nightstand and checked my email while Nicholas slept. Scrolling through my new messages and keeping the ones with the subject line "Review Request" unread for the time being, I opened a new one from Hannah.

Kim!

I just learned Three Monkeys Press passed on your book. I'm quite surprised given the success of their latest titles in the genre, most notably Cut on the Bias.

I'm almost as crushed as you that we won't be part of the same publishing house, but don't give up hope. Felicia can sell anything, and I'm sure she'll find a home for Blogger Girl *eventually. It just takes some books longer, but it doesn't necessarily mean they won't do as well. You waited longer than most to reach five feet, but it happened eventually, right? Haha.*

Please tell your sister the autographed copies of my books are in the mail. She's such a doll.

Hannah

I chuckled. Even though she got the title of my book wrong, and I never did reach five feet tall, I truly believed she meant well. I glanced over at a sleeping Nicholas and kissed the top of his head. I wasn't as bothered by Hannah's knowledge of Three Monkeys' rejection as I thought I'd be. Felicia might not have found a home for *A Blogger's Life* yet, but my own home was as sweet as it could be. After placing my phone back on the table, I curled my body around Nicholas and fell back asleep with a smile.

Chapter 42

Nicholas kept to his word, and things improved dramatically over the next few weeks. We were back to where we were before things went sour. He still worked late hours most nights but always texted to let me know approximately when he'd be home. He made sure to reserve at least two evenings a week for me plus weekends and kept his phone tucked into his pocket and unchecked for what he called "undivided Kimmie time." He involved me in his professional world by sharing stories about his colleagues and the latest in his achievements and answered my questions rather than shrugging them off on the assumption I wouldn't be interested. And, most fun of all, we reinstated our daytime sexting sessions with a vengeance. I was tempted to leave my phone on Daneen's desk open to one of our spicier exchanges, but I decided it didn't matter whether or not she knew how happy we were. The only people who needed to know about our blissful state were Nicholas and me. But the biggest test was still ahead of us. His folks were in town for a family dinner— and I'd be lying if I said I wasn't afraid all it would take to blow our happy home down to the ground was a single face to face with the Big Bad Wolf, a.k.a. Dr. Warren Strong.

The vibe at Catch, a popular Asian-Fusion restaurant in the trendy Meatpacking District, was probably more suitable for a night out with our friends than a family gathering with Dr. and Mrs. Strong, Nicholas's brother Neil and his wife Clarissa, and the two of us, but I was cautiously optimistic the noise level would drown out the tension. I'd considered suggesting we devise a game plan for Nicholas getting through the meal with his ego unscathed at the hand of his father, but Nicholas had promised me he'd handle it.

And when it came to family dynamics, there was only so much an outsider could do.

As the waiter asked if we preferred bottled water, sparkling, or tap, and Dr. Strong took the liberty of responding for us all with "tap," I squeezed Nicholas's hand under the table in silent encouragement. He turned to me and winked before asking, "Should we order a couple bottles of wine for the table?"

After much discussion, we decided on two bottles of pinot noir and several small plates to share, including multiple sushi rolls, mahi mahi tacos, a selection of oysters, and the Seafood Tower.

I was telling Clarissa, who sat on my other side, about *Pastel Is the New Black* and was pleasantly surprised when she whipped out her phone and joined the mailing list right then and there. I had outgrown my reluctance to share my blog with people out of fear they would dismiss the genre of chick lit as being frivolous—to each his own—but I figured her taste in books would lean toward the more intellectual considering her career as a medical research scientist for a major pharmaceutical company. One glass of wine under my belt and tipsy, I told her as much.

She laughed, her blue eyes twinkling. "Not at all. When I'm not reading for the job, the less stuffy the content, the better." From across the table, Dr. Strong belted out a laugh in response to something Neil had said, and Clarissa shifted closer to me—close enough so I could smell the coconut scent of her shoulder-length chestnut hair. Raising her voice to be heard over the din of the table, she said, "My taste has gone quite dark lately, to be honest. Do you review only chick lit?"

With a sideways glance at Nicholas, I said, "Mostly, but not all. Although I do need to protect my brand. *Pastel Is the New Black* is definitely a chick lit blog."

Draping his arm across the back of my chair, Nicholas said, "Did someone mention branding?"

"You can take the guy out of work, but you can't take work out of the guy," I joked. It was such a relief to be able to utter that sentence in jest after everything we'd been through.

"No work tonight. Let's drink to that," Neil said from his chair on the opposite side of the table from Clarissa. He downed what remained in his wineglass in one sip.

"Bottoms up, son. You earned it. How many surgeries did you perform last week?" Warren asked, beaming at his eldest son with pride while refilling his glass.

"This week has been intense as I've been juggling rounds with my reading. And I'm working on a clinical protocol." Neil rubbed his eyes. "But like I said, no work tonight." He winked in Clarissa's direction.

As I noted the resemblance between Nicholas and Neil—both in appearance and mannerisms—I blushed. I wondered if after almost a decade of marriage Clarissa was as hot for Neil as I was for his brother. Nicholas had told me they met at a medical seminar when Neil was an attending physician.

"What about you, son?" Dr. Strong said, directing his green-eyed gaze at Nicholas. "Any headway on the promotion?"

The moment I had dreaded upon us, I tensed against Nicholas's arm, which was still draped across my chair. I took a sip of my drink, hoping the glass wouldn't fall out of my shaky hand.

"Actually, no," Nicholas answered before calmly removing a piece of sushi roll from a platter in front of us and dipping it in soy sauce.

His brow furrowed, Dr. Strong repeated, "No?"

Wishing I could click my Louboutins three times and be anywhere but here, I dared not look at Nicholas. Instead, I took another sip of my wine and stared straight ahead, unintentionally catching the eye of Mrs. Strong. As if reading my mind, she smiled at me warmly as if to say, "No worries."

"My work is under control, Dad. Now, I want to focus on finding the right balance between my career and other equally important aspects of my life." Nicholas found my hand under the table and squeezed. "*More* important, actually."

I sucked in my breath in surprise and, on the verge of tears, locked eyes with him and mouthed, "Thank you."

He nodded, his back straight in a show of confidence.

Remembering we weren't alone at the table, I hesitantly glanced at his mother who dabbed her eyes with her napkin. Then I glanced toward Dr. Strong, fearing the smoke from his ears would burn down the restaurant.

"Son—" Warren began.

"No, Dad," Nicholas said firmly.

"Good for you, little brother," Neil said, breaking the tension.

"To balance," Clarissa piped in, raising her glass.

"To balance," Jeanine echoed. Elbowing her husband, she added, "You might want to take a lesson from your youngest son, Warren. Balance is not your strong suit." Then she kissed him on the cheek. "Although your intensity is one of the things I love the most about you."

Dr. Strong released a reluctant laugh. "Fine. To balance." He raised his glass and took a sip. Clearing his throat, he said, "Speaking of balance, I read an interesting study the other day suggesting a correlation between balance and risk for stroke."

Everyone at the table collectively burst out in laughter. All except Warren, who, looking bewildered, glanced from one person to the next, evidently not seeing the humor in the statement.

After dinner, we lay side by side in bed watching *Behind the Music* on VH1. We were too exhausted and full of food to have sex, but too wound up to sleep. Still glowing in the aftermath of Nicholas standing up to his father and his public proclamation there was more to his life than climbing the legal corporate ladder, I gladly relinquished power over the remote control to him. Too fatigued to pay much attention and not at all interested in the successes and failures of Grand Funk Railroad—I couldn't even name one song they sang—I was content to brush my feet against Nicholas's under the covers.

Nicholas placed the remote control on the part of the blanket that was covering me. "I'm beat, Kimmie. Gonna catch some Zs.

You can watch whatever you want. I won't mind the sound."

Turning off the television, I said, "I'm tired too" and turned on my side facing him.

Nicholas smiled and inched closer to me. "Have a good time tonight?"

"I did. Did you?"

"Yup. Good times with the fam."

"I like Neil and Clarissa."

"Yeah, they're good people."

"Neil isn't what I expected," I confessed.

"What did you expect?" Nicholas asked, closing his eyes.

I swiped two fingers along his forehead. "I kind of figured he'd be all intense like your dad, but he's more like you and your mom."

Nicholas opened his eyes. "He's my favorite brother. Nathan's kind of a jerk sometimes."

I giggled. "He'd probably get along great with Erin."

"You love your sister. Admit it."

"I do. And hopefully you will too." We had planned our trip to Boston for the following month. "I just wish she'd keep her trap shut. I'm afraid to even tell my parents what's going on with my book for fear they'll tell Erin, who will wait half a second before spilling to Hannah."

Nicholas yawned.

"Am I boring you? I thought the days of you falling asleep on me were behind us," I teased.

He gave me a wry grin. "Sorry. Anyway, I thought you made peace with Hannah knowing her publisher rejected you."

"I did. But that was one rejection. I'd prefer to keep her out of the loop for future ones."

"What makes you think there'll be more?"

I bit my lip. "I haven't heard a peep from Felicia in weeks."

"No news is good news."

I smirked at him. "Next you'll tell me rain on your wedding day or getting crapped on by a pigeon is good luck."

"Both of those things are true," he said with confidence.

"Whatever." I moved closer to him, buried my head in his chest, and closed my eyes. "G'night, Nicholas. Thanks for saying what you said to your dad."

"I did it as much for me as I did it for you. But you're welcome," he said, kissing the top of my head. "I love you."

"Love you too," I murmured.

"I'm not going to tell you what happens. You have to keep reading." Nicholas had started reading *A Blogger's Life* and was trying to pump me for information.

"Fine. Be that way."

I chuckled, but when I saw Daneen standing by my desk glowering at me, I put my hand to my mouth. Into the phone, I said, "Hold on a sec, okay?" before addressing her. "What can I do for you?"

"How about we start with your job? Considering your writing hasn't gotten you anywhere, you might want to make a bit more effort. Rob won't let you skate forever." She raised an eyebrow.

My cheeks burning, I said to Nicholas, "I gotta go."

"Put her on."

My belly quivered. "What?"

"Put. Her. On."

I gulped. "K." Turning to Daneen, I said, "Nicholas wants to speak to you" and handed her the phone.

Daneen squeezed into my already crowded cubicle space and smirked at me. "Hello there."

Chewing on my cuticles, I watched as Daneen's upturned lips turned down and her bright eyes went dull. "I didn't know." As her face turned ashen, she scraped a hand through her hair and turned her back on me. "I won't. Yes, I understand. Bye." Without meeting my eyes, she returned the phone to my hand and walked away with her shoulders slumped.

Still watching Daneen's back as she turned the corner, I said to Nicholas, "What the hell did you say to her?"

After a brief hesitation, Nicholas said, "I told her I know you have dirt on her that you've been kind enough to keep to yourself. I told her I've had enough of her cattiness toward you, and if she doesn't start treating you with the respect you deserve, I will use my powers of persuasion to get you to spill all of the dirty details."

"Holy crap." I laughed at my unintentional pun. "Thank you, sweets."

"I know I've urged you to shrug her off, but I can see she doesn't make it easy for you at all. If the secret isn't embarrassing enough to get the job done, I will threaten to pull my work from the firm and blame her as the reason."

"Although I would love for her to leave the firm of her own doing, I don't think I could live with being the cause." Who was I kidding? I could totally live with it.

"Who are you fooling, Kimmie?"

"Ha. You read my mind."

"Speaking of reading, is Henry seriously going to miss Laurel's thirtieth birthday party to take his folks to their bridge game?"

"No spoilers."

Chapter 43

Leaning back against Bridget's couch, I said, "This couch is super comfy, but I'm still glad I don't have to sleep on it anymore."

"Me too."

"Nice, Bridge." I mock glared at her.

"You know what I meant, silly," Bridget said, tossing a throw pillow at me.

I caught the pillow and grinned. "I do." I was about to fling the pillow back at her when I noticed it was designed out of her Instagram photos. I scanned the various images of Bridget and Jonathan both alone and together, as well as a couple of me. "This pillow is awesome."

Beaming, Bridget said, "Thanks," before glancing at her laptop, where an invite to join a video chat with Caroline, who was now with Felix in Morocco, had just popped up on the screen. After joining the chat, we waited for Caroline's smiling face to appear and called out, "Hey Caroline," in unison.

"Hi, girls." When she waved, my eyes were immediately drawn to her ring finger and the sparkling diamond gleaming at us. Of the three of us, I never dreamed Caroline would be the first to get married, considering when she left for her sabbatical, she didn't even have a boyfriend, Bridget lived with hers, and I was nearly at that stage. But I also never imagined I'd write a book, much less get an agent—especially the same agent as Hannah Marshak. The last year had brought many twists and turns, and I couldn't wait to see what happened next.

"Is Felix still your husband?" Bridget asked.

I hurled the pillow at her. "Seriously, Bridget? You couldn't come up with something else to lead with?"

Bridget frowned, her face turning the color of her hair. "Caroline's marital status is going to be first on the agenda for quite a while." Pointing at Caroline, she said, "That's what she gets for eloping with a guy we never met and not allowing us the opportunity to wear matching puffy bridesmaid's dresses." She smiled to show she was only teasing.

"Something most people would thank me for," Caroline said with a chuckle.

"Don't worry, Bridget. You'll get to wear a bridesmaid's dress when I get married. And I'll be nice," I promised.

"Bridesmaid? *Psh.* I expect to be maid of honor when you get married, missy," Bridget said.

"Erin might have a different plan in mind," I responded.

Bridget's face lit up. "I already worked it all out. Erin will be the matron of honor so I can be the maid of honor."

"Unless you get married before me," I said. I quickly added, "Kidding," even though I secretly hoped Bridget and Jonathan would change their minds about getting married one day. Or at least have kids so our daughters could be best friends.

"It's a nonissue," Bridget said, waving me away.

"My getting married should be the last of your concerns right now, anyway. I think we've got time." I giggled.

"I think Bridget has weddings on the mind because of my lack of hoopla. Right, Bridget?" Caroline asked.

"Right. And a new season of *Say Yes to the Dress* started on TLC." Bridget tapped her head. "It's all weddings all the time in here."

I gave her a curious look. "Seriously?" An odd subject to clog the brain of a woman with zero interest in ever planning her own nuptials.

"Kim, what's going on with your book?" Caroline asked.

"Yeah, Kim. What's the latest?" Bridget asked.

I looked at Bridget in surprise. "You already know everything,

Bridget." To Caroline, I said, "As you're aware, I was rejected by Three Monkeys Press. Last I heard, Felicia was going to pitch *A Blogger's Life* at the *Los Angeles Times* Festival of Books, but it's been over a week and crickets."

"Have you followed up with her?" Caroline asked.

"No," I said, biting my nails.

"Why not?" she asked.

"Scared," I mumbled. "At least if I don't know, I can be hopeful. If I ask her, she'll have to break the news that every reputable publisher this side of the equator has turned it down." I shook my head. "I'd rather be blissfully ignorant."

"Except you're clearly not blissful," she said, raising an eyebrow.

"Yeah, K, just drop her a gentle note," Bridget urged.

In truth, I feared too much good fortune had come my way recently, and following up with Felicia would be pushing my luck. How likely was it Nicholas would make things right between us *and* Felicia would sell my book all within such a brief period of time? And it was even less conceivable any update Felicia could provide was one I'd be desirous to receive. Otherwise, wouldn't she have already contacted me unsolicited? My guess was Felicia either had nothing new to report or any update she could provide was contrary to what I wanted to hear. She probably figured what I didn't know wouldn't hurt me. Besides, I wasn't the only author she represented, and I couldn't expect to be her constant priority.

This was how I justified deleting the numerous emails I'd drafted to her over the last week requesting an update. "I'll take your advice under advisement, ladies." Empty promises, as per usual, to facilitate a change in topic. "So tell us about Casablanca, Caroline. Have you been to Rick's Café?" I didn't know if such a venue existed outside of the classic movie, but it didn't matter as long as the question served to take the conversation in another direction.

"In fact, we have. The original was closed down in the eighties, but a new one was reopened by an American ex-pat in 2004. We went there two nights ago. Right, Felix?" Caroline turned her blond head away from the computer, and a moment later, Felix was at her side, crouching down to be seen on the computer monitor. To Caroline, he said, "I put in a wake-up call for tomorrow morning at seven." Facing the screen again, but still stroking Caroline's arm, he said, "We're going to Marrakesh tomorrow and need to get an early start. But enough about us. Hiya, girls." He flashed us a smile.

Bridget nudged my leg with her foot, no doubt in silent appreciation of Felix's European sex appeal. My face heated in agreement. "Hi, Felix. Enjoying Morocco so far?"

Felix nodded enthusiastically. "It's smashing. Rick's Café is nothing like the movie—posh and the cocktails are bomb—but we're glad we went." He kissed Caroline on the head. "Right, babes?"

I glanced at Bridget who looked equally confused, but we both nodded at Felix. "Awesome," I said.

"Brill," Bridget said before laughing.

Caroline yawned. "It's late here, guys, and we should get some shut-eye."

"We'll let you go, then. Good talking to you two," Bridget said.

"Have fun in Marrakesh," I said.

"We will. Keep us posted on the book stuff, Kim. And any other interesting developments," Caroline said.

"As soon as I have something to share, you'll be among the first to know," I assured her.

"No matter where we are. Promise?" Caroline's eyes probed mine as if she wasn't so sure.

"Uh, yeah. I promise," I said, taken aback by her need for reassurance. Along with Nicholas, my parents, Bridget (and Jonathan by association) and Rob, I considered Caroline among the most important people in my life. Rob was a late addition to my A-list ever since his heart-to-heart with Nicholas led to our reconciliation.

Caroline grinned. "Great. Love you guys."

"Love you too," Bridget said.

"Muah!" I waved at the monitor one more time before Caroline ended the call, and her face disappeared from the screen. I stretched my arms over my head. It was five hours earlier in New York City than in Morocco, but I was still beat.

"Caroline was acting odd," I said to Bridget, who had stood up to bring the almost-empty platter of cheese we were nibbling on to the kitchen.

"How so?"

I followed her into the kitchen. "She seemed so concerned with me keeping her in the loop on stuff. Have I been leaving her out?" The woman was on another continent in the throes of her extended honeymoon. Although I didn't want to waste her limited text plan with minutiae, I'd never purposely keep her in the dark.

With her back to me as she returned the container of leftover cheese to the refrigerator, Bridget said, "I didn't notice anything unusual about her behavior."

Standing behind her, I said, "Really? Okay, maybe I'm being paranoid."

Bridget turned around and asked, "Are you PMSing?" just as Jonathan walked into the apartment carrying bags of groceries in each arm.

Placing the bags on the kitchen island, he expelled an exasperated sigh. "I'm beginning to think you plan these 'period' conversations for when I'll be in earshot."

"Yes, it's all a conspiracy, honey bunny," Bridget said, tickling him on his sides. "But seriously, Kim, don't give it another thought."

"Give what another thought?" Jonathan asked, scratching his head where his crew cut was beginning to grow in.

"Nothing," Bridget replied before I could answer. "Are you hungry, Jonathan? Want any cheese?"

Jonathan gave me a puzzled glance, and I shrugged my shoulders. "I should get going. I wanted to work on book two tonight and it's already..." I glanced at my watch. "...almost eight o'clock. I'm so overwhelmed. Between the day job, maintaining the blog, keeping up on my reading, writing, and Nicholas, I have zero energy." Thinking out loud, I said, "Maybe I'll skip the writing and take a bubble bath." I smiled wickedly, remembering the bath I took with Nicholas only a few nights earlier and the subsequent marathon sex. If I wanted a relaxing night, I'd need to take a solo soak this time around.

Jonathan and Bridget exchanged a glance.

"What?" Had I said the part about my bath with Nicholas out loud?

"Nothing," Bridget said, pulling me into a hug. "You don't give yourself enough credit, Kim. You have tons of energy, and I'm positive you could take on another...um...project if you wanted to."

I chuckled. "Thanks for the vote of confidence, Bridge."

A few minutes later, I sat on the downtown train with my head buried in my e-reader hoping to drown out the noise of my fellow commuters (and make a dent in my TBR pile). Despite my attempt to concentrate on the words on the device, my mind kept wandering to the events of the evening. I couldn't decide who'd acted stranger—Bridget or Caroline.

Chapter 44

The following week, Nicholas and I were in our apartment relaxing after a casual dinner of bacon, lettuce, and tomato sandwiches and homemade potato chips. The television was on at low volume in the background while I worked on *Love on Stone Street* and Nicholas read a book—an actual novel, not a legal treatise or twenty-page agreement—he'd come so far.

"Kimmie," Nicholas said, tickling my toes.

I was stretched across the couch with my legs on Nicholas's lap, but my butt lifted off of the couch at the sensation. I giggled. "Stop it. You know I'm ticklish."

"Hence the reason I do it," he said, playing my toes like the keys of a clarinet until I laughed again. "Let's take a walk." He glanced toward the window in our living room. "It's a nice night." As his fingers moved in the direction of my feet once again, I pulled my legs away and sat up straight.

Following his gaze out the window, I queried, "How do you know? It's dark outside." It was almost nine thirty.

Ignoring my question, Nicholas tapped his phone. Then he looked up and grinned. "According to Accuweather, it's sixty-five degrees with only fifteen percent humidity. Perfect weather for a summer stroll around the block." He stood up and reached for my hand.

I allowed him to pull me up. We were in kissing distance so, naturally, I pressed my lips softly against his until he deepened the kiss and reached under my shirt to massage my lower back.

Reluctantly separating from his embrace, I said, "You sure you want to take a walk now?" I could think of other things I'd rather do, none of which included accomplishing today's goal of hitting the forty-thousand word count on book two.

Dragging me toward the foyer of our apartment, he said, "Yes."

Resisting his force, I took a step backward. "Let me use the bathroom first. And run a brush through my hair."

Nicholas stroked his thumb gently across my cheek and kissed my forehead. "Do what you got to do. I have cabin fever. Meet you outside."

Nicholas was right—the crisp dry air outside made walking quite comfortable. Still, I was glad I grabbed my denim jacket as what I thought would be a brief jaunt around the block turned into an on-foot tour of the extended neighborhood. As we walked, we pointed out our favorite buildings from an architectural standpoint and added several restaurants and bars to our to-try list.

"I definitely want to eat there," I said, pointing at La Sirène, a French restaurant we'd still yet to try.

"Then we'll make it happen," Nicholas said with a smile.

We continued to walk hand in hand in contented silence until Nicholas stopped short in front of the Soho Grand Hotel. "What do we have here?" he asked, glancing at the entrance.

"The Soho Grand. Remember the last time we were here together? The only time, actually."

"How could I forget?" Nicholas said with a wink.

My ten-year high school reunion the year before was held at the Soho Grand—when Nicholas and I were first becoming "friends." When I told him about the reunion, he suggested we meet for a drink after since he lived so close to the hotel. Nervous as all get-out, I summoned the nerve to text him. He showed up, and after initial tension—caused by Hannah Marshak both hitting on him and outing Jonathan as my high-school sweetheart and current friend with benefits—we confessed our mutual attraction. We slept together for the first time that night and soon after became boyfriend and girlfriend. I was one of those fortunate women who managed to make love out of what could easily have been a late-night one-time booty call. I still didn't know how I got so lucky. (Aside from my mad bedroom skills.)

Bringing me back to the present, Nicholas motioned toward the entrance. "Should we get a drink?"

"Why not?"

I followed him inside the lobby and up the stairs to the Grand Bar, where we sat in plush oversized chairs and gave our drink orders. "I think I'll stick to prosecco and leave the Dirty Soho for another time," I said, shuddering in the memory of the drink I had the last time. I could still taste the potent cocktail I had ordered after running away from Nicholas in a huff when I thought he was more interested in Hannah than me.

When the waitress brought over our drinks, we clinked glasses. "To the Soho Grand," I said.

"To the Soho Grand," Nicholas repeated. "Where it all began."

I gazed at him adoringly. "Best night ever."

Nicholas cocked his head to the side. "Eventually, yes. But you had me scared there for a while."

Jerking my head back, I said, "I had *you* scared? My hands were shaking when I texted you, asking if you wanted to meet me."

"Why would you be afraid?"

I shrugged. "I didn't know if you liked me the way I liked you."

"What guy asks a girl to meet him for a drink on a Saturday night if he doesn't like her?" Nicholas asked, narrowing his eyes.

"Precisely what Bridget said before she got hammered. And then I wondered if you were only looking to get laid. Why were you scared?"

"You were none too pleased to see me at first, if you recall. Anyway, I did want to get in your pants," Nicholas confessed. "But I was smitten."

"I was too," I said, my voice cracking with emotion. "I was taken aback seeing you talking to Hannah. If you had chosen her, I would have been crushed."

"Hannah who?" Nicholas said with a blank expression.

When I playfully nudged him in the leg, he grabbed ahold of my hand. "I only had eyes for you, Kimmie Long."

We smiled goofily at each other for a moment, not saying anything. Eventually, Nicholas broke the silence. "Kim...I..." Before he could get another word out, my phone rang, startling us both.

"Hold that thought," I said, releasing my phone from my purse. "It's Felicia. I should take this."

Nicholas nodded. "Go for it."

I whispered, "I'll just be a second." Still holding his hand, I answered the phone. "Hi, Felicia." Riddled with anxiety as to the reason she was phoning me, my pulse raced— Felicia didn't do courtesy calls, certainly not at this late hour.

"Is this a good time?"

I glanced at Nicholas and squeezed his hand. "Sure. I'm having a drink with my boyfriend at the Soho Grand." I winced at my tendency to provide more information than was required.

"Nice. The perfect venue for a celebration."

My heart slamming against my chest, I asked, "Is there something to celebrate?" I locked eyes with Nicholas, who whispered, "What?"

I mouthed, "I don't know" and chewed on my lip. "Felicia?"

"I do have some news, Kim," she said in an even tone.

I held tightly to Nicholas's hand like I needed it to pull me out of quicksand. "You do?"

"I promised you I would find a home for *A Blogger's Life*. Did you believe me?"

In a meek voice, I said, "Yes," blinking away the onset of tears. I knew something big was coming. I dug my nails deeper into Nicholas's palm, but he didn't flinch.

"I know you were disappointed when Three Monkeys Press passed, but I'm hoping what I'm about to say will make up for it."

I swallowed hard. "Okay?" She was killing me with calmness.

"Have you ever heard of Fifth Avenue Press?"

I stuttered, "Have...have I ever heard of Fifth Avenue Press?" It was only one of the biggest most prestigious New York City publishing houses. Raising my voice, I said, "Of course I have"

Felicia chuckled. "Well...they've offered you a two-book deal and a thirty-thousand-dollar advance."

I leaped from the chair. "Oh my God. Oh my God. Oh my God." I repeated the phrase in shock and beamed at Nicholas as if he could hear the other end of the conversation. When he called the waitress over for another round of drinks and flashed me one of his brightest smiles, I figured he got the gist.

"I'll go over the details tomorrow, but I didn't want to wait to give you the news. I'm so happy for you, Kim."

I sat back down. "Thank you so much." I wiped a tear from my cheek. "I can't believe this is happening to me."

"Believe it. This is only the beginning. Call me tomorrow, and we'll set up a time for you to come to the office. In the meantime, have a drink for me."

"I will."

"Bye, Kim."

"Bye." I ended the call and looked at Nicholas, my body shaking from the shock. "Fifth Avenue Press offered me a two-book publishing deal complete with a thirty-thousand-dollar advance." I felt detached from my body.

Nicholas blinked back his own tears and pulled me into a hug. Releasing me, he said, "I'm so proud of you, Kim. So unbelievably proud. And since I've actually read the book now, I can honestly say I'm not at all surprised."

I glanced around the room. "This place is good luck. Only amazing things happen here."

Nicholas let go of my hand and exhaled. "Which reminds me..."

I leaned forward. "What?"

He gave me a sheepish grin. "I'm not sure if I can top getting 'the call,' but I'm going to try." He reached into his pocket and removed a small blue velvet box.

My mouth opened.

"Kim," he said, rising from his chair.

"Nicholas?"

In what felt like slow motion, I watched Nicholas get down on one knee. "Kimmie Michele Long, how do you feel about getting a book deal and a marriage proposal on the same night?" He opened the box, revealing the most stunning pink diamond engagement ring I'd ever laid eyes on.

I gulped. "I lied before. *This* is the best night ever." I allowed him to slip the ring onto my finger.

"Will you marry me, Kimmie Long?"

"I will absolutely marry you, Nicholas Strong," I said, before vaulting off the chair and into his arms. As we hugged, I wondered if Nicholas's plan to pop the question was what had Bridget and Caroline acting so strangely. I would be sure to drill them for details at a later date, but first things first—I was engaged.

"I love you so much, Blogger Girl," he said, kissing me with a fire I knew was not the withering flame of a late-night booty call but a heat that could last a lifetime. "Or should I say, Novelista Girl?" He winked at me.

"Neither of the above," I said, shaking my head with my lips pursed.

Nicholas furrowed his brow and looked at me with curiosity. "No? What then?"

I flashed him a brilliant smile. "*Published* Girl."

"I like it," he said with a grin before giving me a pensive look. "So Laurel and Henry."

I cocked my head to the side. "What about them?" Once Nicholas got around to starting *A Blogger's Life*, he finished it within forty-eight hours. He even sent me texts during his commute to work updating me on his progress. He was adorable. He was my *fiancé*.

"Henry nearly screwed things up, huh?"

"He sure did."

"But he learned the error of his ways."

"Yes, he did."

"Just like me."

I gazed into his eyes. "Just like you."

Nicholas smiled, not saying anything.

Leaning toward him, I whispered, "Want a spoiler?"

"You bet," he said, lowering his head closer to mine.

I reached for his hand. "They live happily ever after."

Running his fingers along the pink stone of my engagement ring, Nicholas said, "Just like us."

I nodded. "Just like us."

Meredith Schorr

A born-and-bred New Yorker, Meredith Schorr discovered her passion for writing when she began to enjoy drafting work-related emails way more than she was probably supposed to. After trying her hand penning children's stories and blogging her personal experiences, Meredith found her calling writing chick lit and humorous women's fiction. She secures much inspiration from her day job as a hardworking trademark paralegal and her still-single (but looking) status. Meredith is a loyal New York Yankees fan, an avid runner, and an unashamed television addict. To learn more, visit her at www.meredithschorr.com.

Books by Meredith Schorr

JUST FRIENDS WITH BENEFITS
A STATE OF JANE
HOW DO YOU KNOW?

The Blogger Girl Series

BLOGGER GIRL (#1)
NOVELISTA GIRL (#2)

Henery Press Books

And finally, before you go...
Here are a few other books
you might enjoy:

JUST FRIENDS WITH BENEFITS

Meredith Schorr

(from the Henery Press Chick Lit Collection)

When a friend urges Stephanie Cohen not to put all her eggs in one bastard, the advice falls on deaf ears. Stephanie's college crush on Craig Hille has been awakened thirteen years later as if soaked in a can of Red Bull, and she is determined not to let the guy who got away once, get away twice.

Stephanie, a thirty-two-year-old paralegal from Washington, D.C., is a seventies and eighties television trivia buff who can recite the starting lineup of the New York Yankees and go beer for beer with the guys. And despite her failure to get married and pro-create prior to entering her thirties, she has so far managed to keep her overbearing mother from sticking her head in the oven.

Just Friends with Benefits is the humorous story of Stephanie's pursuit of love, her adventures in friendship, and her journey to discover what really matters.

Available at booksellers nationwide and online

Visit www.henerypress.com for details

LOVE LITERARY STYLE

Karin Gillespie

(from the Henery Press Chick Lit Collection)

They say opposites attract, and what could be more opposite than a stuffy literary writer falling for a self-published romance writer?

Novelist Aaron Mite meets Laurie Lee at a writers' colony and mistakenly believes her to be a renowned writer of important fiction. When he discovers she's a self-published romance author, he's already fallen in love with her.

Aaron thinks genre fiction is an affront to the fiction-writing craft. He often quotes the essayist, Arthur Krystal who says literary fiction "melts the frozen sea inside of us." Ironically Aaron doesn't seem to realize that he's emotionally frozen. The vivacious Laurie, lover of flamingo-patterned attire and all things hot pink, is the one person who might be capable of melting him.

In the tradition of *The Rosie Project*, *Love Literary Style* is a sparkling romantic comedy which pokes fun at the divide between low and high brow fiction.

Available at booksellers nationwide and online

Visit www.henerypress.com for details

A STATE OF JANE

Meredith Schorr

(From the Henery Press Chick Lit Collection)

It's more about finding yourself than finding a man.

Jane Frank is ready to fall in love. It's been a year since her first and only relationship ended and far too long since the last time she was kissed. With the LSAT coming up, she needs to find a boyfriend (or husband) before acing law school and becoming a partner at her father's firm. There's just one problem: all the guys in New York City are flakes. Interested one day and gone the next, they seemingly drop off the face of the earth with no warning and no explanation.

In her misguided belief that life doesn't really start until you get married and have kids, Jane jumps from one extreme to the next trying to force a happily ever after until she breaks. Will she ever find her path, and can she do it without alienating her friends and family and risking her career in the process?

A State of Jane is a hilarious, heartwarming, and honest coming-of-age story of what happens when a good girl discovers there is more to finding love than following the rules.

Available at booksellers nationwide and online

Visit www.henerypress.com for details